GUILT

GUILT

G. H. Ephron

St. Martin's Minotaur
New York

www.minotaurbooks.com

Library of Congress Cataloging-in-Publication Data

Ephron, G. H.
    Guilt / G. H. Ephron. — 1st U.S. ed.
        p. cm.
    ISBN 0-312-33595-4
    EAN 978-0312-33595-3
    1. Zak, Peter (Fictitious character) — Fiction. 2. Forensic psychiatrists — Fiction. 3. Cambridge (Mass.) — Fiction. 4. Bombings — Fiction. 5. Psychological fiction. lcsh I. Title.

    PS3555.P49G85 2005
    813'.6 — dc22

                                                            2004051438

First Edition: March 2005

10   9   8   7   6   5   4   3   2   1

For Don's patients and colleagues
For Jerry, Molly, and Naomi

Acknowledgments

Thanks to our editor, Kelley Ragland, for believing in Dr. Zak and making each book better. To our agent, Gail Hochman, for her enthusiastic support. To Sarah Hanley and Tony Hanley of One Step Beyond Martial Arts Training Center in Hyde Park for giving Hallie a painless introduction to self-defense. To Gus Rancatore for his enduring support and inspirational setting—Toscanini's Ice Cream. To writers and readers who test-drove the book endless times: Connie Biewald, Maggie Bucholt, Patricia and Joseph Kennedy, Pat Rathbone, and Donna Tramontozzi. To Cynthia Lepore, Adriana Bobinchock, and the McLean Hospital for their support. To Katrina, Juliana, Olivia, Sophie, and Emma for inspiration. To Carl Brotman for twenty-five years of support. Special thanks to Susan Florence and Beth Blankstein, who made contributions to Jewish Family and Children's Services in order to attain the dubious distinction of having characters in this book named after their nearest and dearest. We thank them for their generosity and remind readers that names notwithstanding, all characters in this book are fictional. As always, thanks to our spouses, Jerry and Sue, whose love and support make it all possible.

GUILT

1

MARY ALICE Boudreaux paused in front of Storrow Hall. The place oozed Harvard—monumental, aloof. Across the front, clusters of columns supported archways, and above that was a checkerboard band of pale pink and terracotta brick. Back home, everything this austere and grand had been flattened when Sherman marched through.

She read the edict carved in the stone façade:

AND THOU SHALT TEACH THEM ORDINANCES AND LAWS,
AND SHALT SHOW THEM THE WAY WHEREIN THEY MUST WALK,
AND THE WORK THAT THEY MUST DO.

Her daddy would have liked that, a quote from the Bible on a classroom building. He'd been convinced she was heading straight into the arms of the devil. Law school was bad enough. Yankee law school was a sacrilege. Hadn't they given her a good home? Sent her to a fine college? What she was supposed to do now was find a man, get hitched, and settle down to making babies. If she needed intellectual stimulation, well heck, that's what the Junior League was for.

Her parents hadn't a clue what to make of her. Just like she still hadn't a clue what to make of most of her fellow law students. She'd imagined a bunch of briefcase-toting stiffs, hanging around in the custom-fitted pinstripes that were their birthright—not these scruffy kids who, in the middle of this hot September day, lounged on the broad front steps in their shorts and sandals, basking in the late morning sun, using their battered backpacks as pillows and footrests.

Behind her, cars were parked in a small lot, and beyond that, traffic whizzed out of a tunnel and up Massachusetts Avenue—Mass Ave, as the locals called it. She smoothed the skirt of her suit and climbed the steps into the coolness of the portico, aware of heads turning to watch. With her blond hair and eyes the color of a summer sky, she'd been told by more than one intense, cerebral guy that she looked like a "sorority queen"—a pejorative phrase in this neck of the woods. Most of the smart, fast-talking women wrote her off, too. Some even had this crazy idea that being from the South, she came from a hoard of sheet-wearing rednecks that hadn't got the sense God promised a nanny goat. There really should be a law against ignorance.

Mary Alice shifted her briefcase to her other hand and pushed through the double doors, past the signs: NO TRESPASSING; NO SOLICITING. They sure knew how to welcome a stranger.

It was cooler inside—only fitting, given that the place looked like the vault of a medieval castle. Her heels clicked on the polished wood floor as she walked past a cavernous lecture hall, full of students in stadium seats, all focused on a gray-haired professor in the pit.

At the end of the hall, a circular space opened up. Light streamed in through two banks of multipaned windows that stretched from waist-high walnut wainscoting to the ceiling. There, on a low, curved leather banquette attached to the wall, sat Jackie Klevinski. She was perched, like a watchful praying mantis, with her long arms and legs folded, her eyes bright. She had on brown pants and a pullover. Long sleeves hid the scars that Mary Alice knew ran up and down the inside of her arms, needle tracks that would be with Jackie for the rest of her life. She sat there, coiled to spring, the strap of her oversized purse over her shoulder. The scarf covering her dark hair partially obscured a bruise on the side of her face, her husband's latest handiwork.

Jackie's face opened into a smile when she saw Mary Alice. For a moment Mary Alice saw what a pretty girl this woman must have been before her marriage to Joe had hardened her over with fear.

"Mrs. Klevinski—" Mary Alice addressed her formally, the way she did her clients and everyone except her closest friends and relatives. She couldn't get used to the way complete strangers were immediately on a first-name basis up here. Her southern upbringing with its politenesses, its formal ways of addressing older people in particular, wasn't something she could shake. She wasn't sure she wanted to shake it. Shoot, she couldn't stop being who she was. "It's good to see you again."

When Mary Alice extended her hand, Jackie flinched. She was skittish that way. But then, Jackie had the domestic equivalent of shell shock. She'd balked at meeting Mary Alice again at the Legal Aid Bureau. If her husband found out she'd been talking to a lawyer and was getting a restraining order, there'd be all hell to pay.

Mary Alice had suggested they meet here. During classes, it was usually deserted and quiet—an echoey kind of quiet. That was good. No one could sneak up on them without being heard. And it was convenient. Jackie had a job working mother's hours at Harvard's undergraduate admissions office, and Mary Alice had to be there anyway. Her ethics class was the next one meeting in the second-floor lecture hall.

Mary Alice put down her briefcase and sat. She placed her hand on Jackie's arm. "This is a good thing you're doing. I know you know that, and I know it's hard."

Jackie blinked back tears. "I know I've got to. It's just that half the time he doesn't know what he's doing."

You could say that again. Roaring drunk, Joe Klevinski probably couldn't tell whether it was a wall or his wife's face that he was bashing. It infuriated Mary Alice the way Jackie made excuses for the jerk.

Mary Alice took her time explaining the abuse-prevention order. Step by step she went over the process, even though she'd gone over it the last time they'd met. Tomorrow they'd file the paperwork, meet with the judge. Now was the time to get cold feet.

"Once you have the order, he'll have to move out of the house," Mary Alice said. "He'll have to leave you alone."

"And what if he won't?"

"You call the police."

Jackie leaned her head back and gazed at the ceiling.

Mary Alice pulled out a sheaf of papers. "These are the forms we need to file."

Still taking her time, she went over each part of the paperwork she'd completed with the help of her supervising attorney. In cold, bloodless language, the affidavit summarized the years of abuse and injuries. "I don't remember all the beatings, but there were a lot of them," Jackie had said. "I used to cower in the corner. He'd punch, kick, pour beer over me, and tell me how worthless I was. Said no one would want me. I believed him."

The final straw had been when their seven-year-old daughter, Sophie, tried to step between them during one of Joe's rages. Jackie insisted that Joe would never hurt Sophie deliberately. But that night he did hurt her. She wasn't going to let that happen again, Jackie said. Not ever.

Jackie twisted her wedding ring and stared at the final form: "Issues Related to Children." Silence pooled around them. This was the hardest part for her, severing Joe from Sophie.

As Mary Alice sat back and waited, giving Jackie as much time as she could to come to terms with what she was about to do, a man in a dark blue parka came out of the classroom. How anyone could wear a heavy coat in this heat was more than Mary Alice could fathom. Maybe the a/c in the lecture hall was on overdrive. The man dropped his backpack on the floor and disappeared into the men's room under the stairs.

Mary Alice checked her watch. Soon classes would end and the hall would be full of students. She went outside and scanned the crowd on the steps. As promised, a fellow legal aid volunteer, Leah Cohen, was there waiting for her. Leah had agreed to witness the signatures. Together they went back inside.

"Joe won't like this," Jackie said in a hoarse whisper. The pen shook in her hand. "Not one bit."

She braced herself, like someone about to dive into cold water, and signed the forms. Leah witnessed the signatures and left. Mary Alice took the heavy embosser out of her briefcase and notarized the document.

"The hearing. You don't think they'll find out about . . . my past?" Jackie asked.

Mary Alice was pretty sure Jackie's husband would want to avoid any discussion of heroin addiction. He'd had his own run-ins with the law on that count. Still, as Mary Alice's grandma would have pointed out, that man's driveway didn't go all the way to the house.

"If it comes up at the hearing, then we'll deal with it. You've been clean for four years. You've got a good job."

"I do," Jackie said, sounding surprised and pleased. When she smiled, the worry lines vanished from her forehead.

Mary Alice stood. "I'll call you. I'll file these, and then I'll call." She put the papers and the notary stamp back into her briefcase and snapped it shut.

Jackie stood, tucked a strand of dark hair into her scarf, and adjusted her bag on her shoulder. "Miss Boudreaux?"

Mary Alice looked up at her—Jackie was a good head taller. "What is it, darlin'?" She felt her face grow warm. Where had that slipped out from?

Jackie put her hands on Mary Alice's shoulders and held her there, the way Mary Alice's grandma would when she was about to give her a dressing-down. Jackie's face clouded over. "You feeling all right?" she asked.

Uh-oh. Mary Alice knew what was coming. Jackie was into auras and holistic medicine. She wore a crystal on a chain around her neck, two pale purple stones fused together. A healing crystal, she called it. What the heck. Mary Alice's great-uncle had peddled dowsing pendulums and divining rods.

"I'm fine," Mary Alice said.

"But you're—"

"Really, I'm feeling great." Mary Alice glanced at her watch. "I'd better be going. And they'll be expecting you back at work."

"But . . ." Jackie hesitated, then backed away, nearly bumping into the man in the parka, who'd come out of the bathroom and was waiting by the classroom door. "Thanks for everything."

Students began to exit the classroom.

"Let me know if you need help finding somewhere to stay," Mary Alice said, raising her voice to be heard over the growing chatter in the hall. "See you tomorrow."

Jackie left. Mary Alice picked up her briefcase. *You can only do what you can do*—her grandma used to say that, too, and it was the truth.

A second classroom emptied into the corridor. She was about to leave when she noticed the man's backpack still sitting behind the classroom door. She could see him walking down the corridor and heading out. He must have forgotten it.

"Hey!" she shouted. Some nearby students turned around. Mary Alice picked up the backpack and started to run. "Excuse me. . . . Pardon me. . . . Someone left this," she said as she tried to get around students and faculty chatting in the corridor.

"Hey!" she called, outside now under the portico.

The man was in the parking lot, standing there shading his eyes and gazing back at the building.

"You in the blue coat." She held up the backpack. She thought she saw surprise in the man's eyes, but he was too far away to be sure. "You forgot something," she shouted.

Instead of coming toward her, he zipped his jacket, pulled up the hood, and did an about-face. He trotted over to a parked motorbike, jumped on, pushed down on the pedal, and took off, riding over the sidewalk and out onto Mass Ave.

Well don't trip over your feet leavin', Mary Alice thought as she stood there feeling like a chump.

From the pedestrian island in the middle of the street, Jackie was looking back, a questioning look in her eyes. Mary Alice waved her away.

Odd. She was sure he'd seen her. He must have known she was calling him. She looked down at the backpack. It was heavier than she'd have expected, even if it were packed with law books.

That's when she noticed the faint chemical smell. Heard a click. She barely registered the flash that lit up around her like a supernova.

2

EVEN FROM the street, Peter Zak could see that Il Panino, the storefront café on a nondescript patch of Mass Ave about a half-mile from Harvard Square, was packed with its usual lunchtime throng. He admired the way Annie Squires maneuvered into a parking spot out front just barely bigger than her Jeep, perfect on the first try. It was one of many things he admired about her.

Grabbing a weekday lunch together was a rare treat. He took Annie's hand and they started across the street. A guy on a motorbike wearing a hooded blue parka honked and swerved around them. The horn sounded like a quiz show's wrong-answer buzzer.

"Jerk," Annie said.

Il Panino didn't exactly qualify as "fast food," but it was worth the fifteen-minute wait for their homemade mozzarella on crusty bread with summer tomatoes, fresh basil, roasted red peppers, and spicy prosciutto drizzled with a fruity olive oil.

Peter held the door for Annie.

"Well, will you look who's here," boomed a brawny, barrel-chested uniformed cop who was sitting at a table in the corner with a group of Cambridge's finest. "What do you know!" his buddy said. By their expressions of delight, Peter knew they weren't talking to him. A third one sprang up, gave a courtly bow, and pulled over a chair. One chair.

"Be a sport," Annie said, giving Peter a half-apologetic look. He let himself be dragged over. "Hey, you guys. You know Peter Zak?"

"Sure. Hi, Doc," said the barrel-chested cop. His thatch of sandy-colored hair and shirt taut across his belly seemed vaguely familiar; probably involved in one of the forensic cases on which Peter had consulted.

The rest of the officers ignored Peter, giving Annie their full attention.

An unpleasant sensation flickered in the pit of his stomach. Jealousy. He tried to squash it back. What the hell, Annie was one of the guys. After all, she'd grown up in nearby Somerville in a family of cops. On top of that, she was an investigator. She had to deal with police officers on a regular basis. Getting along with them was her job, and she was good at it. They even overlooked the fact that, as an investigator for a criminal defense attorney, she'd gone over to the dark side.

None of them noticed when Peter excused himself and headed for the sandwich line. The menu was on a board overhead. He caught his reflection in the mirror beneath it and tried to erase the sour look on his face. He tugged at his jacket. No, it wasn't his imagination that the shoulders seemed a little snug and the trousers a little loose. He'd been rowing regularly all summer. On the downside, a few new gray hairs had sprouted at the temples and he needed a haircut.

The harried woman in a white apron behind the counter was

taking an order from the man in front of him. Annie hadn't taken the offered chair. She was leaning over to talk to her buddies, her hands on the table. Packed nicely into formfitting jeans, she certainly had a handsome derriere, and her short top had ridden up exposing a few inches of tender back. It was a place Peter liked to kiss, right there in the indentation over her spine. And the nape of her neck, under all that long, curly, reddish-brown hair, and . . . oh, hell, actually most anywhere.

"The guys" were listening to Annie, their faces rapt with attention. One of them put his hand on her shoulder. Now the officer got up and planted himself in front of her. The two of them faced off, he about an inch taller. An instant later, Annie had him turned around, his arm twisted and locked in place behind. The table erupted in whistles and applause.

"You change ya mind about eating?" asked the woman behind the counter.

Peter turned back. She had an eyebrow arched, and seemed unimpressed by his "doctor's clothes"—the navy blue blazer and gray slacks he wore as a uniform whether he was managing the Neuropsychiatric Unit at the Pearce Psychiatric Institute or testifying in court as an expert witness.

Peter ordered a couple of sandwiches, and took their drinks to a table near the window. Annie joined him.

"They were asking about my self-defense class," Annie said. She opened the bottle of water, brushed back a strand of hair, and took a drink. "I was showing them—" The fire truck that screamed past toward Harvard Square distracted her. "Actually, they were giving me a hard time, so what could I do? I had to demonstrate."

Annie strained forward as another siren approached. This time it was a ladder truck, followed by the fire chief's red SUV. Their radios buzzing, all the cops rapidly packed up leftovers and headed out.

"I wonder what happened," Annie said.

The woman at the counter called their number and Peter got up. When he returned, Annie was out on the sidewalk watching a pair of ambulances *whoop-whoop*ing up Mass Ave, weaving around traffic. She tilted after them, as if drawn by a force field.

Peter had a lot in common with Annie, but this was one thing they most emphatically did not share. If fire trucks and ambulances were going one way, he'd be headed the other. Let the pros handle it.

Peter went outside and joined her. He put his arm around her waist and squeezed. "Hungry?" he whispered into her ear.

"Mmm," she said, but it wasn't the kind of *mmm* he'd hoped to elicit from her. It had a decidedly distracted edge. Annie tipped her head back a notch and sniffed the air. "A fire maybe? A big one?" She gazed at the horizon in the direction of the Square. "Or maybe not. I don't see a lot of smoke."

These days, a fire seemed relatively mundane as catastrophes went. A world of awful had been opened up to include all kinds of unthinkable acts by terrorists, zealots convinced of their cause and willing to die in a blaze of glory as long as they took a few infidels with them, all in the name of a god, someone's God.

They went back inside. Peter ate. Annie mostly nibbled, looking up as a pair of police cruisers flew by, blue and white lights flashing, then two more. Next time he managed to inveigle Annie into a shared lunch, Peter promised himself he'd pick a place that wasn't frequented by cops and with no windows on a main street.

Now traffic headed into the Square was at a standstill. Typical Boston drivers, the ones not making U-turns were honking. A man in a big black SUV got out of his car. He scratched his head as he stood on the yellow line looking up Mass Ave.

Pedestrians had stopped and were looking up the street like a pack of hunting dogs. A man in a T-shirt and jeans ran past toward the

Square. A tall, lanky woman wearing a scarf plodded in the opposite direction, the only one oblivious. Her face was smeared with soot, and the knee of her pants was torn and bloody. She cradled one arm in the other.

She stumbled. Peter jumped to his feet.

"Jackie!" Annie cried.

They raced outside. The woman didn't stop until she ran into Annie. Then she stood there blinking and rubbing her head as if she'd hit an unexpected wall. Annie put her hands on the woman's shoulders.

"What happened?"

The woman looked into Annie's face, her mouth open, recognition dawning in her eyes. Her knees gave way. Peter helped Annie prop her up. They half-carried her inside and sat her down.

Annie put her arm around the woman while Peter got a cup and poured some of Annie's water into it. When he offered it, the woman shied away like a nervous horse.

"This is Dr. Peter Zak," Annie said. "He's my friend. Peter, this is Jackie Klevinski. I know her from Slim Freddie's."

Slim Freddie's was the dojo where Annie taught self-defense. This was probably one of her students.

Jackie took the water from Peter and held it in a trembling hand. She sipped and set the cup down. Her face was chalky, her breathing shallow. Sweat beaded on her forehead and her pupils were dilated. Shock. Her pulse would be going a mile a minute. Peter grabbed a chair and put her feet up on the seat.

"Are you hurt?" Annie asked. "Your arm?"

"I'll call an ambulance," Peter said, and started to get out his cell phone.

"No," Jackie said, the words coming out like a small explosion. Others in the café turned to stare. "No," Jackie repeated, more quietly this time, tucking a strand of hair into her head scarf. "I'll be all right."

She pushed up her sleeve and examined a skinned elbow. The inside of her arm was scarred. Looked like she'd been an addict, though the tracks weren't recent. The scars didn't seem to surprise Annie, nor did Jackie's reluctance to go to the ER.

Annie wadded up a napkin and poured some water on it. She dabbed at the scrape, then pressed Jackie's hand over it to keep it in place.

"And your leg?" Annie asked.

"My leg?" Jackie looked down, as if seeing the torn pant leg and blood for the first time.

Annie pushed back her chair, leaned forward, and pushed up Jackie's pants. There was a nasty-looking scrape on her knee.

"Where were you?" Annie asked.

"I was" — Jackie took a few seconds to finish the thought — "at Harvard. At the law school talking to Mary Alice."

Annie seemed to know who Mary Alice was. "What happened?"

Jackie's mouth stretched open, her face twisted in anguish. "B . . . bomb," she said, hiccupping out the word. "On the steps—" Her shoulders shook as she wept uncontrollably.

In halting sentences, she explained that she'd taken an hour off from her job at the admissions office to meet with the legal aid intern who was helping her file a restraining order against her husband. She'd left her and started for the Square, then turned back, thinking she heard Mary Alice calling. She saw her standing on the steps of the building holding something.

Annie turned still, her hands fisted.

"She was standing there" — Jackie's voice broke — "and then there was this flash." She made a little choking sound and put her hand over her mouth.

Annie gasped as the news socked her in the gut. "Mary Alice?" She put her fingers to her lips. "How could that be? I saw her just yesterday. She came by the office . . . she came to go over some paperwork . . . *your* paperwork with Chip. This was going to be her first real case."

Jackie blinked. "I didn't know that. Seemed like she knew just what she was doing."

"You must have been knocked down by the blast," Peter said.

Again Jackie seemed surprised. "I guess so. There were people lying on the steps bleeding. Car windows shattered. There was smoke. Yelling. I didn't know what to do." The words were spilling out. "I heard sirens. Then I . . ." Her voice trailed off. "It was so awful. Seems like the next thing I know, I'm here and you're asking if I'm okay." She stared out the window. Now drivers were standing by their cars and talking to one another. "I guess I must have walked here."

Annie sat forward, her hands unclenched. "You said Mary Alice was holding something. What was she holding?"

Jackie focused her gaze in midair. She held her hands out, palms facing one another about a foot apart. "Something dark. Maybe a backpack."

"Her backpack?"

"No. She had a briefcase. She always carried a briefcase. She was always so proper and professional. A suit and a briefcase, and she—"

"So she had a backpack, not her briefcase?" Annie said, cutting in.

Jackie's face clouded with confusion. "She had both. But she was holding the backpack out in front of her."

"Like she was showing it to someone?"

Jackie nodded. "I heard her calling. She was there, standing on the steps . . . and then she wasn't." Jackie's mouth strained open in a wordless scream.

Annie put her hand on Jackie's arm.

"I *knew* something was going to happen," Jackie added.

"What do you mean?"

"Her aura. Everyone has an aura, you know." Jackie tilted her head to one side and gazed at Annie. "You, too. A pale blue band, right next to your skin. That's protection and strength. When I saw Miss Boudreaux this morning, that's what I noticed. The blue was real faint. I tried to tell her."

They'd never talked about it, but Peter was pretty sure where Annie stood on the subject of auras. Same place she stood when it came to alien abductions and crop circles.

"It's my fault." Jackie's voice was barely a whisper. "I should have made her listen. Warned her. And it's my fault we met there. I was afraid that Joe—" Her eyes widened. "You don't think Joe could have . . . I mean he didn't know where I was going to be. How could he? I was at work. He was at work . . . ." There was a second's pause and her eyes lit up with anxiety. She jumped up, knocking over a chair. "Sophie!"

Peter exchanged a look with Annie. "You go," he said. "I'll find my way back to your office and meet you there later."

He knew as well as she did that Jackie wasn't thinking clearly. But then, sometimes irrational fear called for irrational action. You couldn't always sit around and calmly analyze the situation. Jackie needed to know her daughter was safe.

3

ANNIE WAS already out of her chair holding her car keys. She raced for the door with Jackie after her. They darted across the street, between the stalled-out cars, to her Jeep.

Annie started the car, and Jackie gave her directions to Sophie's school. Traffic going into the Square still wasn't moving. Fortunately, the school was in the opposite direction. She gunned the engine, and the Jeep seemed to leap from its parking spot.

"I'm sorry," Jackie said, staring down into her lap.

Annie squashed the surge of anger. *Don't apologize!* she wanted to scream. It was all of a piece with what Jackie had learned from years married to that abusive louse. Whatever bad thing happened, he managed to make it her fault. If he had to beat the crap out of her, well, that was her fault, too. Peter probably had a fancy term for it. Annie called it "doormat syndrome." At least in self-defense class Jackie was learning how to fight back.

Didn't sound as if Mary Alice had had a chance to fight back.

Wrong place, wrong time. Shit happened—that's what everyone said. It would be a long time before Annie would get to where she could accept this particular piece of shit. She felt herself choking up. She couldn't cry, damn it. Now was not the time. *Focus.*

She punched the radio and news came on. A commentator was on the scene, talking about the explosion. The entire Harvard Square area was closed to traffic. The Red Line subway trains were stopped. Dozens had been hurt, at least one fatality. A breathless witness reported: "It was a woman. I saw her. She shouted something, and then she blew herself up."

Now the commentator was spinning—a female suicide bomber, unheard of just a few years ago, was no longer a shocker. *Suicide bombing my foot.* Annie noticed that her knuckles were going white. She eased her grip on the steering wheel.

"You have to explain what happened to the police," she said, holding Jackie's gaze before turning back to the road.

"I . . ." Jackie started. "The police? No way."

"Jackie, I know how you feel about cops. But this is different. You've got to talk to them."

Jackie stared out the car window, her jaw clenched. "To them I'm just another junkie."

"Ex-junkie."

"Tell them that. They're waiting for me to blink funny so they can call DSS and take Sophie away."

Annie took a breath and counted to ten. "You were there. You saw what happened. Maybe you saw someone or something that will help the police catch whoever did this."

Jackie's look hardened. "I didn't see anything. It was like I told you."

Annie accelerated, barely making it through a light. "You said Jackie came out on the steps with a backpack, or whatever it was, and called out to someone. Did you see who?"

"No, but . . ." The words were barely audible. There was a pause. "Annie, please, don't make me—"

Jackie got enough browbeating at home, Annie didn't want to add more. But she couldn't let it go. "They think Mary Alice was a terrorist."

Jackie swallowed. "There might have been a man. I'm not sure." She strained forward. "Go right at the next corner."

Annie turned and continued along a one-way side street lined with triple-deckers and parked cars.

Jackie kneaded one hand over the other and shook her head like a terrier worrying at a chew toy. "The police. They twist your words."

"All they'll want to know is what you saw." Annie put her hand on Jackie's arm.

Jackie jerked away. "Yeah, right. I don't trust any of them."

Annie pulled the car in the loading zone in front of the school. She yanked the hand brake. "Would it make a difference if the cop was someone I know? Someone *I* trust?"

Jackie stared down into her lap, a muscle working in her jaw.

Annie pressed. "What if I can get him to come to my office and talk to you there? You won't be sorry."

Jackie rolled her eyes, as if she'd heard that one before.

· · ·

Sour milk and pine cleaner—did every school have the same disgusting smells? Annie wondered as she and Jackie entered the rambling, cinder-block-and-glass building. It was not a bit like Annie's old elementary school, red brick with columns and wide front steps. She'd played freeze tag with the boys in the parking lot that doubled as a playground.

VISITORS MUST CHECK IN AT THE MAIN OFFICE said a sign opposite the doors, along with an arrow pointing left. Annie could feel Jackie wanting to break away and run to Sophie's classroom, but she let herself be led to the office.

At least there was no hard wooden bench in the hall. "You're benched, Miss Squires" was what Annie's fifth grade teacher, Mrs. Hathaway, mistress of the hissy fit, used to shriek. Annie couldn't even count the times she'd been thrown out of class for mouthing off and worse. She'd have to sit on the bench outside the principal's office. Everyone who walked by knew she was bad or she wouldn't be sitting there, waiting for Mr. Gross to come waddling up the hall, his comb-over flapping. She no longer remembered if Gross was his actual name, or if they called him that because he was. He'd see her sitting on that bench and his eyebrows would come together. If he'd been a cartoon character, steam would have shot from his ears.

MAIN OFFICE was written on the pebble glass inset in the door in front of them. Annie was about to ask Jackie if she was ready to go in when she noticed Jackie's bloodshot eyes and dirt-streaked face.

"Better make a pit stop," she said, and propelled Jackie to a door marked GIRLS. They went in.

Lavatories hadn't changed, either. Four stalls with swinging doors, pink gelatinous soap that plopped out of a metal dispenser, brown paper towels, and water faucets that you had to press down. Feeling suddenly like the giant Alice after she ate the mushroom, Annie realized that the sinks and toilets were miniaturized.

Jackie rinsed her face and ran her fingers through her hair. She stooped to see herself in the mirror. She took a deep breath and composed her face. Then they headed back to the office.

At the main desk, Jackie explained that there'd been a family emergency and she needed to take her daughter home. A woman with kind eyes asked to see identification. She consulted a computer and wrote out a pass for Jackie to give to the teacher.

Jackie stumbled down the hall, just barely keeping herself from breaking into a run. The classroom was around the corner. Jackie hovered, uncertain, the paper trembling in her hand as she stood in the doorway, breathing heavily, her hand over her heart.

The children saw them before the teacher. A heavy girl with corn-rows in her hair pointed and whispered to the boy beside her. He poked a little girl with shoulder-length dark curls, a slight build, and shoe-button eyes who sat at her desk, gripping a pencil and concentrating as she wrote. The little girl looked up and stared with her mouth open, the questioning look on her face quickly changing to dread. That had to be Sophie Klevinski.

If Annie's mother had come to pick her up in the middle of school, "What did I do now?" would have been Annie's first thought. "Are you all right?" was what Sophie said as they walked out of the school building. She held on to Jackie's hand and slid Annie a wary look.

When Jackie told Sophie she was fine, her schedule was just a lit-tle crazy and she needed to pick her up early, Sophie said, "It's Daddy, isn't it?"

Only seven years old and already *she* was taking care of *them*.

· · ·

Annie drove Sophie and Jackie to her office. It still gave her goose bumps to see SQUIRES INVESTIGATIONS stenciled under FERGUSON & ASSOCIATES on the front door of the law office. For ten years, Annie had worked with attorney Chip Ferguson in the public defender's of-fice. Now they shared this second-floor office in a renovated turn-of-the-century stable near the Cambridge Courthouse, just a half-dozen blocks from the Charles River.

She settled Sophie with a soda and a bag of pretzels at a desk in the outer office where, according to their accountant, they could now afford to hire a receptionist. Annie had posted an ad and had an avalanche of resumes in response, but neither she nor Chip had had time to look through them. They needed an assistant to hire an assistant.

Peter and Chip came out of Chip's office. Chip looked somber and tired in rolled shirtsleeves, his tie loosened at the neck—not at all the slick, suited appearance he presented to a jury. He pressed his lips together and Annie returned his long, sad look with a shake of her head. He'd been supervising Mary Alice's internship at Legal Aid, and Annie had been the one who'd recommended that Jackie go to Legal Aid for help with her restraining order.

Annie went to her office and looked in her date book for Detective Sergeant Joseph MacRae's cell phone number. She dialed. "Mac? It's me, Annie," she said when he picked up.

Through the open door, she could see Peter scowl. She wanted to kick him. *Will you get over it?* She was sick and tired of explaining that she and Mac were friends, old friends, able to support each other in difficult times—but that it would never amount to anything more than that. On the other hand . . . she suppressed a guilty smile. Maybe a little jealousy wasn't such a bad thing. She kicked the door shut.

"What do you want?" Mac said. "I'm in the middle of something."

"I know you are. At the law school, right?"

"Shit. Are we on the tube already?"

"The victim is Mary Alice Boudreaux." That shut him up. She could imagine him grudgingly fishing his pad out of his pocket.

"B-O-U—" Annie started. Suddenly she felt like the floor was moving under her. She needed to sit down to finish spelling the name. She was so used to dealing with violence and murder. She knew how to keep her head down, do her job, and hold tragedy at arm's length—but this was different.

"She's a second-year law student. Was."

"How the hell—?"

"A friend of mine was with the victim right before the explosion." Annie hated that word *victim*. So anonymous. "She—" Annie wanted to rat-a-tat the details but she couldn't. She gasped as her insides seized up. Good thing Mac couldn't see her. *Would you get a grip?* That had been a favorite expression of Mary Alice's, one she often addressed to herself.

"This eyewitness. Her name?"

"This woman, she's in shock, and—" Annie started. The phone crackled static. "Hello?"

"I'm here. Yeah, pretty horrendous thing to see happen. Hang on."

There were voices. Mac barked an order to someone. Then, "I'll need to talk to her." His voice faded, came back. "We need to take her statement. As soon as possible. Bring her over."

Typical Mac, assuming that once he gave an order she'd salaam like a good girl and do as she was told.

"She'll talk to you, but not at the station."

"Annie, we need a statement and we need it fast. You know as well as I do that the first few hours are critical. I haven't got time to hand-hold some flighty woman."

He could be such a pig. "Just because she's a woman doesn't mean she's flighty," Annie said, barely holding on to her temper. "And she"—Annie edited out the word *won't*—"would rather not come to the station. Can't you come here?"

"Shit, Annie, you can be such a royal pain in the ass." There were more back-and-forth asides on his end. There was a pause. "Okay, okay. I'll send someone over."

Halfway home, but not quite. "Mac, she's a friend." She waited a few beats. "And she's had some bad experiences with cops."

Mac sighed with exasperation. On any stubbornness scale, she could match him point for point.

"All right, all right. I'll come over myself."

"Thanks, Mac. I owe you one."

"*Another* one," he said, grunting. He disconnected.

Jackie was standing, her eyes trained on the office door, when Annie emerged. Sophie was on the floor, drawing on paper with whiteboard markers.

"This friend of mine, he's a detective," Annie told Jackie, keeping her voice low. Not low enough. Sophie looked up, her eyes bright. This was a kid used to listening for nuance.

Jackie and Annie stepped into Annie's office, leaving the door open.

"It's all set. He's coming here later."

Jackie stared at the clock on the desk like it was about to explode. "But I can't stay. When Joe gets home and I'm not there, he'll call the office and find out I wasn't at work this afternoon. God knows what he'll do if he finds out where I was."

"Think about whether you should be going home right now." Annie said it as gently as she could. The bomb blast hadn't changed the fundamental fact that Jackie needed to be somewhere safe when her husband got the news that she was throwing him out. "This is why you're getting a restraining order."

"But I—" Jackie sank into a chair. "I know that. Damn. I just wasn't letting myself think about it. Where are we going to go?"

Already Annie was making a mental list of shelters to call. Worst case, they'd come home with her. "First thing tomorrow, Chip will go with you to file the restraining order. He's got copies of the paperwork. I'll find you a place to stay tonight and tomorrow night, until we know Joe has moved out."

Just then Annie remembered. Damn. She was supposed to meet her sister, Abby, for dinner. Abby was finally ready to talk about the new man in her life, the Mr. Wonderful who'd been monopolizing her evenings for weeks. Annie was dying to know, and given Abby's track record, afraid to find out. If she had to cancel tonight, there was always tomorrow, she thought, fingering the white coffee mug on her desk. GOT GRITS, it said in black letters. Mary Alice had brought back a bunch of mugs like it from South Carolina after Christmas break. She'd filled each one with a baggie of what she said were the real thing—stone-ground grits. Something was missing from your life, she'd told them, if you'd never had them the way her mother served them, "hot as Hades" and slathered with butter.

Annie felt a lump rising in her throat, the letters swimming beyond a veil of tears. Then Jackie and Annie were holding each other, trying to muffle the sounds so Sophie wouldn't hear.

4

DETECTIVE SERGEANT Joseph MacRae gave a tight nod as he strode past Peter and into Chip's office. His face was taut, and his red hair cut military-short. He was not a big man, but he filled the space around him like a charged wire.

Peter gave him a throwaway "Good to-see-you." Though not Peter's favorite person, MacRae was a pretty decent police detective.

Annie shepherded Jackie into the office, too, and closed the door behind them, leaving Peter in the outer office with Sophie. Peter checked the wall clock. They were expecting him back at the Neuropsych Unit in a half hour. He didn't like leaving the folks he worked with hanging, and he wasn't thrilled about being left to watch a seven-year-old.

He called Gloria Alspag, the nurse in charge of the unit, to say he'd be getting back late. She gave him a thorough chewing out. Why hadn't he called in earlier? She'd been frantic with worry when she heard about the bombing, everyone had, since they knew he'd been heading over to somewhere in the Harvard Square area. By the time he hung up she'd made him feel thoroughly chagrinned.

Sophie was on the floor drawing. She gave him a frank, appraising look—a man she'd never seen before today—pushed back her hair, and went back to her picture. Peter didn't have a lot of experience with kids, so he hung back. Child Psych 101. Meet them at their level and don't be threatening.

"Hey, that's pretty neat," he said.

Sophie drew eyes on the smallest of three figures. She concentrated and gripped the blue marker, the tip of her tongue visible between her lips. She'd already finished drawing a big black creature with short, pointy ears, and a medium-sized blue one with tall ears. A family?

Peter checked the clock again. Two minutes had gone by. He wondered how long he'd be stuck there.

"Hey, mister, you don't have to babysit me," Sophie said. She looked up with sharp eyes. "I'm not a baby."

He felt properly chastised. Sophie went back to drawing red lines radiating from a red sun. She didn't have a yellow marker. With her nose so close to the paper, he hoped she wouldn't get high off the chemicals that permeated the air. She shifted so her back was to him.

What was the matter with him, anyway, getting intimidated by a little girl? Let's see, introducing yourself is always good. He pulled over a chair and sat near her.

"My name is Peter. You're a good artist."

Sophie ignored him.

"That's a very cool picture," he tried.

Peter could feel Sophie shrinking back into herself. She didn't suffer fools.

If at first you don't succeed . . . He wasn't above bribery. He dug into his pocket. Lifesavers. He set the half-eaten roll on the floor between them.

Sophie gave it a glance and went back to her drawing. She switched to the green marker and drew a few tentative blades of grass. Her eyes flicked over to Peter, then to the Lifesavers.

"It's okay," he said. "Help yourself."

Sophie licked her lips and picked up the pack. She peeled back the paper covering a yellow Lifesaver.

"You like yellow ones?" he asked.

"They're okay." She pried the candy loose and slipped it into her mouth. "Thank you," she said, depositing the words as carefully as she set the package down in the exact same spot where it had been.

"You can have the rest, if you like."

She didn't reach for the pack, but went back to drawing.

"That looks like a bunny." Peter pointed to the middle-sized blue figure.

Sophie considered her picture. The Lifesaver was a lump in her cheek. "That's the mommy bunny. And that's the baby." She pointed to the smallest figure.

"And who's that?" Peter asked, indicating the large black figure with pointy ears.

"That's the big bad wolf," she said, her face solemn.

"He looks scary."

Sophie didn't answer.

Cunning—that was the word Peter's Irish next-door neighbors used to describe their baby granddaughter. It was the perfect word for Sophie Klevinski. She had a round face and dark eyes that gleamed with intelligence.

She put some finishing touches on the figures—a tie around the neck of the wolf and a bow on the head of the little blue bunny. She reached tentatively for the Lifesaver pack and helped herself to a red one. Then she picked up the green marker and drew a horizon line and a hill with tiny houses off in the distance—pretty sophisticated spatial details.

Annie and Chip emerged from the conference room followed by Jackie. Sophie grabbed for the package of Lifesavers and sprang to her feet. She ran to her mother and latched on to her leg. Jackie smoothed Sophie's curls, then leaned down and kissed the top of her head.

Sophie stuck her tongue out and showed her mother what was left of the Lifesaver. "The man gave it to me."

"Did you say thank-you to Dr. Zak?" Jackie asked.

"Peter," Peter said. "She certainly did."

Now MacRae came out. "Well, I'll be going," he said, standing there looking self-conscious in his dark blue suit. This one fit him better than usual.

"Thank you," MacRae said to Jackie, and gave her a stiff handshake. "We'll be able to reach you if we need to follow up?"

Jackie seemed startled. She opened her mouth but no words came out.

"Jackie might not be at home," Annie said, jumping in. "Call me. I'll know how to get in touch."

"Mommy?" Sophie asked, her face clouded over. She squeezed her arms around Jackie's leg and looked up, craning her neck.

MacRae hitched up his pants and started for the door. He looked tired as he wiped the back of his arm over his forehead. Peter walked out with him.

"What kind of sick fuck does this kind of thing?" MacRae asked under his breath.

For a moment, Peter wondered if it was a serious question or just an expression of frustration.

"You people will probably end up defending the bastard," he added, and left before Peter could tell him to go to hell.

• • •

Peter called the unit again. It was nearly five o'clock. Annie was making calls, trying to find a shelter for Sophie and Jackie. Jackie sat sipping a cup of tea and Sophie worked on a new picture.

Dr. Kwan Liu, Peter's longtime friend and partner in running the unit, picked up.

"If it isn't the itinerant bomb squad investigator," Kwan said.

"I'm sorry. I talked to Gloria. I couldn't get away—"

"And you're wondering if we're managing without you? I know it's hard to believe, but we are."

"I'm heading back now," Peter told him. "Should be there in twenty minutes."

"After we've done all the heavy lifting? Don't bother. We'll continue to suffer in silence."

Peter didn't point out how loud, not to mention whiny, this "silence" of his was.

"Peter"—Kwan's voice turned serious—"you weren't there or anything, were you?"

Nothing like kindness and concern to bring out the guilt. He was fine, he told Kwan, and gave a quick summary of what had happened. In return, he heard all the gory details about how Kwan and Gloria and the day staff had struggled through a particularly challenging day. They'd spent the afternoon trying to dissuade one delirious patient from trying out every bed in the place—not a big deal, but upsetting to the patients already occupying them. Kwan had to abandon a group of doctors visiting from China in order to help bring the situation under control.

"What can I do to make amends and assuage my conscience?" Peter asked.

"At least you have one." There was a pause. "Ah, let's see. I'm sure you won't have any trouble being on call for me tonight. And—I know, a chai latté from Starbucks tomorrow morning at, say, about eight?"

"Eight?" Peter shuddered. That was when he was usually just prying himself out of bed.

"And how about something for Gloria, who shouldered this taxing burden with me?" He was on a roll. "Make that a decaf latté. Don't forget, she likes hers with extra sugar. And let me think . . ."

"Don't press your luck," Peter said, his guilt rapidly shading into resentment.

• • •

An hour later, the savory smell of pot roast filled Peter's mother's apartment. Peter watched Sophie, her face flushed and serious as she stood on the chrome, red-cushioned kitchen chair, concentrating on the task at hand: grating potato onto a dish towel. The apron hung down around her ankles. Pearl Zak had tied Sophie's hair back with a pink ribbon.

Peter still wasn't sure how he'd ended up bringing Sophie and Jackie home with him. He'd mentioned that this was the night he usually had dinner with his mother, who lived on the other side of his two-family house. Annie had been on the phone. She still hadn't found a shelter for Jackie and Sophie, and she'd had to cancel her dinner date with her sister. Next thing Peter knew, it was settled.

Extras for dinner was no big deal for Pearl, especially after Peter gave her the condensed version of Jackie Klevinski's predicament.

She usually cooked enough for four anyway, despite the fact that she'd been living alone for the six years since Peter's father died, and Peter and his brother had flown the coop years earlier.

"You're very good at this," Pearl said, as Sophie rubbed the potato across the grater. There was already a good-sized mound of grated potatoes. "Just a *bissel* more."

Peter had been assigned table setting. He got four glasses from the cabinet. Pearl snagged one from him, sniffed it, and pulled a face. It was ridiculous, washing an already-washed glass. But this was her house, and Peter had long ago learned that it was a lot less wear and tear all around if he just saluted and marched. Pearl even ran empty deli containers through the dishwasher before dumping them in the recycle bin.

"There, that's plenty," Pearl said, taking the grater from Sophie and setting it in the sink. She held Sophie's hands under the running water.

"Will they taste good?" Sophie asked. She dried her hands and gave the potatoes a suspicious look. She'd probably grow up to be an expert sniffer of clean glasses herself.

"Not now, but when they're cooked. They're Petey's favorite."

Peter cringed as he rinsed out the last glass. He hated it when she called him that.

"Petey?" Sophie looked around, then at Peter. Her eyes grew wide and a smile tugged at the corners of her mouth. "Petey, Petey, Petey . . ." she said under her breath.

Great. Now he had a first-grader giving him grief.

Peter set the glasses on the table, but from Pearl's sour look he knew they were on the wrong side. He shifted them.

"They taste a little like French fries, only they're shaped like pancakes," he said.

"Potato pancakes," Sophie said, adding a syllable to the middle so it came out pan-a-cakes.

"Potato latkes," Pearl said.

"Do you eat them with maple syrup?" She looked as if she didn't think much of this idea.

Pearl laughed. "Some people like to eat them with sour cream."

"*Sour* cream?" Sophie gave a questioning look over her shoulder to Jackie.

Pearl opened the refrigerator door and took out a container of sour cream. She opened it and spooned out a dollop. "Try. See what you think."

Sophie put out her index finger and hesitated. She poked at the sour cream and put her finger in her mouth. She stood there, thoughtful, her eyes raised to the ceiling. Her mouth widened into a smile.

Pearl was beaming. Nothing made her happier than someone else eating and enjoying. She offered Sophie the spoon. Sophie took it and began to lick off tiny tastes.

Pearl carried the dish towel holding the grated potatoes to the sink. She showed Sophie how to twist it in a bundle, wringing out the milky-colored liquid from the potatoes. Sophie took a turn.

Pearl gave a minuscule head shake when Peter went for the paper napkins in the kitchen drawer. So it was to be cloth napkins. Peter went to the cabinet in the dining room and took out four crisp, ironed, white linen napkins, folded them, and put them on the table.

When the potatoes were wrung out, Pearl shook them into a bowl. She helped Sophie crack two eggs over them, sprinkle on a fistful of flour, and stir with a wooden spoon.

"You'll make an excellent cook," Pearl said, as she heated oil in a skillet on the stove, "but I'm afraid you can't help me with this part. Frying in hot oil is for grown-ups."

Without being told, Sophie washed her hands again. Then she watched as Pearl ladled spoonfuls of grated potato into the hot oil. The kitchen filled with the rich, thick aroma of cooking potatoes, and Peter felt his stomach rumble as the fat sizzled. Minutes later, Peter's mother lifted a round of crispy brown potato pancakes onto paper toweling and started a new batch. As the mound grew, it was all Peter could do to keep himself from sampling one.

Before they sat down to eat, Pearl bustled into the living room and brought back an African violet plant that was bursting with pink blossoms. She set it in the middle of the table.

Every one of the potato pancakes disappeared, at least ten of them into Sophie, who made an art out of icing each one with a thin layer of sour cream. Sophie was a welcome distraction, Peter thought. She kept them all from having to think about backpacks exploding or the need for safe places to spend the night.

After dinner, Sophie sat on the living room rug using the hard candy Pearl kept in a cut crystal bowl to outline the patterns in the oriental rug. Jackie was helping dry dishes and Peter was putting them away when the phone rang. It was Annie. She'd found a place that could take Jackie and Sophie. Peter wrote down the information, but found himself feeling increasingly uneasy about dropping Jackie and Sophie at a homeless shelter. Annie's "It's one of the better ones in the area" wasn't all that reassuring.

When he relayed the news, Pearl's reaction was more precise. "Shelter shmelter," she said under her breath. "They have bed bugs."

"Mom," Peter said, giving the word an extra syllable.

Pearl folded her arms over her implacable front. "We're not sending that nice woman and that adorable little girl out into the street."

"We'll be fine," Jackie said, overhearing Pearl's stage whisper. "It won't be the first time we've stayed in one of those places."

"Foo. Don't be ridiculous. You'll stay right here. There's plenty of room." There was a spare room with the same twin beds Peter and his brother had slept on growing up.

Sophie was in the doorway, listening. She had the lace antimacassar from the back of the sofa draped across her shoulders, and one from the arm of an easy chair on top of her head. She wore a pair of black patent leather high-heeled pumps that must have been Peter's mother's, though he couldn't remember Pearl wearing shoes like that for decades.

"Can we, Mommy? Can we?"

"It's settled, then," Pearl said.

• • •

Peter opened the front door the next morning just as Jackie, Sophie, and Pearl were leaving for Sophie's school. The warm, humid morning felt more like summer than fall. He watched them walk to the street, Pearl holding Sophie's hand on one side, Jackie on the other. It struck him how much his mother would have enjoyed a grandchild, and how much he appreciated her never pestering him and Kate about having kids. Yes, they'd talked about the child they might someday have, but *now* had never been the right time. Then, four years ago, Kate was murdered by a man Peter had helped defend. He sometimes wondered if the loss would have been more bearable if they'd had a child.

Kate would have gotten a kick out of Sophie Klevinski. She'd have had her upstairs in her studio, throwing clay, showing her how to make a graceful shape grow out of nothing. The loss still hurt, but at least now memories brought sweetness with the pain.

Peter walked outside, picked up the *Boston Globe* off the lawn, and opened to the front page. FATAL BLAST AT HARVARD. The picture was of the front of Storrow Hall, the building façade and steps blackened. A chunk had been blown out of the portico overhang.

There was also a photograph of a smiling young woman wearing pearls and a sweater—a typical yearbook picture. Mary Alice Boudreaux.

Peter scanned the story. For all the inches of newsprint, actual information was scant. Apparently, had the device gone off inside the building, dozens would have been killed. Instead, it had only been Mary Alice. There were dozens of injured.

MacRae's question taunted Peter—*What kind of sick fuck does this kind of thing?* Had Jackie's husband found out where she was meeting her lawyer? More likely it was something else, and Mary Alice was a random victim. Bad luck, wrong place, wrong time. Peter wondered who or what was the intended target. Some*one* or some*thing?* Perhaps the institution itself?

Peter recoiled from his next thought: They'd know more after the next bombing. And more with the one after that.

IT SEEMED appropriate to Annie to be giving a final exam to her self-defense class three days after the law school bombing. Freddie Mancusi, the owner of Slim Freddie's, a martial arts school in the basement of a bowling alley behind Union Square in Somerville, was unrecognizable in full-body, padded, red-plastic armor, complete with helmet and faceplate. Born Freda, Freddie looked like a cross between the Michelin tire man and a mutant lobster. It was Annie's turn to be spotter and Freddie's turn to wear the red-man suit.

Molly Kennedy, an athletic college student with short dark hair and a turned-up nose, pretended to be walking down the street. She wore protective gear, too—a helmet plus knee pads, elbow pads, and a face mask. Freddie took a step closer to Molly, and waved her arms menacingly.

"Stay back!" Molly shouted at Freddie.

The large basement with its padded floor and mattresses wrapped around the lolly columns was the perfect place for a self-defense class.

No windows meant no one could watch from outside. They didn't want to inadvertently train offenders, like Molly's ex-boyfriend, who was stalking her.

Freddie made a grab for Molly.

"Stop! Get away from me," Molly yelled, loud and from the diaphragm, the way they'd been teaching her. "No!" She took a defensive stance, one foot ahead of the other, hands raised.

Freddie came at her again. Molly jabbed gloved fingers into Freddie's face mask and kicked at her padded groin. Annie knew Freddie couldn't feel a thing, and she couldn't see down over the throat guard. So she gestured to show Freddie where she'd been kicked so she could react.

With Freddie off balance, Molly tried to take off, but Freddie recovered and grabbed her from behind.

Molly came down hard with her heel on Freddie's instep. Annie yelled to let Freddie know she'd been stomped on. When Freddie loosened her grip, Molly broke free. She raced to the wall and stood there, panting for breath and exhilarated.

"Free free free!" she cried, like this was a game of hide-and-seek. She pumped her fist in the air. "YES!"

Freddie pulled off her helmet and faceplate. Her face was almost as red as the plastic suit. She shook out her dark hair, sending out a spray of sweat. Then she leaned over, hands on her thighs, and took some deep breaths. Annie handed her a bottle of water.

"Great way to lose weight," Freddie said, grinning. She chugalugged from the bottle. The deceptively slight woman had won every single one of the person-sized trophies that lined one wall of the dojo.

Annie told Molly she'd done great, and reminded her how timid she'd been when she started taking the classes. She'd had no idea how to defend herself, and could only raise her voice to a shrill scream, the kind of sound people tend to ignore.

Annie followed Molly to the closed office where the other women were waiting their turn to take the final test. They were huddled together on folding chairs in the office, deep in conversation, and didn't look up when Molly and Annie came in. Everyone was there except Jackie. It was already a quarter past. Jackie hadn't missed a class before. In fact, she'd never been more than five minutes late. Annie hoped she was all right. The restraining order would have been served yesterday, and Jackie had planned to move home today.

"I'm afraid to get on the subway," one woman said.

"What do you think this guy looks like?" another asked. "I mean, could you tell by looking at him?"

"I get the heebie-jeebies driving through the tunnel," a third one said. "I mean what if there was a car bomb? You wouldn't have a chance."

By contrast, fending off a rapist seemed like a walk in the park.

"Hey, guys," Annie said. "Who's up next?"

Geneva Devaille stood. She was a plump woman with skin so dark it was almost blue, a lilting Jamaican accent, and enormous dark eyes that gave away the fear she'd lived with since she was robbed and raped in her own apartment. At first she hadn't wanted to take the final test—no one had to. For women who'd been hurt, it could bring back what they were trying hard to forget. But Geneva had come in that morning and announced she'd try.

Molly took off her padding and handed Annie the helmet. Annie spritzed the interior with disinfectant and wiped it clean.

Sonya Mckay, a twenty-something in tight jeans, a short top, and a sun tattooed over her navel, said, "There was a bomb scare at my daughter's school. Turned out it was a volleyball in a paper bag. But they didn't know that until after they'd evacuated all the classrooms and—"

She stopped in the middle of the sentence and the place turned silent, the only sound a thud, then a rumble as a bowling ball rolled down one of the alleys overhead.

"I just want to talk." The man's voice came from the main room.

Annie went to the doorway and the women crowded behind her. Jackie Klevinski was backing up into the room. Coming at her was a man in a dark blue work uniform. He was of average height, with dark hair, clean-shaven except for a scraggly mustache and a little triangle of hair under his lower lip. He had the body of a man who worked out, lots of upper arms and chest, bullnecked, with a slight bow to his legs like they had trouble supporting all that bulk. Had to be Joe Klevinski, Jackie's loving hubbie.

"Come on, Jackie. It's not fair. You can't just—"

He froze when he saw them all.

"Joe, I'm sorry, it's just that I can't go on like this," Jackie said.

She had on the same pants she'd been wearing three days earlier, cleaned and the knee mended. Her long hair was tied back, low at the neck.

"Give me a chance to make it up to you," he said, lowering his voice, the tone pleading. "You know how much I love you and Sophie. Please, don't do this."

Jackie turned and saw them all watching.

"Come on, baby. I just want to talk," he said, his voice wheedling, his arms outstretched as he closed the space between them.

Jackie scrambled back. "I can't. It's too late."

"Honey—" Klevinski started. His voice had a flinty edge. That sound combined with that word brought back a memory from childhood. *Honey, don't make me hurt you,* delivered in just that tone of voice, was what her best friend Charlotte Florence's father used to say to Charlotte's mother. Annie shuddered and stiffened.

"Mr. Klevinski," she said, shooting for a loud, confident tone. She strode over. "I'm going to have to ask you to leave." She kept her voice calm as a telemarketer's. "You're not supposed to be here."

He dodged to one side. Annie blocked his way. He tried to go around her but Annie was in his face. He strained to see around her. When he saw Freddie, he gawped. "What the hell is that supposed to be?" he said. She'd removed neck guard and chest plate and was trying to strip off the rest of the gear. The damned red-man suit made it impossible to move.

"I need you," Klevinski shouted to Jackie. "You know I'm no good without you. Sophie needs a father. You're destroying me—"

Right. It was her fault.

"Joe, please stop," Jackie said, tears running down her face.

That's what they did, the bastards. Laid the guilt on thick, like it was Jackie's fault that he drank and had to use her as a punching bag to prove he was a man.

"She's not . . . going . . . with you," Annie said. With each word, she felt adrenaline pump through her. Her vision turned sharp. She became aware of the space between his crooked front teeth, the slight paunch hanging over his belt, the hairs on his knuckles.

He blinked at Annie, his lower lip curled with disdain. He gave her a slow once-over, up and down. "Why don't you just mind your own business?"

The women had closed ranks around Jackie. Klevinski eyed each of them, leering. *Just a bunch of women,* his look said.

Annie held up both hands, palms facing him. "You're interrupting our class. I'm asking you to leave."

"Cunt," Klevinski said, and faced off opposite her.

Go ahead, Annie thought, *make a move. I'd just love to wipe your smug expression off on the floor.*

"You slimy-assed bitch." Klevinski raised his hand to grab Annie's wrist.

Before she was even aware of her own movement, Annie had

grabbed his arm at the elbow and pulled him off balance. In an instant, she'd pivoted behind him. She had his elbow anchored, and was pressing down hard on the back of his hand. It was a very effective hold and excruciatingly painful.

"What's the matter?" Annie said. "Not as much fun, is it, when you're on the receiving end?"

He struggled to get loose, but Annie had his arm locked in place. She increased the pressure on the back of his hand, harder and harder until he screamed in pain. Such a satisfying sound. Just a little harder and the bone would crack. It didn't take much, if you knew where to press.

"Annie!" Freddie shouted. She'd managed to get free of the padding. "Ease up." Her voice was calm, authoritative, but her eyes were tense with alarm. The women stood in stunned silence.

Annie eased the pressure and felt Klevinski go slack.

"Someone call the police," Annie said.

No one moved.

Annie strained over her shoulder to see. Jackie was leaning on Molly and weeping. "Annie, let him go, please," Jackie begged.

"You know what's going to happen. He'll be back another time, another place, looking for you. It's just a matter of time before—"

"Let him go," Jackie said, louder this time. "Please. I can't do this."

Annie couldn't hold onto Klevinski and argue with Jackie at the same time. He let her propel him out into the hall.

Still holding on, she said under her breath, "If it were up to me, I'd have broken your arm and had you thrown in jail."

"And I'd have sued the crap out of you," he said. "For Christ's sake, she's my wife. I just wanted to talk to her."

"The restraining order says you can't. But you think you're special, don't you? That none of this is your fault. I know all about men like you."

He gave Annie a hard look, like he was trying to memorize her face. "I'll bet you do." He ran his tongue over his lips. "Like it rough, don't you?"

It took everything Annie had to keep from losing it. "You sonofabitch. Stay away from her."

"You know, this is none of your fucking business."

Annie wanted to grab one of Freddie's trophies and whack the bastard across the head with it. Instead, she renewed the pressure on his wrist until he was up on his toes, swearing and howling with pain.

"All right, all right. I'm going," he managed to say.

Annie knew she was going to regret this, but she had no choice. She loosened her hold and he broke away.

She followed him out to his truck. He stood out there massaging his wrist, his eyes a pair of burnt-out coals. Finally he turned and left. The winch on the back of the disappearing truck reminded her—wasn't he a mechanic? Wouldn't that give him easy access to whatever it took to make a bomb? Annie made a mental note to call and make sure Joe Klevinski was on Mac's list of suspects.

"What the hell's the matter with you, girl?" Freddie asked her when Annie came back inside. "You better be careful or you'll find yourself with a great big bull's-eye across your back."

• • •

After class, Jackie and Annie sat on folding chairs in the empty studio. Jackie had dark smudges under her eyes. She explained that she'd been afraid to go home. She and Sophie had spent another night with Peter's mother. She'd walked Sophie to school, then taken the subway to Slim Freddie's. Joe was waiting for her when she got there, so she walked around the block. When she got back, she thought he'd gone.

"Has he moved out?" Annie asked.

"I think so. I was going to go back later today."

"Is he bothering you at work?"

"I called in sick the last three days. I've been too afraid. I mean anyone can come into the admissions office. What if he comes back?"

Which *he* did she mean? The husband or the bomber? Or were they one and the same?

"I can't keep calling in sick. If I miss another payment, I'll lose the condo for sure. But I need to be where I feel safe."

Jackie would never feel safe working at Harvard as long as Joe knew where to find her. But finding a new job wasn't that easy. Suddenly it occurred to Annie. She and Chip needed to hire someone, that was for sure—someone to answer the phones, take care of the filing, run the occasional paperwork over to . . . well, Jackie wouldn't be able to do that, not for a while at least. But she'd be safe until Joe figured out where she worked, and hopefully he'd have cooled off by then. Hiring Jackie would sure save a whole lot of time, not having to go through a gazillion resumes and interview candidates. Seemed like a slam dunk.

She told Jackie her idea. "We can't afford to pay a huge salary. But you'd get health insurance, and—"

Jackie was staring at her, wide-eyed, like she'd been hit by a two-by-four.

"What?" Annie asked.

"It's just that no one's ever . . . I mean . . . Yes is what I mean. Yes, I'll take the job. And thank you." She hugged Annie. "You won't regret this. I promise."

Annie hoped to hell that Jackie was right.

6

PETER WAS stuck in traffic. He'd been on his way to the Cambridge Courthouse to testify in a purely routine case, quoting research, work he could do on two cylinders—he'd only taken the work because Chip convinced him that his young defendant deserved a break. Detours were still in effect around Harvard Square four weeks after the bombing, making traffic a world-class nightmare. To avoid the mess, Peter had crossed the Charles River into Boston and taken Storrow Drive. *Wrong.* Apparently, everyone else had the same brilliant idea. Traffic crept toward Leverett Circle.

He called Chip on his cell phone and left an update on his progress. He suggested Chip and Annie go up without him. He'd join them as soon as he could.

Then he sat back and tried to relax. There was nothing for it. He rolled down his window. The heat spell had long since snapped with a few resounding thunderstorms, and today the air was crisp with fall, the surface of the river flat as glass. Maybe he'd get out of court in time to get in some rowing.

Too bad Annie didn't love to row the way he did. She adored blading—a form of public humiliation, not a sport, as far as he was concerned. Skating killed his feet, he needed trees to stop, and when he fell down, which he did frequently, he couldn't get up without an inordinate display of klutziness. Annie said he should give it a chance. He'd grow to like it. *Right, when pigs fly.*

Annie kept telling him how "just fine" Jackie Klevinski was working out. Not only did she like the work, she was talking about enrolling in a program to become a paralegal. Not at Harvard, she said. That place had bad karma, and she'd known it all along.

Annie invited him to butt out when he dared to question whether hiring Jackie was such a hot idea. Jackie needed to learn to take care of herself, he'd suggested, not continue to be taken care of, and maybe Annie was letting herself get too involved. It worried Peter, too, that his mother was babysitting Sophie after school. What if Joe Klevinski found out where they lived and showed up one afternoon in a rage? When Peter mentioned this to Pearl, she said to stop *hakken* her—Yiddish for "butt out." She reminded him that she was the resident noodge.

By the time he got into East Cambridge, the trial was due to start in ten minutes. Parking spots were scarce, and there'd be a backup at the metal detector at the entrance. With their official IDs, Chip and Annie could zip through without waiting on line. He hoped they weren't still waiting for him.

He squeezed his Miata into a space on the top floor of the parking garage on Third and didn't bother to wait for the elevator. He ran five flights down, then cut across Bullfinch Square. If he hadn't been in such a hurry, he'd have slowed down to enjoy the refurbished century-old courtyard, an oasis of calm surrounded by early nineteenth-century red-brick court buildings.

He started down the steps to the street. Across the busy intersection stood the modern, nondescript Middlesex District Court, a building whose only virtue was to remind the good citizens of the Commonwealth that progress wasn't always a good thing. The structure had so much less appeal with its ugly concrete and—

Peter never got to finish the thought. A powerful shock wave forced him back. Time seemed to slow down as he felt himself lifted off the ground. Somewhere in midair he registered the sound of an explosion. Next thing he knew, he was flat on his back in the courtyard.

He lay there, sounds suddenly muted. Scores of pigeons flapped against a blue sky. They must have been blown out of their roosts. A deep shadow fell, like a hand had reached out to blot the sun. The air hung thick with sulphur.

Peter lifted his head. Car alarms clanged. He could make out raised voices. Somewhere a woman was screaming.

Trying not to move too fast, he propped himself on one elbow. The ground sparkled with broken glass. His back and his head hurt like hell. He touched his forehead, his head. No blood. He looked down. Legs and arms seemed intact. The only thing missing was his briefcase.

Peter started to get up, but a wave of dizziness forced him down again. He rolled onto his hands and knees and crawled to the top of the steps. From there, he looked down at the devastation. Traffic had come to a halt. Black smoke billowed from where the glass doors had blown off the front of the courthouse. People were lying on the sidewalk and in the street, blood everywhere. If he hadn't been running late, he'd have been one of them.

A man in a business suit was on his knees a few feet away, talking on a cell phone. Peter could only make out the occasional word: "injured. . . . explosion. . . . Thorndike Street."

More slowly this time, Peter got to his feet. He saw his briefcase lying on a step halfway down. It was open, and the papers spilled out. He'd have to gather them up before they all blew away, Peter thought distractedly; otherwise he wouldn't have what he needed to testify. That's why he was here. To testify about the effects of alcohol on judgment. The trial should be getting under way—he looked at his watch—any minute. Chip and Annie should be waiting for him. . . .

The situation snapped into focus, and Peter stared at the smoking lobby, emptiness edging on nausea in the pit of his stomach, a cold sweat on his back. Were Chip and Annie somewhere in there?

"Is THAT adorable or what?" Annie's sister Abby asked as she tucked a strand of long red hair behind her ear with a manicured finger. Once upon a time, it had bothered Annie that Abby was perfect—five-foot-five, silky straight hair, hourglass figure, turned-up nose. And no freckles.

They were outside a grassy enclosure in a part of the Franklin Park Zoo closed to the public. Jackie, Sophie, and Abby's boyfriend, Luke Thompson—the guy Abby had been keeping under wraps—were pressed up against the chain-link fence watching a six-foot-tall baby giraffe stand on spindly legs alongside its two-story-tall mother. Annie had gotten a reprieve from going to court with Chip so she could attend this private viewing and finally meet Luke. She'd invited Jackie and Sophie to come along. When Jackie fretted about leaving the office untended, Annie reminded her that they'd survived for a year armed with only voice mail and beepers.

Who dated a zookeeper, anyway? Annie wondered as she watched

Luke telling Sophie about the zoo baby that had been front-page news in the Boston media, a welcome change from articles about fear and bomb threats. With his blond, wavy hair and strong chin, Luke seemed like the type who'd watch himself in the mirror over the bar while he tried a new pickup line. Annie hoped she was wrong. It was about time her sister got a break in the man department. Abby had been married once. That guy had been a bad cliché from start to finish and, after about six months of wedded bliss, took off with a stripper. The other men who'd appeared and disappeared from Abby's life had been a pitiful bunch. There was the accountant who raised pit bulls. The chef who worked nights and weekends, and whose apartment had no furniture in it except a bed and a ceiling-mounted mirror. Every one of them was good-looking as hell, and after each one dumped her, Abby disintegrated.

You hurt my sister and I'll break off your arm and beat you over the head with the bloody stump, Annie wanted to tell Luke, but she stifled the impulse.

The mother giraffe's slender stilt legs angled apart so she could lower her head. The flesh in her neck bunched up as she nuzzled the youngster. Annie found herself mesmerized by the sheer size and grace of these creatures, their bodies a patchwork of brown and white velvet.

"Doesn't it look just like one of those stuffed toys we lusted after in FAO Schwartz in New York?" Abby said.

Annie vividly remembered that visit to Manhattan. She had been ten years old, Abby was five. There were pictures in their family photo album of her and Abby wearing matching navy blue wool coats and berets trimmed with red ribbon, standing on the steps of the Plaza Hotel. It had been one of the few times their parents took them on a family vacation anywhere other than Cape Cod, where Uncle Jack and Aunt Felicia had a cottage.

"Remember the ice cream sundaes?" Annie asked, remembering the old-fashioned ice cream parlor their mother had taken them to across from Central Park. It was all marble and brass, and smelled like malted milk and cotton candy. When Annie returned to New York years later she couldn't find the place.

"We didn't go for ice cream," Abby said.

Annie knew better than to argue. It was just like her sister to be so definite and so wrong at the same time. *You better pick your battles with that one,* her mother used to say.

"Sophie's going to remember this," Annie said.

"Know what we call a baby giraffe?" Luke asked Sophie. "A calf."

"So what's the mother?" Sophie asked. "A cow?"

Annie could relate to Sophie, as smart as she was sassy.

"That's right," Luke said. "Actually, lots of animal mothers are called cows. Mother elephants. Hippos."

"Dolphins, too," Sophie said, looking serious.

Luke smiled. "That's right. And do you know how old this baby is?"

Sophie shook her head.

"She's three *days* old."

Sophie gasped. She was as much in Luke's thrall as Abby. So what was not to like?

"Her name is Jamila," Luke said.

"Jamila." Sophie breathed the name, pressing herself up against the fence.

"That means 'love' in Swahili," Luke added, winking at Abby. This was giving Annie a toothache.

Sophie scrambled up the chain-link and peered over the top as the mother giraffe licked the baby's face.

"Get down from there!" Jackie cried, and went to pull her away. But Luke motioned to her that it was all right.

Sophie was so bold and fearless while Jackie was afraid of her own shadow. Kids could be so different from their parents. How on earth, Annie wondered, would Abby ever deal with a fence-climber? Annie would probably end up with a girlie girl who wanted to be a cheerleader. If she and Peter had a little girl, what would she look like? Annie nearly choked on the question. What was she thinking, anyway?

Sophie climbed down and tugged on Jackie's elbow. "Did you see? Did you see? The mommy's got a black tongue. Luke says it's more than a foot long."

Luke explained how the mother giraffe gave birth standing up, and the newborn dropped all the way to the ground. The mother had to kick and prod her so she'd get up and walk.

"Her fur," Sophie said. "It looks so soft." She wiggled her fingers through the chain-link. "Can I touch her?"

"Right now the mother is feeling pretty protective," Luke said. "So I think we'd better respect that. But in a few weeks you can come back and I'll take you inside."

Maybe this guy *was* different.

"I don't want to screw this one up," Abby whispered to Annie, crossing the fingers of both hands. "You like him, don't you?"

It shouldn't matter what I think was what Annie started to say. But she knew it did. It always had and probably always would. As much as they'd become friends, Annie was still the big sister.

Annie's cell phone rang. She fished it out from her leather backpack.

"Annie?" It was Peter. "You're okay?"

"Well of course I'm—"

"Where are you?"

"I'm at the Franklin Park Zoo. Why?"

"The zoo? What are you doing at the zoo?" He sounded out of breath.

"My sister Abby—" Annie's throat went dry. Peter wasn't the type to check up on her. "Why do you want to know?"

"Where's Chip?"

Annie could hear shouting and sirens in the background. Something had happened. "I thought he was in court with you."

"I was late getting here—"

"Here?"

"I'm outside the courthouse. Annie, there's been another bombing. Looks like it went off in the lobby."

Annie felt cold, barely able to breathe. *Calm down*, she told herself. Chip was just late. He always underestimated how long it took to get places, never factored in time to park. Or maybe he had decided to walk. Nah, he never walked anywhere.

Peter went on. "I was hoping he'd called you."

No, the message light on her phone wasn't blinking. Suddenly the smells inside the giraffe house were nauseating. She stumbled toward the exit and pushed through the door. Outside, she leaned against a bench and took gulps of fresh air. The static on the line felt like a pointed stick drawing a jagged line down her back.

"Annie? Are you there?"

"You've got to find him."

"I will. I'll call you back as soon as I know something. Call me if you hear anything."

"Is it bad?" Annie asked, not wanting to know the answer.

"It's pretty grim."

Peter's eyes stung. He didn't know how long he'd been standing there, just looking at the cell phone. One ring and his call had gone directly to Chip's voice mail. Did melted cell phones ring? Did one-legged ducks swim in a circle? He squashed the comedy routine that threatened to erupt in his head. *Stay anchored,* he told himself as he pocketed the phone and tried to refocus. Thank god, at least Annie was fine.

Chip was probably fine, too. There were loads of reasons why Chip wouldn't be answering his cell phone. He could be using it, or have it turned off. He'd have to have turned it off if he'd gone into the court-room. The upper floors of the courthouse looked unscathed in the acrid haze that hung over the area. At the base of the building, a steady stream of people were exiting, falling over each other as they tumbled out the door, coughing and covered with soot. Peter squinted through a gray scrim. Didn't look as if Chip was among them.

The intersection was rapidly filling with emergency vehicles and men in uniform shouting orders, herding people into groups, taking names, clearing the way for orange-clad emergency-services personnel, who were trying to get to the wounded or rush them out on stretchers. A firefighter in a yellow rubber raincoat emerged from the building, propping up a woman who was bent nearly double, coughing. He yelled for oxygen, and an EMT with a portable tank rushed over.

A breeze kicked up and an empty file folder skittered across the asphalt. Papers—pages from printed documents—were flying around like someone was celebrating end-the-bureaucracy day for City Hall.

Peter started across the street. A woman sat dazed at the curb, blood on her white T-shirt. A man in a business suit was facedown on the sidewalk. The back of his head was bloody. Dark pinstripes, dark hair. About Chip's height. Peter rushed over. The man's fingers were moving, and he wore a wedding ring. Thank god, not Chip. Peter felt a twinge of guilt at the thought. Peter crouched beside him. The man's eyes were glazed but he was conscious.

"What happened?" the man asked, pushing himself over onto his side.

More emergency vehicles converged on the courthouse from both sides. Peter got out his handkerchief and pressed it to the man's bleeding scalp. "Looks like you have a head wound. There was an explosion."

The man blinked and his eyes focused. "Another one?" It was the question everyone would soon be asking.

"Peter!"

The voice came from behind Peter. He turned. Relief flooded through him as Chip hurried over, his briefcase flailing.

"Jesus, I thought you were in there," Peter said.

Chip stared across at the charred lobby. "That's where I thought you were."

Emergency personnel had set up a triage center at the end of the block. An EMT came over and started to take vital signs from the man Peter had been helping.

"I had to take care of something at family court," Chip said. "If the clerk hadn't been so inept, I'd have been here." Chip gave Peter a careful once-over. "Don't tell me, you ran late, too. You sure you're all right?"

Peter looked down. His shirt and suit were stained with soot and his jacket sleeve was torn at the shoulder. An empty, bloody Nike lay a few feet from where they were standing. That put things in perspective.

"I'm fine."

A police officer asked them to move behind where other officers were putting up sawhorse barriers. Peter remembered his briefcase. It was still on the steps. While Chip called Annie to tell her he was fine, Peter gathered up the papers that hadn't blown away.

A dark sedan pulled up. Peter recognized MacRae getting out. MacRae spoke briefly to a uniformed officer, who pointed at a lamp-post. MacRae went over and examined a flyer posted there. He pulled on a latex glove, reached up, eased off the tape, pulled down the flyer, and tucked it into a plastic bag.

Peter looked over at the mailbox nearby. There were flyers stuck there, too. A fluorescent green one for a local jazz group that was appearing at the Ryles. Below that was one that said, ANXIOUS? UNABLE TO SLEEP? It was a call for volunteers for a clinical study at Mass General. Peter looked around at his fellow bystanders. More than a few of them would soon qualify.

• • •

Bullfinch Square seemed oddly untouched as Peter and Chip crossed through. It could have been a quiet twilight in the protected area of green foliage and red brick not a hundred feet from the chaos of the courthouse. They continued up to Cambridge Street and around the corner to a coffee shop. There, the owner was using duct tape to attach clear plastic sheeting where there had been a window. Broken glass had already been swept away and the place was doing a brisk business. They got the last empty table.

Chip and Peter and Annie had often met at this greasy spoon with its too many coats of dark green paint on the walls. Over breakfast or lunch, they plotted strategy during a trial. Now it seemed like everyone in the place was talking on a cell phone.

"I was walking over from the T. She was supposed to meet me . . ." said one hollow-eyed, middle-aged man in a rumpled suit, probably an attorney.

"Looks like Armageddon," said another.

"Yeah, I'll be home early. Sure. A half gallon of milk," said a bearded fellow in uniform, probably a court officer. "Anything else?"

Chip cleared his throat. He was eying Peter's coffee. "You sure you're all right?"

Peter looked down at the two sugar packets he'd emptied into the cup. He was adding a third one. He didn't even like sugar in his coffee.

Chip sat there musing, his eyes troubled. "I hope the prisoners got evacuated safely." His client would have been up in the twelfth-floor courtroom, awaiting the trial. Chip would also be wondering about the people he knew who worked at the courthouse—who'd made it out in one piece and who hadn't.

"First the law school. Then the district court," Peter said. "Maybe someone's ticked at lawyers."

"Wouldn't be the first time," Chip said. "Odd coincidence, don't you think? The first bomb takes out the law school intern I happen to have been working with. This one just misses me and you, and could have gotten Annie if she'd been here."

Peter shrugged. There was no point in speculating.

"You think I'm paranoid?" Chip asked.

"You ever read about that man in Pennsylvania who got struck by lightning three times? Sometimes it's really just coincidence."

Peter opened his briefcase and began sorting through and straightening the papers he'd stuffed inside. The pages had gotten out of order, but everything seemed to be there.

"I wonder when they'll reschedule the trial," Chip said. "And where."

Peter flattened out the notes he'd planned to review while he was waiting to testify. His crib sheet with a table summarizing the main research findings about the effects of alcohol on judgment had been torn nearly in half. Under that was a rumpled piece of paper that looked as if someone had stepped on it. The top corners were torn. Peter's stomach rolled as he read the words printed in big black letters. He rotated the page to show Chip.

Chip's lips moved as he read.

There is no god. No right or wrong.
The law prevents Us from pursuing Our destiny.
Nothing but violent resistance can ever overcome the selfishness
which is the basis of the present organization of society, which
the few willingly perpetuate to exploit the many.

A pudgy man in a suit at the neighboring table peered around his newspaper through horn-rimmed glasses. Peter had an instant of eye contact with him before the man adjusted his paper in front of his face.

"I wonder if this is what MacRae was pulling down," Peter said, keeping his voice low.

Chip ran his finger under the words and held on the final sentence

"This sounds familiar. Some kind of quote, maybe. And did you notice this?" He pointed to a handwritten symbol near the bottom of the page. It was a circle with the capital letter A inside it. Peter didn't recognize it. "Stands for anarchy."

"Hey, you!" the waiter, an older man in dark trousers and a white shirt, shouted after the man who'd been sitting at the table next to them, but the man was already out the door. "Sonofabitch," the waiter muttered. "Didn't pay for his coffee."

"So, Peter, where'd you say you picked this up?" MacRae asked the next morning, gazing poker-faced at the flyer Peter had brought to his office.

"Across from the courthouse. Thought it might go with the one you pulled down off the lamppost?"

MacRae did a double take.

"I was across the street, up on the plaza, on my way to court. Late, thank god." Peter told him that he'd been knocked down and his papers had gone flying. "I didn't realize until I got back that I'd picked it up. When I read it, I realized I should bring it to you."

MacRae slipped the flyer into an evidence bag. "Flyers just like this were all over the immediate neighborhood."

Peter told him that Chip thought he'd recognized the quote, and that the symbol at the end stood for anarchy.

"I know. It's un-fucking-believable," MacRae said. "Cambridge. *Pff.*" He blew air out between his teeth.

In a nutshell, that was what Peter loved about the place where "mainstream" thinkers were considered a fringe element. When Peter first moved there, a scruffy, amiable group of old-style radicals who called themselves the Anarchist Drinking Brigade held regular meetings at the Green Street Grill. Last year, a church in the middle of Harvard Square hosted a book fair where they sold anarchist manifestos alongside vegan cookbooks.

"You think this could be the same person who did the law school?" Peter asked.

MacRae looked impassive.

Peter recalled the way MacRae had dismissed him after the law school bombing. *You people will probably end up defending the bastard.* The hell with him. Peter's conscience was clear. He'd brought in what he'd found. He started to get up, then paused at the sound of MacRae clearing his throat.

MacRae opened his top desk drawer and pulled out a piece of paper. He held it facedown on his desk. "I'd like to show you something. We haven't given this to the press, so I don't want to hear about it on the evening news."

MacRae could be such an arrogant sonofabitch. "You want me to sign something?"

"No. I just wanted to be clear. I'm showing you this in confidence."

He handed Peter the paper. It was a Xerox of a flyer. Looked as if the original had been weathered and torn.

Freedom from oppression!
The law prevents Us from pursuing Our destiny.
Civil government is in reality instituted for the defense of the
rich against the poor. When people fear government, there is
Tyranny. When government fears the people, there is liberty.

There was the same symbol at the bottom, a circled A.

"Was this one found near the district court, too?" Peter asked.

MacRae shook his head. "Law school. Must've been up for weeks. Unfortunately, we didn't find it and more like it until this morning, when we knew what we were looking for."

"How do you think he got past courthouse security?" Peter asked.

MacRae stood there chewing his lower lip. He hated to part with information but he knew the dance—you had to give a little to get a little. "All we know is he did."

That was unsettling. Meant the bomber could blend in. Might have come dressed like an attorney, had an ID pass to get in. It would be easy to leave behind a briefcase with the bomb in it, then disappear into the neighborhood. Could have been one of the people on the sidewalk, or in the coffee shop. The man calling to say he'd be getting home early and bringing a half gallon of milk. The one who bolted out of the place without paying. Maybe it was the man on the sidewalk Peter had tried to help. Peter couldn't remember if the man had a briefcase, or even what he looked like. A suit, that was about all Peter could bring back. Big help, everyone around there wore suits. It was an odd thing about suits—when you weren't concentrating on noticing, sometimes that was all you saw.

MacRae's next question took Peter aback: "So, is this guy crazy?"

Not exactly a plea for help, and certainly not an apology for being rude and unpleasant, but Peter savored the moment—MacRae was actually asking his opinion and offering the tiniest acknowledgment that maybe he didn't have all the answers.

Unfortunately, neither did Peter. "You think it's the work of one person?" he asked, sidestepping the question.

"Suppose, just for argument's sake, that this is one person. What are we looking for?"

Peter didn't answer right away.

"Hey, it could have been you in that building," MacRae said, misinterpreting Peter's reticence. He'd hesitated because he wasn't a profiler. When he evaluated a suspect, it was based on an in-depth evaluation. He interpreted the results and extrapolated backward. This was different. He had no interviews, no test data. Still, there was behavior. That was something. The same principles could be applied.

"This is just informal, right? I mean no one's going to subpoena me to testify, right, because I'd just be shooting from the hip."

MacRae held up two fingers. "Scout's honor."

What *did* he think, assuming, as MacRae suggested, that it was one person who did both bombings, and assuming the flyers were his?

"Whoever it is, he's not a big fan of the government," Peter offered.

Duh. MacRae didn't say it, but his expression did.

"And based on the messages, the targets don't seem random."

MacRae still didn't seem overly impressed.

Peter went on. "He's planning. Thinking things through. It takes time to compose these messages, print them, and put them up, to gather what he needs to make the explosives. And he's interested in more than making noise and communicating a message. He's picked times and places that guarantee casualties."

Peter took off his glasses and rubbed the bridge of his nose. What were the options? "Could be schizophrenic, someone like the Unabomber with some convoluted logic behind the point he's trying to make. He could even have a legitimate gripe. Maybe he's someone who should have been protected by the judicial system but wasn't, and he's conflating larger social issues with his own personal issues, maybe to the point of being delusional about them. Could be a sociopath, using anarchist rhetoric as a cover. Or a terrorist, with an organization behind him."

Now MacRae looked exasperated. He was getting questions, not answers.

"This is pure speculation, right?" Peter said.

"You don't see me taking notes."

"Okay." Peter put his glasses back on. "I'd say it's a man. Bright. Well-read. Disenfranchised. Educated. White. Unmarried. Probably not in a committed relationship. Only child." MacRae reared back as Peter reeled off his ideas. "Possibly a childhood abuse victim. Maybe a history of fanaticism or cult involvement. Probably reads sci-fi or spy novels."

MacRae's eyebrows went up in surprise. "Sci-fi?"

"I'd say this is someone whose grip on reality is a little bit loose or distorted, who might think he can engineer change all by himself."

MacRae fished out his pad and cocked his pen. "You mind? No subpoenas, I promise."

Peter didn't protest as MacRae wrote.

Peter went on. "To set up something like this, knowing people will be randomly killed, suggests an individual who doesn't connect emotionally to other people. No empathy. That's where the abuse comes in. Kids who were physically abused learn a different way of relating because the people who are supposed to take care of them don't."

"How the hell do you know he's white?"

"I told you, I don't know squat. This is pure blue-sky speculation."

"Yeah, yeah, yeah. But?"

"But you don't get lots of anarchists of color in the U.S. these days."

MacRae's pen scratched on the paper.

"Local. Urban. Narcissistic," Peter said, rattling off some more half-baked but educated guesses. "He has to announce what he's do-ing. To have time to do all this—plan it, make the bombs, set them up to blow on a weekday morning—he's probably not working. Un- or underemployed. May have a criminal record of some kind."

MacRae gave Peter a look of genuine appreciation. "This gives us some new avenues to explore."

"Motive. That's the key. He's smart, not impulsive, and he's got an agenda. Figure out why and you'll be a lot closer to knowing who." Acting as if this were an aside, Peter added, "Chip mentioned the possibility that he or Annie might be the target. Chip was working with Mary Alice Boudreaux, and Chip and Annie were due to be at the courthouse when the bomb went off."

Peter thought MacRae would dismiss the idea out of hand but he didn't. "I'd thought of that, too," he said. "Something to rule out."

10

"Sorry, I was vacuuming," Annie admitted when it took her five rings to pick up Peter's call that night.

"You were doing what?" Peter sounded stunned. He was right. Annie usually avoided anything that smacked of housekeeping. But when she got home from the zoo she'd straightened, dusted— including the windowsills and ceiling moldings—and sorted her underwear drawer.

Yes, she knew what it was about. Anything to keep from facing how devastated she'd be if Peter and Chip got erased in an instant. As Annie cleaned, she'd found herself thinking about Mary Alice, remembering her voice, the drawl, the salt and vinegar that seasoned her sweetness, the unflinching way she appraised others.

"After that I scarfed down a bag of potato chips and a Sam Adams."

"That sounds more like it," Peter said. Then his voice turned serious.

"Listen, when this kind of thing happens, the only sane response is to go a little nuts."

If anyone else had told her that, Annie would have found it patronizing. Instead, she found the observation calming. Peter was solid, grounded, and so perceptive about everyone's inner turmoil except his own.

"Nothing can happen to you out on the river," he pointed out. "How about meeting at my house after work tomorrow? We'll go for a row."

In a weak moment she'd agreed. But as she drove over to Peter's house with Jackie the next afternoon, she was having second thoughts. What had she been thinking, anyway?

Peter loved everything about rowing—the rhythm, the way the boat glided across the water, the two of them working in perfect synchrony, the sun glinting off the Hancock Tower.

Not to put too fine a point on it, she hated everything about the sport. It made her cold and wet, she couldn't see where she was going, and the boat got all tippy when she so much as changed her mind. The worst part was Peter telling her to watch the set, raise her starboard oar, and make sure she caught at the same time he did. She couldn't stand taking orders, especially from a man, even Peter. You'll grow to like it—Peter kept telling her. *Trust me, I won't*, she was tempted to shoot back.

Maybe she could talk him into a run along the river instead.

Sophie was with Pearl that afternoon—that's why Annie had Jackie along. She glanced over at her. Jackie still seemed listless, her face tired and drawn as it had been all day.

"You okay?" Annie asked.

"I'm tired. I guess I'm not sleeping very well. I thought I was getting over it, but the new bombing brought it all back." A tear slid down her cheek. She scrounged a tissue from her purse and blew her nose. "I know this is going to sound weird, but I've been seeing Mary Alice."

"I keep thinking I see her, too," Annie said. It had happened day before yesterday. Annie was walking to her car after work. A young blond woman crossed the street, dressed in a suit and carrying a briefcase. Before she could stop herself, Annie called out, "Mary Alice!" Of course, Annie caught herself right away. She felt foolish and very sad.

"Not thinking that I see her. Really *seeing her* seeing her," Jackie said.

They were stopped at a light. Jackie fingered the crystal she wore around her neck. Annie knew she was into holistic healing and auras—but talking to the dead?

"Don't look at me that way," Jackie said with a tired laugh. "You don't have to worry. I'm not going crazy or anything."

The light changed and Annie accelerated down Prospect Street toward Mem Drive. "So you saw her?"

Now Jackie had her hands in her lap. She was kneading one over the other. "It happened this morning. I woke up with this strong feeling that I wasn't alone. It was dark in the room, but I could see something, a shadow at the foot of my bed. I had this really strong sense that someone was there. I got scared. I mean, what if it was Joe?

"Then I heard her. Not a sound, really, more like sparks passing through me, like she was channeling words to me instead of saying them. She was calling my name."

Annie listened, driving on automatic pilot as traffic crawled along Mem Drive. She almost didn't see the man in running shorts who was trying to cross the street in the crosswalk—a foolhardy thing to do in this town. Jackie braced herself against the dashboard as the car lurched to a halt.

"But here's the thing," Jackie went on. "I know this is crazy because she's dead, but I wanted to ask her if she was all right. I tried to say something but I couldn't make a sound. I couldn't even raise my head. My chest felt heavy, like someone poured cement all over me.

"Then Sophie came into my bedroom. She asked who I was talking to. Did I have a bad dream? I could tell she couldn't see Mary Alice. She crawled into bed with me. By then, Mary Alice was gone." Jackie held a trembling fist to her mouth. "Sophie said, 'Who were you talking to, Mommy?' Annie, do you think she heard Mary Alice, too?"

Annie turned up Peter's street. She didn't know what to say. The rational part of her knew this was nothing more than Jackie's heart playing tricks on her. Still, there was something intoxicating about the possibility that Mary Alice wasn't simply gone, forever gone from existence, that she might be watching over them from another place and trying to communicate.

Annie pulled up in front of the house. Peter's car wasn't there yet. Pearl was sitting on the front steps wearing lavender sweatpants and a matching zippered sweatshirt. Mr. Kuppel, Pearl's long-time "friend," who was semiretired and worked part-time at a local video store, was raking leaves. Annie was glad they weren't huddled inside watching the news, which was undoubtedly reporting every bomb threat and pundit's theory.

She tooted the horn and got out. Mr. Kuppel paused and waved. He leaned against the rake, took off his cap, and ran his arm across his forehead. His zippered tan jacket stretched across his ample middle and his face was flushed. Jackie got out of the car and shaded her eyes.

With a shrill, kamikaze scream, Sophie came tearing out from the side of the house, took a flying leap, and landed in the leaves. Annie laughed. Jumping into leaf piles used to send her sister, Abby, into sneezing fits, but that never stopped her.

Sophie lay there in a fit of giggles, tossing leaves in the air. Jackie could try all she wanted, but no amount of pink ruffles and hair ribbons was going to get the tomboy out of that little girl.

"She's helping," Mr. Kuppel said, poker-faced.

"Such a help," Pearl said, heaving herself to her feet. She unfolded an oversized paper bag and went over to the leaf pile. "Okay, young lady," she said. She opened the bag and set it on the lawn. "In here."

Sophie did a somersault. Then she stood and dutifully began gathering armfuls of leaves and loading them into the bag.

"How come I can't get her to do that at home?" Jackie asked.

Jackie went over to Sophie and brushed the leaves out of her hair. When she came back, she was holding a fancy pink barrette, festooned with ribbons and beads, one even Annie would have loved when she was Sophie's age.

"Joe gave it to her," Jackie said.

Annie knew from Jackie's guilty look that it had been a recent gift. It was easy to tell Jackie to turn her back on Joe, drive him out of her life—obviously it was a whole lot harder for Jackie to do it.

"Oh, he's not bothering us or anything. He left it at school for Sophie. He misses her."

Men like Joe were so much more appealing at a distance, and they knew just which strings to pull. If he couldn't get Jackie to talk to him, he'd seduce Sophie; if he couldn't do it in person, he'd do it with gifts.

"She misses him. Sleeps in one of his old T-shirts. She won't even let me wash it. Says it'll wash out his smell." Jackie brushed away a tear. "She thinks it's her fault. I keep telling her it's nothing she did."

Just then Peter pulled up. Annie wasn't used to seeing him driving the silver Miata. He had that guy-thing about cars. Used to drive a really cool antique Beamer, which unfortunately was no longer among the living. Since then, he'd been through a couple of rentals and a boring Subaru. The Miata suited him, though it was hilarious when all six-foot-plus of him climbed out of that itsy-bitsy car, like a humongous clown getting out of a miniature fire truck. Annie hadn't told him that, though she had to agree, the car was a blast to drive. It hugged the road on the nastiest curves, and stopped on a dime.

Sophie ran over as he came up the walk. "Petey! Petey! Petey!" she cried. To Annie's shock and amazement, he grinned. Even Annie couldn't get away with calling him that. Sophie took a flying leap into his arms. He lifted her over his head, twirled around once, and gently put her back down.

Sophie tugged at his trouser leg until he bent over. She whispered something. He thought for a moment, rummaged in one back pocket, then the other one, then his jacket pocket. Made a big show of finding nothing. Finally, he reached into a hip pocket and, in mock amazement, drew out a roll of Lifesavers and gave it to Sophie.

Poor Peter. He was completely smitten. Annie could just see it, he'd be feeding their kid candy, Pearl would be plying her with potato latkes, and Annie'd be wondering how in the hell she'd gotten herself knocked up.

Solemn-faced, Sophie opened the package. She took out a red Lifesaver, held it up to the light, and then slid it into her mouth.

Jackie put the barrette back in Sophie's hair. She took Sophie's hand. "We'd better be going," she called over to Pearl. "Thanks for everything."

"Daddy," Sophie squeaked, watching a dark pickup truck with a winch on the back pull up at the curb. The window rolled down.

Annie exchanged a look with Peter. How the hell did Joe Klevinski know Jackie and Sophie were there? Peter went over and said something to Pearl and Mr. Kuppel.

The door of the truck complained with a metal-on-metal noise when Klevinski opened it and lumbered out. He looked bedraggled, with his shirttails hanging out, his dark hair lank and greasy, and his face covered with stubble. Annie wondered if he was drunk.

"Hey, sweetheart," he said to Jackie. He turned back to the car and pulled out a bouquet of roses.

Slick routine. He'd be all sweetness and light until Jackie dropped the restraining order and let him move back in.

Jackie was standing there, rooted to the spot, her eyes wide and mouth open, as if she didn't know which way to go. She gave a strangled cry as Sophie broke free and ran to her father.

Klevinski crouched and held his arms open. "Who's my little girl?"

"I am! I am!"

He scooped her up and pressed his face into her hair. He drew back and took a good look at her.

"What's that in your mouth?"

Sophie swallowed. "Nothing."

Klevinski examined one side of her face, then the other. He took one of her hands and turned it over, examining the fingernails. He frowned. With men like him, it was about control, right down to what you could eat and when you could go to the bathroom. Annie was relieved when he let Sophie slither out of his grasp and she ran back to Jackie.

Jackie crouched and put her arms firmly around Sophie's waist. She gave Annie a quick glance, as if for a shot of courage. Then she fixed her husband with a hard look. "You're not supposed to be here."

He held out the flowers. You had to give him credit, the pale yellow, oversized roses, the petals' tips tinged with raspberry, looked like the kind you paid a bundle for at one of those fancy florists in Harvard Square.

He moved in what seemed like slow motion toward Jackie. "I got these for you. At least you could let me drive you home."

Annie moved to intercept him on one side, Peter on the other.

Klevinski hesitated and stared hard at Annie. "Who the hell are you, and why don't you mind your own business? This is between me and my wife."

"Jackie, why don't you take Sophie inside to wash up," Peter said.

Sophie struggled to see over her shoulder as Jackie and Pearl hustled her away, into the house.

Klevinski eyed Peter, then Annie. His eyes flickered recognition. "You . . . you're the bitch who—"

Annie wanted to kick him in the balls and see him double over, then chop him behind the head and drop him to the ground. Instead, she took out her cell phone and gave him what she hoped was a placid stare. "Violating a restraining order. You know what that means? Go directly to jail."

Klevinski tossed a look toward the house and raised his voice. "She's my wife. Sophie is my daughter. They belong to me."

"*Belong* to you?" Annie said, outrage coursing through her. "Your shoes belong to you. Some poor Doberman pinscher might have the misfortune of belonging to you. Your wife and daughter are human beings. You don't own them."

She started to dial. With a swipe of his arm, Klevinski sent the cell phone flying. He pushed past her, heading for the house.

Now Peter was blocking his way with Mr. Kuppel for backup, the rake gripped across his body like a lance.

"It's my wife in there," Klevinski brayed, getting in Peter's face and poking him in the chest.

Peter shoved him. "It's my home in there. This is private property, and you're trespassing."

Klevinski came back sputtering. "Jackie!" he bellowed. He hurled the roses on the lawn, reared back, and swung wildly.

Peter caught his wrist and held it. "Your daughter is in the house." His words had a quiet intensity. "She could be watching right now. Is this what you want her to see, you brawling and behaving like a thug?"

"Jackie . . ." Klevinski said, more of a plea this time. He seemed chastened for the moment.

Peter let go of the wrist and Klevinski stumbled back.

"You're leaving," Peter said. "Now!" The word dropped like a stone in front of Klevinski.

Klevinski gave Peter a hostile glare. He rubbed his wrist and fisted and unfisted his hand. His gaze slid over to Mr. Kuppel and he gave a smirk of contempt. Then he shifted to Annie. She could smell his sour breath. His look was one of pure bottled rage. His gaze traveled down, lingering on her chest.

Peter came over and put his arm around Annie. His strong hand squeezing her shoulder was all that kept her from smashing her knee into the SOB's groin.

"I think you'd best be on your way," Peter said.

Klevinski gave one final look toward the house before turning to go. Annie felt her heart pounding as he sauntered back to his truck. She could imagine him reaching inside for a tire iron or wrench, and coming back swinging. She hadn't brought her gun, and Mace was in her backpack on the floor of the car. She didn't relax until his truck disappeared down the street.

• • •

They never did get to the river. Instead, Annie and Peter sat in Pearl's kitchen with Jackie, drinking hot tea. Sophie napped on the living room sofa.

"He says it's dangerous for me to be working in a lawyer's office, what with courthouses and law schools getting blown up," Jackie said.

"You told him where you work?" Annie asked.

"Well, not exactly where. But he knows it's an attorney's office." Jackie picked at the cake on her plate. "I'm sorry, Annie. He was worried that I was still working at Harvard, that I could get hurt." She blinked back tears. "I don't know how he found out about Sophie coming here after school."

"He's not supposed to be calling you," Annie said.

"He didn't. I called him." Jackie crossed her arms over her chest. "I'm sorry. I had to ask him about—"

Annie felt more sad than angry. Something compelled Jackie to continue her dance with this man, enabled her to convince herself that something good could come of it. Annie shrank from the look Peter was giving her, though she knew she deserved it. She'd never forgive herself if something happened to Pearl. And it would be only a matter of time before Klevinski figured out where Jackie worked. Then he could visit anytime the spirit moved him. Jackie would be a sitting duck, and Chip and Annie would be sitting right there with her.

"He says he's going to take classes," Jackie said. "Anger management. And he's joined AA. He's trying to change."

Was she kidding?

"People *can* change, Annie. Really they can."

Annie didn't trust herself to say anything.

• • •

"So can someone like that change?" Annie asked Peter.

Jackie and Sophie had gone home, and Peter and Annie were at

Toscanini's, Annie in a chair, Peter with his butt perched on the windowsill. Apparently no one was afraid of a bomb in an ice cream parlor, even one wedged midway between the Cambridge Courthouse and Harvard. There was a line out the door.

"Sure, some people can change," Peter answered in that noncommittal tone of his that drove Annie bonkers. "With the right help."

"You really believe that?"

Peter gave her an indulgent smile. "Sure. It's possible. Treatment is like peeling an onion. Anger management is the top layer. It helps control behavior. Then there's got to be substance-abuse treatment. Alcohol and drugs lower inhibitions."

"He's a heroin addict," Annie said. "*Was*, according to Jackie. But then, so was she, and she's clean now."

"Going a level deeper, talk therapy helps. If the person can understand where the anger is coming from, he might take a moment and say: 'Is what I feel really appropriate to this situation, and do I really want to engage in this behavior?'"

Annie took a lick of burnt caramel ice cream. With its toasted-marshmallow-skin taste, add some chocolate sauce and graham cracker crumbs and you'd have yourself a s'more. S'mores made her think of Girl Scouts. In Girl Scouts she'd gotten introduced to gourmet goodies like s'mores and Rice Krispy Treats. She'd also learned useful stuff like how to hook potholders and make a rice-and-bean mosaic of swans. Indirectly through Girl Scouts, Annie first found out about the unspeakable things wives and children kept quiet about, because that was where she met Charlotte Florence. Charlotte was as tall as Annie and quiet . . . in fact, she reminded Annie a whole lot of Jackie Klevinski, except that her long hair was black, not brown. Until then, family violence was something Annie had witnessed only on TV.

"You are such an optimist, and I am so not," Annie said.

"Ah, and vhen did you first start having dese feelings?" Peter asked, affecting a bad Sigmund Freud accent.

Annie smiled, but she was remembering Mrs. Florence's battered face, the nose broken and the skin around the eye purple from new bruises, yellow from old ones.

"Tell me what you're thinking," Peter said.

Annie told him about Charlotte, and how her parents would fight whenever Annie slept over. Annie and Charlotte would hide under the bed and listen, Annie terrified that at any moment the door would crash open and Mr. Florence would come looking for them. Charlotte had been embarrassed and humiliated. She'd made Annie promise never to tell anyone.

Mrs. Florence died when they were in high school. No one ever said if she got sick, or committed suicide, or if Mr. Florence killed her. She just "passed away," and Charlotte stopped coming to school.

Annie still had dreams about them, she told Peter, nightmares really. She dreamed she was under the bed with Charlotte, listening to the Florences fight. Then Mr. Florence would come stomping into the room, yelling for Charlotte. He'd raise the bed skirts . . . that's when Annie would try to wake herself up.

Peter reached out and touched Annie's hand. "Dreaming. That's one of the ways the mind helps us deal with unresolved issues."

Annie took another bite of ice cream. Now it tasted bitter.

There was laughter from a group of college-age kids up at the counter. Then a woman's voice, "Now y'all quit makin' fun of me." Annie looked up, expecting to see Mary Alice standing there in the group.

"Do you believe in ghosts?" she asked Peter.

Peter's eyebrows shot up. "Have I ever mentioned that a person can get whiplash talking to you?"

"Like to keep you guessing."

She told him about Jackie "seeing"—she drew quotation marks in the air around the word—Mary Alice at the foot of her bed. "Jackie says she was awake, but she couldn't move."

Peter nodded understanding. "It's something called cataplexy, or sleep paralysis. She was in a hypnopompic state." Only Peter could make fancy words sound reassuring. "That's the transition of semi-consciousness between sleeping and waking. For some people, it's a time of hallucination."

"Like dreaming?"

"Sort of. Intense dreaming, a little more like hypnosis. There's often the same hyperintensity of imagery. It's this contradictory thing where your eyes are open and you're seeing visions at the same time." Peter leaned forward, gesturing as he explained. "When you think about it, Mother Nature is pretty careful with us."

He had an endless capacity to be fascinated by the intricacies of the human mind. Annie felt a rush of tenderness. She wanted to reach out and touch his face, outline his jaw and chin with her fingertips.

"While she's given us dreams to help us deal with our feelings, she's also disconnected the motor system during sleep. Otherwise, we might go running around, smashing into walls in our sleep. But sometimes, when you're in the borderland between sleep and wakefulness, your dream factory continues full blast. You're awake, but you feel like you can't move because your motor system is still disconnected, and at the same time you can get these very intense visions. It's not uncommon."

Another memory came back to Annie. She was young, maybe six years old, and it was right after her grandfather died. She'd be trying to fall asleep and there he'd be, sitting at the foot of her bed. He'd had on his favorite red-and-green plaid flannel shirt, and she could smell his pipe. It wasn't scary at all. He sat there and told her the story of Rumplestiltskin, her favorite fairy tale, and she fell asleep.

"It can happen when you're falling asleep, too," Peter said when she told him about it. "We've got another twelve-syllable word for that. When you're under stress and your defenses are lowered, like when you're grieving, you can become more susceptible. Did it upset Jackie?"

"She was excited, actually. Do you think she needs to see a shrink?"

Peter gave her a funny look. "A woman married to an abusive husband for seven years, who's still calling him on the phone, and you're asking me if she needs therapy?"

"You know what I mean. To deal with these visions."

"Probably not. It's pretty normal. Sounds like she's working them through by herself." There was a pause, and Peter looked away. "Actually, seeing someone you care for who's died can feel like a gift."

Annie didn't ask, but she was pretty sure Peter was talking from firsthand experience. She knew she'd never have him one hundred percent as she might have if he'd never been married to Kate, and she knew the feeling of loss was something he'd never be without. That was okay. If Kate visited him from time to time, that was okay, too.

THE NEXT morning, Peter left home in what should have been plenty of time for morning meeting. He made a stop at a crowded Starbucks, then drove to the Pearce, where he sat waiting his turn in a line of cars backed up at the gate. For the first time in the ten-plus years he'd been working there, a uniformed guard stood outside the gatehouse Peter had mistaken for a telephone booth the first time he'd driven onto the grounds. The guard was checking IDs before letting anyone drive in. Seemed like a ridiculous precaution since the grounds went on for unfenced acres. Anyone with the determination and stamina could wander in on foot, armed with as many Uzis as he could carry.

By the time the guard eyeballed Peter's ID and gave the inside of his car a perfunctory glance, Peter was officially late. Then he had to poke along at the required ten miles an hour over the road that snaked across the rolling grounds, past manicured lawns and geometrically shaped bushes.

Peter wasn't surprised to find the parking lot nearest the Neuro-psych Unit full. He had to park in the big lot and hike back.

"It's your fault I'm late," he told Kwan when he arrived and handed Kwan his chai latté. "You're the one who got me started on yuppie coffee. What a mob at eight in the morning."

"I've been here since six," Kwan said, sounding surly. His impec-cably tailored suit did look a bit rumpled. "Catch up on your beauty sleep?" He opened the container. "You'll put this on my tab?"

Peter peeled back the lid of his double espresso and took a sip. There was nothing like that first strong, solid hit of caffeine. He checked the whiteboard. There were the names of eighteen patients. That meant the unit was full. Full was good. It kept hospital bean counters off their backs.

Sunlight was trying to make its way in through the conference room windows, which, like the windows of most psychiatric hospi-tals, were covered with mesh screening. With its massive fireplace and ornate mantel, the narrow room seemed lopsided. It was half of what had once been an elegant sitting room in the good old days when the rich and famous spent months at the Pearce getting their beaks clipped and their feathers soothed.

Peter took Gloria's latté out of the bag just as she arrived, breathless.

"Sorry. Trying to get a few things sorted out," she said, digging into her pocket for money. Peter waved her off.

Gloria had been in early, too, but the collar of her white oxford shirt was stiff, and the crease was still in her khaki trousers. It was her short hair that was going in all directions, the comb lines long gone.

She removed the lid and took a sniff. She sat and drank, then sat back and sighed, a look of contentment on her face. How on earth could decaf be that satisfying? It was like drinking nonalcoholic beer. Why bother?

When the rest of the staff arrived—social worker, occupational therapist, a couple of interns, the new psych fellow, and two mental health workers—Peter started the meeting. They did a quick once-around of what was up. Everyone agreed there was an extra level of agitation on the unit. The bombings remained the *topic du jour* in the common room and it was coming up in every group.

"No matter how I try to steer them to individual work, the focus keeps shifting back to these bombings," said the social worker.

Even the demented patients were affected, Gloria told them. Take Mr. Sanchez, for example. He had no idea what year it was, where he was, or whether he'd eaten breakfast. Now all of a sudden he was talking nonstop about the time he and his brother had been attacked by a machete-wielding robber in Colombia fifty years ago.

"If you ask him specifically about the bombing, he hasn't a clue. But it's as if he's channeling everyone else's anxiety."

Peter wasn't surprised. The emotional component survived long after dementia destroyed short-term memory. Mr. Sanchez had probably forgotten whatever he may have heard people say about the bombings, or even that there had been bombings; what stuck was the aroma of fear, which in turn hooked itself onto scary events in the past that he could recall.

They settled down to work, starting with the new admission. Peter pulled the file from the rack and read out the salient points. "Rudy Ravitch. Male. Thirty-five years old. Security guard at the Cambridge Courthouse. He was on duty day before yesterday." Around the table there was a collective murmur of sympathy. "Struck in the head by debris. Unconscious for a brief period. Ten at the scene on the Glasgow Coma Scale." Mild head injury. That hardly rated a trip to the Pearce. There had to be more.

"He was taking a break when the bomb went off," Kwan explained. "A chunk of debris came down on his head. EMTs treated him at the scene. Took him to the ER. Kept him overnight, then released him. Yesterday he shows up at the ER at the Faulkner. Dizziness. Shortness of breath. Severe chest pain."

He went on. "They worked him up. CT scan. EKG. Blood tests. Nothing. Now they've got him attached to a Holter monitor. No doubt about it, there's something going on, but it doesn't look like a heart attack. They release him. On his way out, he collapses again. This morning they ship him to us to rule out PTSD."

Ruling *out* post-traumatic stress disorder involved ruling *in* an insult to the brain that could account for the symptoms. "No history of seizure?" Peter asked.

Kwan shook his head.

"Not on any meds? No drugs in his system?"

"Nothing to write home about. He'd taken a couple of Advil, but that was—" Kwan broke off and sat forward, alert. There was a commotion in the hall.

Gloria and Kwan exchanged a look, and everyone headed for the door. A heavyset man Peter hadn't met before was in the corridor, bent nearly double and groaning. One of the nurses was propping him up, helping him in through the doorway from the screen porch.

A well-practiced team, they sprang into action. Peter and Kwan rushed over to assist the patient, while Gloria went for a wheelchair. The man had his hand clutched to his chest and his face was glazed with sweat. A three-inch gash in his head, lined with stitches, was purple against his pale skin. This had to be their new patient, Rudy Ravitch.

His face twisted in agony as they eased his rigid body into the wheelchair. "Oh, god, it hurts. I can't breathe. My back—" he said, gasping. "I'm dying."

Kwan listened to Ravitch's chest while Peter crouched in front of him.

"Just keep breathing and try to relax," Peter said. He could smell cigarette smoke. The nurse had probably taken Ravitch outside for a smoke. "You're going to be all right."

After examining Ravitch, Kwan called a technician to administer an EKG. Later that morning Kwan called Peter in his office. As they'd both suspected, test results ruled out heart attack. That left the default diagnosis: panic attack. The symptoms were nearly identical to a heart attack, just as painful and terrifying to experience but not life-threatening. After what Ravitch had witnessed, panic attack seemed an entirely appropriate aftermath.

The standard treatment for panic attacks would have been an anxiolytic such as Xanax and a few weeks of behavioral therapy, but Ravitch's head injury complicated things. Kwan ordered an MRI. They needed a closer look at Ravitch's brain before deciding what to do next.

• • •

"I heard this place was a country club. So where's the first tee?" Ravitch asked with a nervous chuckle. He and Peter were sitting opposite one another in the examining room. Peter had asked him if he'd be willing to talk to MacRae, and he'd agreed.

"So, you play golf?" Peter asked. Ravitch nodded. "Unfortunately, you're fifty years too late. There used to be a golf course right on the grounds."

Ravitch looked around the room, taking in the floral watercolor on the wall. His look said: How the hell did I end up here?

"You a shrink?" he asked, addressing a blue-and-white Chinese vase lamp base.

"A neuropsychologist. That's someone who studies the relationship between behavior and what goes on in the brain."

Ravitch's jaw tightened. "I'm not crazy."

"Yes, well, that's our working assumption as well."

He seemed startled, and for the first time he looked right at Peter.

"And since your problem doesn't seem to be heart disease, either, the likeliest scenario is that you're having panic attacks."

Peter told him he wanted to hear more about what had happened to him, and then he was going to administer some psychological tests to help determine the best treatment.

"I smoke," Ravitch said. It sounded like a non sequitur, but it wasn't. "That's what I was doing when it happened. I was out in front of the building, lighting up. My buddy, Leon, he's an ex-smoker, so he's sympathetic. The other guys, they're all a bunch of stiffs.

"So Leon tells me it's okay, he'll cover for me." He grimaced and shook his head. "You know what happened to Leon?" His voice broke and his shoulders heaved. Tears flowed down his cheeks. For a few moments, he couldn't say anything. "Pieces. He got blown into pieces. His wife won't even get a whole body to bury. Jesus Christ, what a shitty thing to happen."

There was a box of tissues on the counter. Peter got it and put it between them. Ravitch took one and wiped his eyes, then blew his nose. Peter waited before going on.

"And what happened to you?"

Ravitch held the tissue tight in his fist. "Me?" He blew his nose again. "I'm outside, and the next thing I know I'm on the ground. I can't see. I'm sitting there, trying to figure out what the hell just happened. It's really quiet and I realize I can't hear anything. I clap my hands and I can't hear them. Even after I wipe the blood out of my eyes I still can't see straight. But I can see enough to know that there must have been a bomb, and I can tell it was in the lobby. I try to stand up and the place starts spinning and I'm back on my ass again." His voice shook with emotion. "All I know is I've got to find Leon and I can't fuckin' see, I can't fuckin' hear, and I can't fuckin' stand." His face contorted and his eyes screwed up. Tears started again. He bent double and put his face in his hands.

Peter sat back and waited. Ravitch would need to return many times to the moment of the explosion, to the minutes before and after, and to all the surrounding events before he'd be able to talk or think about them without breaking down.

Finally Ravitch sat back. He stared into his lap, the tissues clutched in his fist.

"Sounds like a pretty harrowing experience. How long before your hearing came back?"

"I'm in the ambulance, on the way to the hospital, when I realize, thank god, I can hear the siren. I ask the guys in there with me about Leon but they don't know anything. They take me to the emergency room and stitch me. My head's hurting like hell. They keep me overnight.

"Next morning, I get Leon's number from information. Call his wife. That's when I find out, Leon passed away." His body went slack and he stared out in front of him with vacant eyes.

Ravitch roused himself. He gestured. "I went over to Leon's house. Christ almighty, there's a FOR SALE sign on the lawn. Leon was retiring and they were moving to Florida." He kneaded his hands together. "I'm sitting outside on the porch, taking a smoke. You can't smoke anywhere anymore. For chrissakes, gotta go to New Hampshire to have a beer and a smoke."

"So you're outside?"

"Right. I need a smoke, but I'm trying to make it quick. I light up. Inhale. And that makes my head hurt, so I'm taking little puffs, and all of a sudden I can't breathe. My heart is pounding and chest feels real tight. And my back—it's like someone's driving a knife in be-tween my shoulder blades, driving it and banging it in there. I'm sure I'm having a heart attack."

"So you went to the hospital?"

"Again. They put me on the machines. Doc comes in later and says I'm all clear. My heart's fine. Then what the fuck was it? Stress, he tells me." Ravitch raised his eyebrows. "Can you believe that? And I'm wondering how many martinis this idiot had for lunch. They want to keep me for a couple more hours, just to be on the safe side. So I get to lie there, bored shitless, there's not even a TV in the room. I can't walk to the bathroom by myself because I get dizzy every time I get up.

"Finally they let me go. I'm walking out of the building and wham, it happens again."

"Doing anything in particular at the time?"

"Nah," he said. Peter knew what was coming next. "Just having a smoke."

12

MacRae came by the hospital that afternoon to interview Ravitch. Afterward, Peter walked MacRae outside.

"He's just like that woman we interviewed at Annie's office. Doesn't remember a damn thing that's of any use," MacRae said, pausing under the portico overhang outside the unit. "Is that because of the head injury?"

MacRae knew all too well about head injuries. He and Peter first met when MacRae was questioning a surviving witness who'd spent weeks in a coma after being shot in the head. After weeks of questioning, the days-long hole in her memory shrank and she claimed to remember who shot her. But was the memory genuine? Peter and MacRae had been on opposite sides of that question.

"This guy has only a minor head injury. I don't think it's affecting his memory," Peter told MacRae. "Yes, he was unconscious, but only for a few minutes. I'll be surprised if the MRI we've got scheduled shows any significant injury to the brain. His amnesia is more likely due to emotional trauma."

"Emotional trauma? That's good news, right?"

"I'd say. There's a fair chance that he'll recall more over time."

"How much time? We can't afford to wait around. It was four weeks between the bombings. If there's going to be another attack, it could be in a week or two. Isn't there some way to kick-start his memory?"

Too bad MRIs didn't show memories the way they showed blood flow and tumors. But there were other ways.

"Hypnotism," Peter said.

MacRae gave Peter a surprised look.

"What?" Peter asked.

"I don't know, you endorsing hypnosis. Seems kind of 'out there' for, uh, someone like you."

For a stuffy, pointy-headed academic like you was the part MacRae didn't say.

"You're right. I'm not a big fan of hypnosis. It's too easily abused. But in this case, it's possible that Mr. Ravitch actually remembers something significant, he just doesn't know what it is. Maybe he saw the bomber, even the bomb itself, but it had no significance to him. So the memory got stored but it didn't get specially tagged, so now it's not easily accessible. If he's hypnotized, put into a relaxed, hyperalert state, allowed to rescan the entire scene without his normal inhibitions, he should remember all sorts of information, and some of it might be just what you're looking for."

Peter didn't mention another benefit. Hypnosis was sometimes used as a treatment for panic disorders, enabling the victim to revisit the frightening event and, with help, master his own response. That was what repetitive nightmares and repetition compulsions were all about, too—nature's way of revisiting trauma.

"Good." Peter could almost see MacRae's notions about Peter getting reshuffled. "So let's say he's hypnotized and he remembers stuff. How do we know he's not making it up on the spot? Might not even know he's doing it."

Peter was impressed that MacRae recognized this possibility— tough, blue-collar muscle-head that he was. "Bottom line, you can't. Anyone in a hypnotic state is susceptible to suggestions. The one thing you can do is be very careful about how questions are posed. Some people are highly suggestive. You need an expert."

"Can you do it?"

The request brought Peter up short. Despite hypnotism's sideshow reputation, there was really nothing special about it. Just another tool, another way to take advantage of the amazing capabilities of the human mind. He'd been trained in hypnosis. Still, he'd rarely used it, and then only as a therapeutic tool.

"We can pay you, if that's what you're worried about," MacRae said. He wasn't being snide, just stating a fact. "And you won't have to testify. That stuff's not admissible in court anyway. What do you say?"

Peter had worked on plenty of cases, but he'd never assisted police in an ongoing investigation, never hypnotized a witness. But it took him barely a heartbeat to agree. All it took was reminding himself that if he and Chip and Annie had been in the courthouse lobby as scheduled, that would have brought the death toll to an even dozen.

• • •

"Promise you won't make me quack like a duck," Ravitch said, giving a wary look around the treatment room, a small, pleasant space with four easy chairs and a coffee table.

Ravitch had been reluctant to be videotaped being hypnotized. Peter had talked him through it, what it would be like, how the police needed all the help they could get. What sealed it was the promise that Ravitch could see the videotape of his own session. Only then, and with his permission, would Peter give the tape to the investigators.

Ravitch rubbed the palms of his hands on his pant legs and gave a quick glance at the video camera on the tripod behind Peter. "I don't know about this," he said, shifting in his chair as he eyed the microphone on the table as if it were an alien being.

Peter realized he'd better get started before Ravitch changed his mind. He checked the camera one last time and adjusted the lens to compensate for the backlighting from the window behind Ravitch. "You'll see. There's not much to it, really. Just pay attention to what's going on, and try to have the experiences that are suggested to you."

Ravitch rolled his head around and the bones in his neck cracked. He resettled himself in the chair.

Peter sat facing him. "Ready? Here we go. See that bit of black tape on the wall? I'll be referring to that as 'the target.' I'd like you to relax, look steadily at the target, and listen to my voice."

Ravitch stared at the tape, his back stiff, hands gripping the arms of the chair. After a few moments, he gave Peter a nervous glance.

"Try to relax. Look steadily at the target," Peter said, keeping his voice low and even. "You can be hypnotized only if you want to be. Just do your best to concentrate on the target, pay attention to my words, and let it happen. Hypnosis is perfectly normal and . . ." As Peter droned on, Ravitch sank back into the chair. His grip loosened. Relaxation in hypnosis was a lot like the first stages of falling asleep, only Ravitch would still be able to hear Peter's voice and direct his own thoughts.

"Now I want you to imagine you're at the beach on a warm summer day." Ravitch did a slow blink as Peter continued painting an idyllic scene. "You're so relaxed. Your eyes will get heavy, and you will wish strongly that they were closed. Then they will close, as if by themselves. When this happens, just let it."

Ravitch's eyelids began to lower. More, then more. Just when Peter thought he was there, his eyes startled open. It wasn't surprising that someone who worked in security would have a hard time letting down his guard.

Ravitch shifted in his seat. His gaze wavered, then anchored on the target.

Peter tried some relaxation exercises, focusing on different sets of muscles. Ravitch's eyes began to close again. This time his eyes stayed shut. His palms rested open on the chair arms.

"That's good. Now I'm going to count. You will feel yourself going down, down, farther and farther into a deep, restful sleep. One . . . two . . ." Peter counted slowly, his voice like a boat rocking gently in still water. At twenty Peter had to fight drowsiness as his own eyelids began to feel heavy. By thirty, Ravitch was slumped over, his eyes closed.

"Now I want you to realize that you can speak, move, and even open your eyes if I should ask you to do so, and still remain just as hypnotized as you are now." Ravitch stirred in his seat. "Now open your eyes. Can you tell me your name?"

Ravitch slowly sat up and opened his eyes. He ran his tongue over his bottom lip. "Rudy Ravitch."

"Now I'd like you to think back to Tuesday. Three days ago. You're going to work. Can you tell me about that?"

"Damn Green Line. Nowhere to sit, as usual." Ravitch's voice was calm, not quite a monotone.

"Who else is on the train?"

Ravitch's eyes shimmied from side to side. "Some jerk's jabbing his briefcase into my side. Old man in the corner. He's nodding off.

Drooling. Girl next to him gets up. She's got a ring in her belly but-ton." Ravitch sniffed as he watched the imaginary girl walk by. "She smells like lemonade."

"Okay. You're getting off the train. Tell me what happens next."

"I'm walking down Cambridge Street. Crossing the street. The traffic is backed up going into town. I stop for a newspaper. The idiot doesn't want to break a twenty but that's all I've got."

"Good. Okay, now you're at the courthouse."

Peter paused, waiting for the pictures in Ravitch's head to sort themselves. Bit by bit, he took Ravitch through his day, revisiting the time when he'd arrived at work and punched in, flashing forward to his morning break, to lunch in what sounded like the same greasy spoon where Peter had gone with Chip after the explosion. Next he took Rav-itch back to work after lunch. This was the start of the critical half hour during which the police thought the bomb had been planted.

"It's getting crowded," Ravitch said. "People are backing up at the metal detector. I'm watching the new scanner. People swipe the key cards we just started using. There's a woman lawyer. She hasn't got a card yet so she shows me her driver's license and I've got to look her up."

"Can you remember what she looked like? What she was carrying?"

Ravitch's eyes seemed to focus. "Long blond hair, short skirt. Fuck-me sandals." He chuckled. "Legs like a pair of tree stumps."

"Who else do you see?"

"There's a young guy with red hair, a beard, and mustache. Works for the DA. He's talking to his friend and laughing. Swipes his card."

"The redhead. He carrying anything?"

"He's got a briefcase. Big. Leather. Bulging."

"What about the man he's talking to? Has he got anything in his hands?"

"Coffee."

"What time is it?"

"Ten to one. Jeez I need a smoke." Ravitch took a sharp inhale. "I'm trying to get Leon's attention. He's confiscating someone's micro-cassette recorder."

"Can you see who?"

Ravitch screwed up his face, straining for the memory. "Just a dude. Dark hair. Blue jacket. Briefcase."

"Have you seen him before?"

"Maybe. Yeah. Looks familiar. I'm trying to talk to Leon and the guy swipes his card. First time it doesn't take. Must have put it through upside down.

"Leon won't look at me." The cords in Ravitch's neck stood out and he grasped the arms of the chair. "There goes a court officer. A cop. A guy in pinstripes. He's a smoker, I can smell it. God, I need a cigarette.

"Line's shorter now, most everyone that's got to be in is in. *Leon?*" He pantomimed putting a cigarette to his mouth. His face relaxed. "Leon says to go ahead."

"So where do you go?"

"Outside. To one side of the doors. I'm lighting up. My hands are shaking. Jesus Christ, I gotta cut back. This is insane." Ravitch closed his eyes and took a long inhale and exhale. In an instant his shoulders relaxed, his face went slack. He sat back in his chair. He held his hand as if he were holding the cigarette between his thumb and forefinger.

"What do you see?"

"One of the secretaries up on the fifth floor. She's coming in. Low-cut sweater. Jeez, what is she, giving it away? She waves at me. Couple of people, a man and a kid, leaving the building. He's got on a tan windbreaker. Another man walks out the door. A reporter. He's got press tags around his neck."

"You recognize him?"

"Dunno. Maybe. Now there's more people leaving. A couple of lawyers maybe? I can't see their faces. And a police officer. He's running out the door." Ravitch inhaled sharply through pursed lips, like he was taking one final drag. "I gotta get back. I stick the butt in the sand in the container by the door and . . ." Ravitch's voice trailed off.

Peter waited for him to go on, but he just hung there looking perplexed, his mouth agape.

"What's the next thing you remember?"

Ravitch coughed and clutched at his throat. "The smoke. I can't breathe." He put his palm to his temple and grimaced. "My head. Christ almighty, my head hurts."

"Where are you?"

Ravitch's face screwed up and there was fear in his eyes. "On the ground. What the hell happened? There's a guy in an orange suit, poking at my eyelid."

There was no point in continuing forward in time. Peter doubled back and asked Ravitch to return to the time before and during his cigarette break and focus on each of the people he saw entering and leaving the building. Then he had him go back again. Each time through there was a new detail or two, but for the most part the story was the same. Just a lot of innocuous comings and goings. And then the bomb. Who knew what was significant.

• • •

That next afternoon Peter brought the videotape over to MacRae at the police station. They met in a large room that looked like a deserted command post. A conference table was littered with empty coffee cups and smelled of the pepperoni pizza MacRae had sprung for. Tacked to the walls were maps and crime-scene photos, rows of mug shots of men, presumably suspects, and pictures of victims.

According to a timeline drawn on the whiteboard, flyers had been noted first by witnesses in Harvard Square three days before the law school bombing, in East Cambridge two days before the courthouse went. The bombings had happened on Tuesdays, exactly four weeks apart. Peter wondered if that would turn out to be a pattern.

MacRae surveyed the room. "I'm supposed to have a dozen officers working on this case. Know what most of them are out doing right now? Checking 'suspicious packages'"—MacRae drew quotation marks in the air—"called in by vigilant citizens."

Peter's mother had been complaining just that morning that their local Shaw's market had security guards checking people entering.

"Never thought I'd say it," MacRae went on, lifting a piece of pizza out of the box, "but I'm grateful for the suits the feds sent over."

Peter helped himself to a triangle of pizza. Not half bad. Put enough pepperoni and melted mozzarella on cardboard and that wouldn't be half bad, either.

"Top brass can't jerk them around like they can the rest of us," MacRae added.

MacRae wiped his hands on a napkin and inserted the videotape Peter had brought into the VCR. The monitor flickered. Then Ravitch came into focus. *Promise you won't make me quack like a duck.* MacRae began taking notes.

They watched it through. As the tape rewound, Peter said, "For a while there, I was afraid he wasn't going to go under."

"You sure he did?"

MacRae's skepticism didn't surprise Peter. "Some people are harder to hypnotize than others. But yeah, I think he was hypnotized."

MacRae shifted in his seat. "I don't know. Just seemed too easy."

"It *is* easy," Peter said, gesturing with a pizza crust. "You're awake, but you're relaxed and much more able to remember details."

"Or make them up."

"There's always that risk."

MacRae ejected the tape. "So what do we know now that we didn't know before? Not much."

Peter got up and went over to the lineup of photos on the wall. Any of them could have been one of the men Ravitch saw.

"I sure would like to know if any of these guys showed in the security video that got blown away in the blast." MacRae scraped off a glob of cheese stuck to the pizza box. It was all that was left.

"Have they been able to salvage the computers?" Peter asked. "You could track down anyone who used a key card to get in that morning."

"The bomber might have used a stolen one."

"So talk to anyone whose key card got scanned that morning, then find out if any of them weren't there. Maybe the person can tell you where and when the card got lost. You'd have one more point to put on your map in terms of where this guy hangs out, one more place you know he blends in."

MacRae looked mildly impressed. "They're working on retrieving data from the computer's hard drive. We should have it soon. Still, sure doesn't feel like much to go on. I'd feel a whole lot better if we had more hard evidence tying this bombing to the first."

"There's the posters."

"Corroborating witnesses would be better. If we can put a suspect at both crime scenes . . ." MacRae got a toothpick out of his pocket and began to pick one of his back teeth. "What about the woman I interviewed who was at the law school and knew the first victim? You think she'd go for being hypnotized?"

Peter thought about Jackie with her auras and conversations with the dead. She'd probably be eager to be hypnotized, maybe a little too eager.

"Annie might be able to convince her. She's working for Annie and Chip."

"I didn't know that," MacRae said, writing himself another note. "I'll talk to Annie about it."

"No, I will," Peter said, the words coming out louder than he'd intended them to.

MacRae's pencil froze midword. His smile said *you poor sucker.*

"Annie wants us to keep putting pressure on that woman's estranged husband, Klevinski," MacRae said, indicating one of the photos. "Poor guy. I sure as hell wouldn't want to be on Annie's shit list."

Peter examined the photograph. He barely recognized Klevinski from their confrontation in front of Peter's house.

MacRae went on. "Anyway, we checked. One interesting thing— turns out he had demolition training in the army."

Demolition training? Peter wouldn't have pegged Joe Klevinski as the bomber. Married (twice) and not all that bright—that was two strikes against him.

"I told Annie, if that second bomb was planted at the courthouse when we think it was, then this Klevinski guy has got an alibi," MacRae said. "He was at a job interview."

"I thought he had a job."

"Got fired. Maybe cops coming back time after time to check up on him made his boss nervous. Losing his wife, his kid, and his job—he's one angry SOB." MacRae shrugged. "I keep telling Annie, you can't arrest a guy for being pissed."

Peter scanned the rest of the ten or so other sullen faces tacked up on the board. Several looked familiar. The Middle Eastern–looking fellow with a bald head and a bushy mustache and beard looked a lot like a physics professor he'd had. The guy next to him resembled the manager of Peter's local deli. Peter knew he'd make a lousy eyewitness. Besides, he'd found out the hard way that appearances could be deceiving. Ralston Bridges had had a baby face and an engaging smile. The cold, dead eyes were the only giveaway to his true psychopathy. Peter's stomach wrenched as he thought about Kate. She was never far from his thoughts. He took out a handkerchief and blew his nose.

MacRae gave him a sideways look. "Maybe you've got some time to talk about these characters?"

"You mean look at their records?"

"Why not? Even interview a couple of them? And we could use some help developing a fuller profile." MacRae looked down at his shoes. "Actually, the profiler who's supposed to be helping us is stuck on a case down in Texas. Will be for a couple of weeks. I told one of the federal agents what you said about the kind of person who'd be capable of a crime like this. He suggested we have you look at the suspects." MacRae eyed Peter and tucked the toothpick into the corner of his mouth. "So, you got time?"

Peter took off his glasses and rubbed the bridge of his nose. "Sure." *In for a penny, in for a pound.*

13

Annie was surprised when Peter asked her to find out if Jackie would be willing to undergo hypnosis. She knew his opinion of hypnotists: bunkum artists. It was pretty weird, too, Peter and Mac working the same side of the street for a change, maybe even appreciating what the other one brought to the table.

Annie called Peter Monday morning to tell him Jackie was looking forward to it. "She wondered if maybe you could help her remember her past lives. Did you know that Shirley MacLaine was Charlemagne's lover?"

"Yes, well, I don't think we'll be going that far back." Annie could imagine him saying that with a perfectly straight face.

Annie glanced out her office window. There it was again, a florist delivery van double-parked in front of their office. Joe Klevinski was pulling out all the stops, trying to worm his way back into Jackie's affections. If it had been up to Annie, she'd have broken off the flower

heads and sent the stems back to the sonofabitch with an appropriately worded note telling him just where he could stick 'em.

Out of the blue, it occurred to Annie that Peter had never given
her flowers. Plenty of bottles of wine, but not a single rose, long-
stemmed or otherwise. She'd brought him flowers once, a bunch of
daisies, after he mangled his ankle tackling a man who'd been pointing a gun at her. That act of bravery trumped flowers any day of the
week. Still, Annie couldn't resist ragging on him.

"Hey, how come you never give me flowers?"

She looked out into the reception area. The flowers were coming
through the front door. The delivery man was nearly hidden behind
the elaborate arrangement. Jackie was at her desk with her hand over
her mouth, obviously wowed.

"Why bother? Flowers couldn't possibly be as fair as you."

She smiled in spite herself. He was such a consummate bullshit
artist.

The delivery man put the flowers on Jackie's desk. She cupped
her hand around a white lily, bent over, and smelled.

"I guess I'm just too easy," Annie said.

That cracked Peter up.

Now Jackie picked a little envelope from among the flowers,
opened the flap, and slid out the card. She smiled and her eyes
glowed. She was falling for it.

"So all I have to do is give you flowers and I can have my way with
you? Is that how it works?" Annie could just see him twirling an
imaginary mustache. "I'll have to try that. We're on for tomorrow
night?"

"Tuesday, right," Annie said, drawing back as Jackie glanced in
her direction. Jackie knew what Annie thought about her husband
and his dogged attempts to win her back.

After Annie hung up, she went out and admired the flowers. She leaned over to smell them. She gagged on the cloying, sweet, over-ripe odor of the lilies. It was the smell of something rotting. She had a vision of a funeral home with heavy mahogany furniture and Scarlett O'Hara window drapes. She remembered the first time she'd been to one. It was her friend Charlotte's mother's funeral. Lilies, white ones, had flanked the coffin where Mrs. Florence lay, her face the unnatural pink of pancake makeup. Charlotte was there, pressed up against her father, his arms holding her tight.

"He hasn't been bothering us," Jackie said in response to nothing. She handed Annie a handwritten note on a slip of paper. "Luke Thompson called while you were on the phone."

Annie read the note. "Meet them at Trattoria Pulcinella tomorrow night 7:30. Call him today if you can't." Below that it said, "Don't tell Abby."

That was sweet. Maybe an early birthday surprise for Abby? Annie tucked the note into her pocket. She'd bring Peter along. He wouldn't mind the change of plan. He loved Pulcinella—he'd introduced her to the place.

Annie glanced at the card from the flowers lying on Jackie's desk. All it said was: "Missing you. I'm sorry." He probably meant it, too.

• • •

It was drizzling out and the air smelled of wet leaves when Annie and Peter got to Pulcinella. Tiny lights twinkled around the window of the storefront restaurant, tucked into a residential Cambridge street.

"Mmm, smell that garlic and tomatoes," Peter said, as he pushed open the heavy glass-paneled wood door for Annie, "and rosemary and olives."

All Annie could smell was fresh bread. "Show-off," she said, giving him a light kiss on the cheek as she brushed by.

The restaurant was just as Annie remembered, a warm, cozy space, one wall bare brick, the opposite wall yellow and hung with oil paintings. Exposed roof rafters made it feel like an Italian country villa. Annie had treated Abby to dinner there about six months earlier when Abby was getting over the accountant/pit-bull owner. That night, Abby had eaten only olives and drunk her way through a bottle of wine. Annie had awarded herself points for not saying how lucky Abby was to be rid of that loser.

Luke waved from a table in the back near the open kitchen. Blond, tan, Luke was as handsome as ever. He wore a loosely constructed khaki sport jacket and a white shirt. All he lacked was a pith helmet. Annie introduced him to Peter.

"Where's Abby?" she asked as they sat.

"She just called to say she'll be late. She's stuck in traffic."

"And she still doesn't know we're here?"

Luke grinned and shook his head.

"So why *are* we here?" Annie asked.

"You'll see. Patience."

Peter choked on his breadstick.

"I can too be patient," Annie said.

"Sure you can. Here, chew on this." He handed her a piece of bread. To Luke he said, "So you run the zoo. I heard all about the baby giraffe."

He didn't exactly *run* the zoo, Luke explained. You might say he ran the animals, but sometimes it felt as if they ran him. And the young giraffe was doing fine, thank you very much. Now they were dealing with a new challenge—an orphaned kangaroo.

"It's this big," Luke said, holding his palms about eight inches apart.

Luke and Peter were deep into a fascinating discussion of neonatal kangaroo behavior when Abby came charging into the restaurant looking frazzled and damp, her hair in disarray.

"Sorry I'm late," she said, shedding her raincoat and leaning over to kiss Annie. Luke pulled out a chair for her. "Traffic is disgusting out there. I forgot Mass Ave through Harvard Square is still shut down. Why do they have to tear up every single damned road between here and . . . ?" She stopped. "What?" she said to Luke who was still standing, his hands laced across his middle and his thumbs tented. Then she looked at Annie and Peter. "Hey, you guys. What are you doing here, anyway?"

"Some of us were talking about baby kangaroos," Annie said.

Abby's face broke into a grin. "It's a little bitty thing, and it needs to be fed every two hours. Did you hear about the artificial pouch —?"

Her voice died when Luke put his index finger to his lips. He cleared his throat and said, in a ringing voice, "I've called you all together for a reason. I have something to say, and I wanted witnesses."

Abby looked at Annie, as if to ask if she had a clue what was going on.

Luke took a breath and continued. "Abby, I know we've only known each other for, uh"—now that he had their attention, he seemed to lose his momentum—"four months." He grabbed the glass of water from the table, took a gulp, and set it down again.

"Four months, three days"—he looked at his watch—"and thirty minutes. And I, uh . . ."

He gave a nervous glance at the couple at the next table, who were watching. One of the waiters had turned around and was staring, too.

Luke took a breath. "My love"—he reached out for Abby's hand—"with all my heart . . ." Abby made a little choking sound.

He fished out an index card, scanned it, then crumpled it up and tossed it on the table. "Oh, the hell with it."

Omigosh, Annie thought, when he actually got down on one knee.

"Here's the thing. I never thought I'd find someone who felt right, the way you do. I mean, who else would be up in the middle of the night, feeding a baby kangaroo?"

He reached into his jacket pocket and pulled out a small silver box with a white ribbon around it. "Always and forever," he whispered, and held the box out to Abby. "Will you marry me?"

The words were pure Hallmark, so why were Annie's eyes misted over and suddenly it felt like someone was sitting on her chest?

Abby's hands trembled as she reached for the box. She slid off the ribbon and opened it. Inside was a black velvet ring case. She opened it.

"I . . ." Abby looked over at Luke.

Now the entire restaurant was watching. Jeez, this guy had guts. What if she turned him down?

She didn't. Abby drew Luke up and threw her arms around him. "Yes," she said. "Yes! Yes! Yes!" The room erupted in applause.

Luke took the diamond solitaire from the case and slid it on Abby's finger. They kissed.

Annie hugged Abby and then Luke. Peter shook Luke's hand. The waiter appeared with a bottle of champagne and four champagne flutes. He uncorked the wine and poured.

"You had this planned, didn't you?" Abby said.

"You weren't going to get any if you said no," Luke replied, grinning.

Peter got his glass in the air first. "I'd like to propose a toast," he said. "To Abby and Luke . . ."

As Annie listened to the toast, she tried to remember when she'd seen Abby this happy. Maybe when she got married the first time. Up to that point, it had been Annie who did things first. Getting her period. Smoking. Driving. Cracking up the car. Annie had broken their parents in, so it had been a whole lot easier when Abby came along. Abby had been nineteen when she'd tied the knot. That had one-upped all of Annie's firsts. *There but for the grace of God go I*, Annie remembered thinking, and thanking her lucky stars that she wasn't the one walking down the aisle. She so wasn't ready. Here was Abby gearing up to marry a second time and Annie *still* wasn't ready.

Everyone was clinking glasses. Annie held up her glass.

"To the two of you," Annie said, and took a sip. Then a swallow. The bubbles must have gone down the wrong way because she was choking. She tried some water but it didn't help. She doubled over, coughing into her napkin, tears streaming down her face.

She got to her feet and excused herself. Abby asked if she wanted her to come along. "No, I'm fine," Annie told her, and stumbled, half-blinded, to the ladies' room.

Annie held on to the edge of the sink, coughing and gasping, still unable to catch her breath. Finally, the coughing stopped. A blurry image stared back at her from the mirror. People said that she and Abby had the same eyes, but it was their mother's eyes that stared back at her now. Annie shivered.

She splashed her face with water and leaned forward. Thirty-five years old and already she had crow's-feet. She ran her fingers through her hair. No gray at least. Not yet.

Annie looked down at the naked ring finger on her left hand. Damn. She didn't need a man to complete her. Really she didn't.

When she got back, Peter reached for her hand under the table. His raised eyebrows asked if she was okay. She tried to smile. It *did* feel good to have his hand to squeeze back. She picked up her champagne glass and drained it.

After dinner, Peter and Annie went back to Annie's apartment. He followed her up the stairs to her place on the third floor. She fumbled for her keys.

"Annie," Peter said. He was looking at her, his eyes full of questions. With his fingertips, he traced her forehead, down her face and jaw. Annie closed her eyes, savoring the gentleness of his touch. He put his hand behind her neck and massaged.

"You okay?" he asked.

Why did he have to keep asking? She opened her eyes. His face was inches from hers. She pulled away.

"I already told you. I'm fine." It came out sharp and strident. "But . . ."

Peter held on. "But what?"

"But I . . . I don't know what I want."

He drew her into an embrace and they kissed. She wanted to melt into him, but she couldn't. He nuzzled her neck. Her knees went weak and she found herself holding on to him, weeping uncontrollably. What the hell was going on?

One thing she knew for sure: she didn't want to be alone tonight.

THE NEXT morning, Peter left Annie sleeping. Neither of them had gotten a good night's sleep. After they left Pulcinella's, Annie had snapped at him when he asked if she was okay. At her place, they took a shower together. That usually relaxed them both. But afterward, Annie paced the floor like a nervous feline. Reluctantly, he gave up trying to entice her into bed.

When he woke up in the middle of the night, Annie was in the living room sitting on the couch, her arms hugging her knees. She still didn't want to talk. Peter sat beside her, put his arms around her, and stroked her head. She relaxed into him and they made love. After that, Peter sat up and watched her sleep. He thought about how simple and straightforward their relationship had once been.

He'd have liked to sleep in the next morning but he'd promised to meet Jackie Klevinski early. He left Annie sleeping soundly, tangled in sheets like she'd been fighting with them all night.

Jackie was at his office waiting for him. He ushered her in and set up the video camera. Then she sat there, her eyes wide and watchful, as he explained how he'd be hypnotizing her. "Hypnosis is really pretty straightforward. There's nothing supernatural about it."

"I believe in the power of the subconscious. Don't you?"

The question stumped him for a moment. He had a pretty good idea that his notion of the subconscious and hers were slightly different. Better to err on the safe side and answer with a simple "Yes, I do."

"Annie said she told you about my visitations."

"The hypnosis might even help some."

"You mean make them stop? But I don't want them to stop."

"It's been happening more?"

"It happened yesterday night again." Jackie's eyes were shining. "I was watching TV, dozing off, kind of, then I heard my name. It was Mary Alice's voice. All I could see was a shadow, but I could tell she was holding something out to me, a dark bundle, like that backpack she had on the law school steps. I knew she wanted me to take it from her, and I thought, *That's my bag she's holding. I must have left it somewhere and she found it.* I wasn't scared or anything, I just kept thinking, *It's my bag she's holding and she needs me to take it.*" Jackie looked puzzled. "Sounds weird, doesn't it?"

If she'd been Peter's patient, he'd have asked her to talk more about "weird," to explore what she was feeling, to think about what might be in that bag. Grief and guilt, Peter suspected, were at the core of these visions.

"Not so weird," Peter said. "You've been through a lot. The mind sometimes takes strange paths to get to the truth." He needed to push on with the business at hand. "You ready to get started?"

It had taken fifteen minutes to get Rudy Ravitch into a trance state; Jackie was there in five. Peter took her back to the day of the law school bombing, up the steps of Storrow Hall, and to her meeting with Mary Alice Boudreaux. *Let her set her own course,* Peter reminded himself. Anything she comes up with should be the product of her memory, not her imagination fueled by his inadvertent suggestion.

"Where are you?"

"I'm sitting on the bench."

"Tell me what you see."

"Miss Boudreaux. She's wearing a nice suit, it's kind of a tan color. Her nails are a real pretty shade of pink. She's got her briefcase open on the floor. She's showing me the papers, reading them real slow, but I can't follow what she was saying. I'm thinking about Joe. He'll go ballistic when he sees them."

"Now look around some more. Listen."

Jackie cocked her head. "They're laughing. In one of the classrooms. The door is open and I can hear someone, a woman, saying something. I can't hear what. A man, answering. There's a hushy, kind of squeaky sound. Sneakers. It's a man going into the men's room across the hall."

"Good. What happens next."

"Miss Boudreaux gets up. Says she'll be right back. She's got someone waiting outside to help with the paperwork. I can hear her heels on the floor, getting quieter, gone. I'm there alone. I look at the papers and I'm afraid. Why am I doing this? It's crazy. I start to get up, to get out of there quick, but Miss Boudreaux is back."

Jackie went through how she'd signed the papers and the other woman left. People started coming out of the classrooms.

Jackie straightened in her seat, her face tense. "I got scared. I knew it didn't make any sense, but I thought, *What if Joe is in one of those classrooms? What if he's hiding down the stairs, or in the men's room.* I put on my scarf. I had to get away." Her look clouded over.

"You feeling all right?" Peter asked.

She gazed off in midair in front of her.

"What do you see?"

"Miss Boudreaux. She looks . . . she doesn't look right. Her aura. Maybe it's the light."

"Tell me about her aura," Peter said.

"It's usually bright yellow with a pale-blue energy band next to her skin. That's what's wrong. The blue isn't there, just a band of red. I start to say something to her, I want to tell her to be careful, but there's people all over the place and I don't like staying there. He could be watching.

"I go outside." Jackie blinked her eyes. "It's hot. Sunny. And it's late. I've got to get a sandwich and get back to the office. There's kids on the steps. One in a gray T-shirt and jeans looks up at me. What a jerk. Doesn't bother to move his leg, so I step over him. People are coming the other way. I'm out on the sidewalk. I run to make the light but I only get halfway across to the traffic island before it changes."

Jackie's head jerked up. "She's calling. Miss Boudreaux? She's there at the top of the steps holding something, a black bag, there's a strap dangling from it. She's waving."

"Who is she waving to?"

"I can't see. There's lots of people on the steps and out in front of the building. A bus is going past . . ." Peter could almost smell the swirl of diesel exhaust as Jackie recoiled and paused for a moment. "It's gone now. I try to get her attention. She lowers the bag. She sees me. She waves back. Then—" Jackie tilted her head to one side, her brow creased with confusion. "There's a flash, right there where she's standing." Jackie's cheeks were wet with tears. "I feel like someone's shoving me hard, throwing me into the traffic. Then it's like time stops. I'm in the middle of the street. The cars are stopped. I've gotta get away from there." She sobbed. "I know I should have told her about the aura. I should have warned her."

It was hard to watch her in so much pain. "I know you feel terribly sad about this, maybe even guilty, and it's difficult to replay it. Just take your time. There's no rush."

Jackie swallowed and wiped her eyes with the back of her hand.

Peter waited a few moments more for Jackie to collect herself. "Do you think you can continue?"

"I want to go on." She shifted in her seat and set her shoulders.

"Good. Okay then, I'd like you to go back to the moment when Miss Boudreaux is on the steps. Concentrate on the people standing opposite her."

"There's so many people."

"She's holding up the bag. Who's she showing it to?"

Jackie squeezed her eyes shut. Peter hoped it wasn't a mistake to press.

"Could be that man. Dark jacket. He's getting a . . . a bike. He's rolling it over the sidewalk, over the grass."

"Does he look familiar?"

"I can't see his face. He's wearing a hood."

"Skin color?"

Jackie shook her head. "He's got gloves on. Black gloves. He's riding over the curb. He takes off—" A little noise escaped from her throat as she stared out in front of her, as if surprised. "His hood blows back and I can see . . ." Lines of anxiety etched her forehead. She flinched. "There's a bus going by and I . . . it's blocking my view." She covered her ears. "It's so loud, harsh-sounding." Slowly she lowered her hands from her ears. "What the . . . ?" she said, looking puzzled. "He's gone."

Peter was on the edge of his seat. If only for an instant, Jackie may have caught a glimpse of the bomber. He tried to keep his voice calm.

"The man you saw on the bike. Go back to that moment when his hood blew back. Try to see. What does he look like?"

"Glasses. He's wearing glasses. Dark hair. And"—she squinted— "maybe a short, dark beard."

"Is he a big man?"

She shook her head.

"How old?"

"I don't know. Not old-old. Thirty or forty."

"Can you describe the bike?"

"It's fancy. White. Handlebars. A big light in the front. The wheels are kind of small."

. . .

"Small wheels and a big light—what the hell kind of bike is that?" MacRae asked later that morning at the police station after Peter showed him and two other detectives the videotape. MacRae had been equally unimpressed by Jackie's description of a dark-haired, not big, not small, not young, not old, hood-wearing guy with glasses who might or might not have had a beard.

They were in the meeting room at the police station, where the pizza smell had been replaced by the smell of stale coffee, and the room had a whole new crop of dirty Styrofoam cups. Peter was only mildly tempted by the lone, semisquashed, glazed donut that sat looking forlorn in the box on the table.

MacRae introduced two other officers, Officer Tozzi and Agent Neddleman.

"Yo," Tozzi said, and shook Peter's hand. The bald, heavyset man was in his shirtsleeves and looked as tired as MacRae.

Neddleman, a slight man with sharp, intense eyes, and skin the color of coffee loaded with cream, didn't say anything. He was a pretty cool character in his dark suit, white shirt, and blue tie. He just slid his eyes at Peter and gave a slight nod.

"Maybe it wasn't a bike at all," Peter said. "I wonder if what she *may have seen*"—he carefully used that phraseology—"is something like a white motor scooter. That would have small wheels and a big headlight. And she said the bus sounded funny when it went by. Maybe that was the sound of the scooter and the bus combined."

MacRae frowned. "And that would explain why she didn't see the bike emerge after the bus went past. The bus would've run blocking for the scooter."

MacRae conferred with Neddleman and Tozzi for a moment. Tozzi left the room.

MacRae picked up a whiteboard marker and began adding items. The list already had on it:

> Male
> White
> Local
> Only child
> Intelligent
> Educated
> Under or unemployed
> Childhood abuse victim
> Criminal record
> Reads sci-fi/spy thrillers
> Lack of empathy
> Delusional
> Anarchist (maybe)

He added:

Dark hair
Beard?
30–40
Bike or motor scooter, no helmet

On another whiteboard, Neddleman wrote:

Cross-check suspects for bike/scooter

and drew a big circle around it.

Taped to the wall were the two flyers Peter recognized from the bombings plus dozens more of the typical flyers you'd find posted on your average Cambridge lamppost.

"Turns out this guy's not very original," MacRae said. "He's quoting Vanzetti and Thomas Paine."

An anarchist fish peddler and a patriot—interesting choices. "He's smart," Peter said. "Educated, probably well-read."

"Though these days anyone can get quotes like those off the Internet," MacRae pointed out. "That's how we identified them."

Peter looked at the rest of the miscellaneous flyers, each one marked with a different Cambridge intersection where presumably it had been found.

"We've been bringing in anything that looks like it might be connected," MacRae explained. He shook his head in disgust. "He couldn't pick some nice, quiet, conservative town like Andover to bomb. No, he has to blow up the People's Republic of Cambridge where every other nut is a frustrated guru."

One flyer began IS THE WORM TURNING? JOIN US IN OUR STRUGGLE. It was signed AAA ANONYMOUS ANTI-AUTHORITARIANS.

"That doesn't look like the work of your bomber," Peter said.

"Why not?" MacRae asked. Neddleman was watching from the corner like a gray shadow.

"Doesn't strike me as a joiner."

"Why don't you have a look at the others. See if any of them leap out at you."

Peter examined the next flyer. JESUS SAVES. Unlikely, too. The messages they knew were his sounded decidedly atheist. Another one began: GE KILLS. Maybe. It wasn't a huge leap from legal institutions to corporate leviathans.

The next one was a drawing of a woman with a ball and chain around her ankle. It read WAGE SLAVERY OR STARVATION? Nope, not his concerns.

The next one gave Peter pause: STOP PARTICIPATING IN THE RUIN OF CREATION. PARTICIPATE IN THE CREATION OF RUINS. Beneath the words was a drawing of a cop's head with a pistol pointed at it. It had come from the corner outside the police station.

"Pretty sick, huh?" MacRae said.

"Sick all right. But I doubt if someone who's quoting Vanzetti and Paine would be so crude."

Peter scanned the rest of the flyers. None of them felt like the first two. "Sorry, wish I could be more help."

More head shots had been taped up. Joe Klevinski was still there. One of the new faces looked familiar. It was a man with a longish beard and a prizefighter's nose squashed against his face. Peter wondered if he'd acquired the nose defending the ears that stood out from his head like a pair of mud flaps.

"That's one of our local celebrities. Harvard Harry," MacRae said. "He's missing."

Now Peter remembered where he'd seen that face. It belonged to one of the more colorful characters who'd hung around the Square for years. Always polite, relatively clean, he'd stand across from the Coop holding an American flag and hand out literature.

Among the mug shots was a piece of paper with the black outline of a head with a question mark in the middle of it.

"That's just there to remind us, could be person or persons unknown," MacRae said.

Neddleman had slipped out of the room. MacRae gave a nod toward the door and mouthed, "Fed."

"No kidding," Peter said.

MacRae lifted a stack of files from the top of a file cabinet, set them on the table, and handed Peter one.

"This one's being picked up for questioning."

Peter opened the file. There was a mug shot that matched one on the wall, a man with disheveled, sandy-colored hair who looked like he'd just been yanked out of bed and had a light shone in his face. Peter read the summary sheet on top. James Tietz. Unfortunate name—kids in school must have tortured him.

Peter read down. Thirty-three years old. Father deceased. He'd been arrested once for driving under the influence. Once for speeding. Another time for disorderly conduct outside a police station— apparently he'd been part of some kind of demonstration.

There was a high school transcript, mostly Cs, some Bs. Ds in physical education. Then a transcript from a local community college. Bs, along with a fair number of incompletes. Looked as if he'd dropped out after three semesters.

After that, he'd been in the military, served under a year in the navy. Peter read the discharge papers. "Demonstrated Unreliability" was the navy's verdict. There was a check in the box beside "Apathy and/or defective attitude or inability to expend effort constructively." Euphemism for what? Peter wondered.

Then there were copies of letters dated four years earlier to the

Cambridge police chief, demanding $200,000 for fire damage to a home.

"Your officers are responsible for the damage," began the rant in one of the letters. "Or should I say irresponsible." *Irresponsible* was underlined three times. Peter scanned the two additional pages of neat, densely packed writing. The tone was almost threatening, but not quite.

"What happened?" Peter asked.

"His mother owned a house in Cambridge that caught fire. Apparently someone left food on the stove unattended. Shouldn't have been a big deal, but it was a comedy of errors. The police cruiser that got there first backed over the fire hydrant, so firefighters had to get a longer hose. By the time they got water in there, the fire was out of control. The insurance company wouldn't pay—his mother had been late sending in the last premium. He sued the insurance company and lost. Sued the police department, the fire department, the city, and when he lost he sued his lawyer for malpractice." MacRae gave a tired smile and shook his head. "Poor schmuck."

No doubt about it, here was someone with a legitimate bone to pick with the justice system. Peter turned back to the mug shot. Not bad-looking. Though the eyes looked funny, pupils dilated, like maybe he was on speed.

"Any incidents with the police before the fire?" Peter asked, as his mind flooded with other questions. Had Tietz been active politically? What kinds of assignments had he had in the navy? Why had he been discharged? Had he been abused as a child?

There was shouting outside the building. Through the window Peter could see reporters swarming three police officers who were escorting a man into the station. The man had his arms up over his face as cameras flashed.

"That's Tietz," MacRae said.

He gave Peter a piece of paper. It was a confidentiality form, promising to keep anything that he learned confidential. MacRae offered a pen. Now raised voices were coming from the lobby. Peter hesitated. Did he really want to be doing this? He glanced back at the rows of photographs on the wall and wondered how many people in the greater Boston area were going to get dragged in for questioning because they were angry with the courts and read sci-fi novels.

That's when he noticed a map of Cambridge on the wall with an area outlined in red. Damned if the outline didn't include Peter's house.

"YOU PEOPLE have got some nerve," said a fuming James Tietz, his arms folded across his chest as he sat ramrod straight in his chair in the police interrogation room. Peter watched through one-way glass in a setup similar to the side-by-side treatment and observation rooms at the Pearce. But this was a different universe, with its uncomfortable-looking chairs, stark walls with chipped paint, and flickering fluorescent lights.

Tietz sat across from MacRae and a woman police officer whom MacRae had introduced to Peter as Jean Mulberry.

The compact, wiry man was sputtering indignation. "Who told you to pick me up? Harassment, that's what it is." His face was pitted with what must have once been a raging case of adolescent acne, and he wore a crisp white dress shirt, cuffs rolled. "I know my rights. Am I under arrest?"

"No, but that can be arranged if you'd rather not answer our questions, which I know you're eager to do because you're a law-abiding citizen, aren't you?" MacRae said.

Tietz looked back and forth from MacRae to his partner. "Why me? I haven't done anything."

"Last Tuesday. Where were you?" MacRae shot the words across the table.

Tietz gave several rapid blinks. "It's none of your business where I was. You people think you can—"

"You can spare the drama. Just answer the question. What were you doing a week ago Tuesday?"

Tietz shifted in his chair, his fists clenching and unclenching.

"At about two o'clock," MacRae added.

Tietz loosened his fists. "Tuesday. That was the day—" His eyes went wide, as if he'd just thought of something. Peter realized that his eyes were just very dark, making his pupils appear to be dilated. Tietz muttered something.

"Pardon me?" MacRae said.

"I was at work," Tietz said, his face impassive.

"Um-hmm," MacRae said in a neutral voice while Officer Mulberry wrote. "Can you tell me where you work?"

"Sound City. In Somerville. I'm a repair tech."

"Who saw you there?"

"I don't know. Everyone who works there—"

"When are you going to stop bullshitting me?" MacRae said, cutting him off. "We've already talked to the store manager. He says you weren't there."

Tietz gripped the table, his knuckles going white. "You went to my work? You talked to my boss? You bastards. It's not enough that you destroy my home? Now you're trying to get me fired?"

MacRae seemed unmoved. "It would be a whole lot better for

you to come clean, get this off your chest. I can help you." His tone had turned urgent. "But if you don't tell me where you were and what happened, the truth this time, then I can't do a thing for you."

It was quiet, except for a rhythmic creaking sound as Tietz jiggled his knee under the table.

"We know you didn't get back from your lunch break until after two-thirty. So where were you?"

"I don't have to put up with this," Tietz said, getting to his feet. He picked up his jacket from the chair back. "You stay out of my life, you, you sons of bitches. It's none of your goddamned business where I was." He swore under his breath.

"Actually," said MacRae, standing and putting both hands on the table, "it is our business. When a bomb goes off—"

"Bomb?" Tietz reared back. He went a shade paler, and his jacket dropped to the floor. Either he was a very good actor, or he hadn't seen this coming. "And you think I . . . ?" He stared goggle-eyed at MacRae. "I had nothing to do with that. I wasn't anywhere near—"

"So, where were you? Why not just cooperate with us and tell us? It will make things go so much easier for you."

Tietz looked steadily at MacRae. "Cooperate," he said. "The Third Reich had euphemisms for what they were doing, too. But it's still persecution. 'Just doing our job,' that's what they said, too."

"And what about September fourth, Tuesday at noon," MacRae said, ignoring the diatribe. "Your boss says you weren't at work then, either."

"Four weeks ago? How the hell am I supposed to remember—" He broke off. "September fourth? Actually, I do know where I was. I was at home. With my mother."

"So I'm sure she'll be able to verify your story."

Tietz gave a thin smile. "You're welcome to ask her. Though you'll have to bring in bigger guns to pull that off." His look turned into an angry, sullen stare. "Stupid bumbling idiots. You've got your heads up your asses."

MacRae sputtered an oath and turned purple. He looked as if he was about to grab Tietz by the neck, but Mulberry pulled him back.

"Hey, back off. That's enough," she told him. "Why don't you go somewhere and cool off."

MacRae glowered at Tietz. "If I find out you're the one responsible, I'm personally going to make your life miserable. And believe me, I can."

MacRae slammed out of the room, and a moment later joined Peter. For all the fireworks, his interrogation had gotten nowhere. That's what happened when you backed someone like Tietz into a corner.

Peter started to say something to that effect when he realized that MacRae's color was back to normal and his face relaxed. He had a lazy smile on his face. Of course, it had been an act.

Mulberry, the proverbial good cop, apologized to Tietz. She was a thickset woman with a pleasant face. Her wavy brown hair had streaks of blond through it.

"Sorry. He can be a bit much," she said. "We're all pretty frustrated, trying to catch this guy before . . ." She leaned forward. "Hey, you okay? Can I get you something to drink? Coffee?"

Tietz sank into his chair. He folded one arm across his chest and put the other fist to his mouth and chewed on a knuckle.

"Cigarette?" Mulberry asked.

Tietz shook his head. "I just want to get the hell out of here."

"I know, I know," Mulberry said, sympathy in her voice. She

looked down at her notes, flipped back to the previous page, then the one before. She underlined something. "So all we need to do is talk to your mother to verify your whereabouts on September fourth?"

"My mother . . ." Tietz's face contorted. "She's dead."

"I'm so sorry. Was it sudden?"

"No." Tietz took a ragged breath. "She lived with me. Had ever since the fire. She had nowhere else to go. Then she got emphysema. She died that day."

"Mmm," Mulberry said, and waited for Tietz to collect himself. "And last Tuesday?"

He glared at her. "I was nowhere near that courthouse, and you'd be wasting your time trying to find someone who can place me there. Just like you're doing right now, wasting your time talking to me while this terrorist, or whoever he is, plans his next move. Maybe he'll do me a favor and blow up this police station."

"You think we might be the next target?" Mulberry said, not missing a beat.

"It sure as hell would be mine."

• • •

"He's hiding something," MacRae told Peter after the interview.

That much had been obvious. But what? "There are a million reasons for getting back late from lunch that you wouldn't want to share with your boss," Peter said. "An affair. A two-martini lunch."

"Appointment with a shrink," MacRae added. "But we pulled him in for questioning about a bombing. You'd think he'd come clean."

"He doesn't trust you. And why should he?"

MacRae shrugged agreement. "We'll find out one way or another."

"You could be wasting your time." Peter flipped through Tietz's file. "He seems pretty broken up about his mother's death. Said he'd been taking care of her. That's not the kind of person you're looking for. Not in my opinion, anyway."

MacRae went over to the mug shots of the other suspects, running his finger over each of them in turn. Last, his finger lingered on the empty outline.

There was a knock at the door. Tozzi stuck his head in. He handed MacRae a manila folder. MacRae opened it and showed Peter a stack of motorbike ads. Peter agreed to ask Jackie Klevinski if any of them looked like what she'd seen.

"He wants to be noticed," Peter said. "I suppose that's a good thing."

"Well, he's certainly got our attention." MacRae said, scratching his head.

"You going public with the profile?" Peter asked.

"We're discussing it." He squinted at Peter. "If we do, you up for it?"

Surely he wasn't serious. The last time Peter had talked to a reporter, it had been a deliberate attempt to smoke out a killer. It had worked all too well.

"Me? That's not what I signed up for."

"Not an official press conference or anything. Just be available to answer questions about what the crimes tell us about the personality of the perpetrator. Why it's probably one person, not an organized terrorist group—stuff like that." Hale and hearty, he clapped a hand on Peter's back. "We need your help. Remember, that's how they finally caught the Unabomber. His brother recognized him from the psychological profile."

"And from his writing," Peter pointed out.

"We'll publish the flyers, too. What do you say?"

Despite Peter's natural aversion to any kind of publicity—he'd had a bellyful of notoriety after Kate's murder—he couldn't say no.

He glanced outside. Another news van had pulled up. A photographer was taking a picture of the entrance to the police station while a group of reporters watched. They looked bored and restless, a pack of hungry lions.

Peter wasn't looking forward to becoming their next meal.

16

ANNIE OPENED her front door and peered out. She held her robe closed as she darted out barefoot and grabbed the newspaper off the bottom step. The streetlights were still on, and the sidewalk was icy. She could hear her mother's voice in her head—*Annie, you can't go outside half-dressed.* She ignored it, but the voice went on hectoring: *You could at least put on clean underwear. What if you slip and fall and the ambulance has to come for you?*

A-BOMBER PROFILED, the headline said. A-bomber? So he'd earned himself a moniker. He'd joined the likes of Son of Sam and the Zodiac Killer, criminals who taunted the police with messages. No doubt he was basking in his newfound celebrity status.

Shivering, Annie came back inside and locked the door behind her. Slowly she climbed the steps, reading as she went.

Columbo, the cat Annie had inherited from her Uncle Jack, was pacing the landing when she got back to the third floor and complaining loudly. Where was breakfast?

Annie brought the newspaper into the kitchen and set it on the counter, shoving aside two nearly empty Chinese take-out containers. Columbo jumped up, stuck his head into one of the containers, and licked the inside. He sat on the newspaper, licked a fastidious paw, and resumed his yowling. All right already.

A few minutes later, Columbo sniffed suspiciously at the cat food Annie put in a bowl on the floor, and Annie sat down at her old but not-quite-vintage Formica-top kitchen table to read. Her stomach rumbled. If only she'd gotten dressed and walked to the corner for a coffee and a muffin.

The front page had a picture of Mac at a press conference, surrounded by reporters. Alongside the photo was the text from flyers that the police had found at the bombing scenes.

Annie read the story.

> Saying this man has too much time on his hands and is secretive and organized, authorities Monday released a personality profile of a bomb-maker who, they believe, is responsible for two Cambridge bombings, one at the Harvard Law School and another at the Middlesex County Courthouse, resulting in the deaths of nine people and injuring twenty-three.
>
> Following Monday's press conference, authorities also released text from flyers found at both bombing scenes in hopes of getting tips from the public, said Detective Sergeant Joseph MacRae of the police department in Cambridge.
>
> "Somebody out there lives next door to the suspect," MacRae said.
>
> While authorities have plenty of leads, MacRae said the case remains "perplexing."

She scanned down.

The bomber is "probably a white male, over 30 years old," said psychologist Peter Zak of the Pearce Psychiatric Institute. Zak is a frequent expert witness for defense counsel in criminal cases, and said he based his analysis on the content of the flyers and evidence from the bombing scenes.

Zak said the bomber is probably an intelligent under-achiever, and is aloof or does not want to talk about how he spends his time.

"The bomber may have had prior run-ins with law enforcement, and may have suffered abuse," said Zak.

"He's a self-absorbed loner, believes the world should revolve around him. It's not clear if he has a political agenda. If not, then he's a murderer with a moral masquerade. He's got a pseudo-political rationale for deep-seated psychological issues, and a sense of impotence that has attained delusional proportions."

Had Peter seen this? Annie wondered. She knew he'd hate the teaser in the middle of the page: PROFILER PIECES TOGETHER POSSI-BILITIES. He'd told everyone who'd listen, in no uncertain terms, that he was *not* a profiler. To be fair, *forensic neuropsychologist* would never have fit in the margin.

She dialed his home number and waited. There were two inches of old coffee sitting in the coffeemaker. She took a sniff, and wondered if its statute of limitations had expired.

There was no answer. She tried his office.

"You're in early," she said when he picked up. "You saw this morning's paper?" She poured the coffee into a cup.

"Seen it? Kwan's got it tacked to the bulletin board in the staff room. Idiots. I *told* them I wasn't a profiler. I get to my office and the phone is ringing. Guess who?"

"A reporter."

"You got it. From the *Boston Phoenix,* asking me all these questions. It's eight in the morning and I haven't had my coffee even."

"Most reporters are good guys. I hope you were polite at least."

"Yeah. Sure I was. I gave him two minutes and then told him to email the rest of his questions—when I had time, I'd get to them. He wouldn't give up, so finally I just hung up. I log into the system, and sure enough I've got his email plus fifty-two others, mostly from strangers. How do these people find me?"

You didn't have to be a detective to figure out Peter's email at the hospital. It was basically his name at PEARCE.ORG. Annie put the cup in the microwave and punched the buttons.

"Listen to this." Peter cleared his throat. " 'You call yourself a profiler? Give me a break with your tired clichés. People who don't get along with other people are not bombers. They're . . .' Yadda, yadda. 'Loners aren't sickos.' It's from a woman who says she belongs to the Social Anxiety and Related Disorders Association. Didn't even know there was such an organization. She ends with 'Sincerely, which Crackerjacks box did you get your degree off of, Bozo?' " Peter groaned. "It's not even grammatical."

Sounded like he was stabbing his keyboard, hitting DELETE DELETE DELETE. The microwave dinged. Annie got the coffee out and took a cautious sip. Ick. Maybe a whole lot of milk would help. She checked the fridge. Not *that* milk.

"Oh, here's another winner. 'What is it with you bleeding heart liberals? Underachiever? Victim of abuse? Give me a break. This guy deserves to be blown up, one part at a time. The death penalty is too good for scum like that.' "

"So, maybe you have a new career?" Annie said, sitting at the kitchen table and ladling sugar into the coffee.

"What? Radio shock jock?"

"Well, it does sound as if you've struck a nerve."

"Move over, Howard Stern."

Columbo rubbed against Annie's leg. She reached down and scratched him behind the ears. He closed his eyes and purred.

"Oh, here's a good one. 'You're wrong about the A-bomber.' Jesus Christ. Right, wrong, now everyone's a profiler. 'You overeducated imbecile. This is not a masquerade. You're like all the rest of them, ignoring our message because you're not ready to . . .' "

Peter's voice died out. Annie could barely hear what sounded like him reading under his breath.

"Holy shit," he said. "The rest of this reads like something out of a Ph.D. thesis from Mars. He's got this convoluted explanation of the bomber's mind. The thing goes on for pages."

Annie set down her coffee. "Do you think it could be him?"

There was a brief silence. "Damn right it could. I better call MacRae," Peter said, and hung up.

. . .

Annie was in her office later that morning with Jackie sitting opposite her across the desk. Jackie had on a pink sweater and a matching shade of lipstick. She was wearing perfume, too, a spicy scent.

"You look nice. New outfit?" Annie asked.

Jackie's hand fluttered to her throat. "Sort of."

Annie had promised Peter that she'd show Jackie the pictures of scooters and bikes and have her pick the one that looked most like what she'd seen at the law school. Of course, she couldn't just spread the pictures out and have Jackie choose one. Oh no, she had to do it *his* way, the complicated way.

She hoped this would go quickly. She had to be on a conference call in fifteen minutes, and after that she had an appointment with a client.

"I'm supposed to ask you to relax and think back to the moment when you saw the man riding away from the law school, just before the bombing," Annie said, feeling silly. "Now close your eyes."

Obediently Jackie closed her eyes and took a long inhale. Annie felt like a crafty Svengali. All she needed now was a turban on her head.

Annie read from her notes. "Good. I want you to try to picture what he was riding on, and when you've got that as clearly as you can in your mind, open your eyes."

After a few moments, Jackie opened her eyes and sat forward.

Annie set two pictures on the desk. One was a white mountain bike, the other a basic motor scooter that looked as if it were made of white PVC piping. "Okay, here we go. Which of these is the closest to what you remember?"

Jackie tilted her head and examined the pictures. "Neither one of them really."

"Can you pick the one that's closest?"

Jackie's hand hovered, and then she pointed to the scooter. Annie discarded the picture of the bike and pulled out a new picture. This one was a futuristic motorbike with a back-slanting windshield. Annie laid it alongside the PVC-piping scooter.

"I'll hold," Jackie said, sticking with the scooter. This was starting to feel like a poker game.

Annie pulled out a new picture. Nothing fancy, just your basic scooter with a molded front panel. A pair of truncated handlebars sprouted from where a light was mounted in the front. The seat was broad, molded to fit two behinds, and there was a flat floorboard.

Jackie fingered her earrings, pink crystal roses. She sat there for a few moments, eyes darting back and forth between the pictures, before pointing to the new picture. "That one's closer."

"Nice earrings," Annie said.

A red streak flared on Jackie's neck. "Oh, these. They're nothing." She slipped off the earrings and dropped them in her pocket.

Annie took out the next picture. She knew what was up. New sweater, earrings, and maybe perfume. Add to that flowers and a fancy barrette for Sophie.

"Jackie—" Annie started, but she didn't know what to say that wouldn't get Jackie's back up. Still, she couldn't stand by and watch Jackie race, lemminglike into the flood. "From Joe?"

Jackie waited for the next picture, as if she hadn't heard the question.

"From Joe?" Annie asked again, trying to keep her voice even.

Jackie flinched, like she was afraid she was going to get hit. "He's going to AA meetings. Four weeks and he's still going. That's something, don't you think? Sophie misses him."

He's a scumbag, Annie wanted say. *He'll get you back, and then how long do you think it'll be before it starts all over again, only this time it'll be worse because he's got more to be angry about.*

They went quickly through the rest of the pictures. Jackie's final choice was a generic-looking white scooter. There were probably a million of them in the Boston area. She got up, looking relieved.

"So, are you seeing him?" Annie asked.

"I . . ." Jackie held her hands open in a mute plea for understanding. Annie could see that the answer was yes. "I know what you're thinking, Annie. And don't think I don't appreciate all the help you've given me. But give me a little credit at least."

Annie didn't say anything.

Jackie looked off into space. "You know, he wasn't always like this. When I first met him, he was gentle. Brought me flowers all the time. It's all because of his first wife. She's the one who changed him."

Joe would probably foist that lame tale of woe off on the next woman in his life, too—Jackie that bitch, she was the one who made him go crazy. Whatever went wrong, it was always someone else's fault.

Jackie gave Annie a wry smile and shook her head. "I know you think that's a crock, but she ran off with her boyfriend and took little Joey with her. It happened when Sophie was little. Joe hasn't heard from either of them, not once since then. What kind of mother takes her son away from his father like that? That's when Joe changed. Started drinking heavy, got into drugs, started hitting me."

Jackie's willingness to be blinkered left Annie struggling for words. Why did she think Joe's first wife had to disappear in order to get away? Wasn't it obvious that there was no "getting away" from this man otherwise?

PETER GRUMBLED as he drove to the police station. Again. He'd called MacRae right away because they'd want to know about the email message. What he didn't know was that MacRae would want him to get down there and go over it with them. Kwan had given a disgusted snort when Peter said he'd have to leave after morning walk rounds. "Well, at least you'll have the bad suits to go with your new job," he told Peter.

Gloria took him aside as he was leaving. "Pay no attention to Mr. Fussy. We're all behind you. Help them get that lunatic before he destroys any more lives."

MacRae had the text of the email message blown up and taped to the wall of the conference room alongside the two flyers from the bomb scenes. Agent Neddleman, dressed again in a dark suit and shirt, slid out of his corner and pored silently over the email text. The sender was CANARY911. The subject: FOR WHAT IT'S WORTH. There were two full pages of text beginning:

You overeducated imbecile. This is not a masquerade. You're like all the rest of them, ignoring Our
message because you're not ready to consider the
possibilities that lay before Us.

The legal system is corrupt, the agent of the Maw.
A raptor, tearing holes in the ozone layer. Laying
waste to forests. Searing the land with acid rain.
Succoring corporate pillagers in the name of consumerism.

Peter glanced at one of the flyers.

The law prevents Us from pursuing Our destiny.

You didn't need to be an expert to see the similarities between the
flyers and the email. Both had that idiosyncratic use of capital letters.
Both spoke in the "royal we." Of course, anyone could have copied
that style, now that the flyers had been reprinted in the newspapers.

"We'll get a linguistic analysis," Neddleman said. "See what the
experts say." His voice was a low rumble. It was the first time Peter
had heard him speak. Neddleman stroked his chin, his face inches
from the words. "Philosopher King. Marshal. The Maw." He rolled
his eyes. "What is this shit, anyway?"

Peter picked up a whiteboard marker and drew three concentric
circles. In the outermost ring, he wrote, "MARSHAL." In the next
inside ring he wrote, "PHILOSOPHER KING." In the bull's-eye he
wrote, "THE MAW."

"It's how this guy sees the three parts of the bomber's mind.
Bizarre, but nevertheless logical. This part"—he underlined
PHILOSOPHER KING—"is apparently at war with this one"—he
underlined THE MAW.

He read aloud the writer's explanation, how the Philosopher King pursued the "highest ideals" of learning and the intellect, while the Maw subverted those high ideals and had to go out and rapaciously consume in order to be satisfied. The Marshal mediated between the two and kept the peace.

Peter had to admire the structure. He mused aloud. "Philosopher King and Maw. That's roughly analogous to what Freud thought of as the superego and the id. The Marshal is like Freud's ego, serving as traffic cop."

"Yeah, right," Neddleman muttered. "A government conspiracy to make us all go shopping."

"Something like that," Peter said.

"So you think all this anarchist stuff is a smokescreen?" MacRae asked Neddleman.

"Pure and utter bullshit," Neddleman said. "If you ask me, he's throwing around a lot of big words, trying to make us think he's a crazy."

Smokescreen? Maybe, but Peter didn't think so. "I can't say for certain that this guy is your bomber. But he sure as hell sounds quote-unquote crazy to me. Could be he's an organized schizophrenic."

"I thought you said the shrink wasn't a profiler," Neddleman said, pointedly ignoring Peter. Here was a guy who didn't like to be contradicted. Hell, Peter thought, if they weren't going to listen to him, then why was he here?

"I'm not. And I'm not a shrink, either. And I'm right here, so you can talk to me."

Neddleman turned his gaze on Peter. He made passivity into an art form.

"Unlike some of us," Peter went on, "I do know something about pathology. I know what crazy looks like, and it's not as easy to fake as you might think. This could be your bomber. And if he is, then

• 141 •

you're not going to be able to negotiate with him. Challenge him and you could reinforce his paranoia."

Neddleman made a fist and massaged the knuckles with his other hand. "Then how . . . Who the hell is he? We've got people working on tracking this email, but that's going to take time. Besides, he's probably using public computers. We need more information to go on."

"He emailed me. Presumably I could reply."

Peter could almost see the cylinders falling into place as Neddleman weighed the suggestion.

"The more we get him to tell us," Peter went on, "the more likely he'll let slip some detail about himself, something that reveals who he is. A part of him wants to brag, tell the world how smart he is. Maybe if we let him, he'll spill what he's planning to do next."

"Or goad him into performing, killing more people," Neddleman said.

"There's that risk."

Peter glanced at the timeline scrawled on the whiteboard. There'd been four weeks between the first two bombings. A few more days and it would be two weeks since the last one. Neddleman was probably wondering the same thing—did they have two weeks' grace? Peter knew that a sudden outbreak of violent behavior could be precipitated by something that had been percolating for years, and it could accelerate in frequency.

A few minutes later Peter was on a laptop MacRae had brought in. He accessed his email at the Pearce and checked to be sure CANARY911 hadn't sent him another message. Then he pulled up the message he'd received that morning and clicked REPLY.

"Dear Mad Bomber," Neddleman said as he watched over Peter's shoulder.

Peter ignored the sarcasm. "If he's schizophrenic, the way to engage him is to get into his world, enter his reality, give a kind of pseudovalidity to what he's saying, and more importantly, to what he's feeling. If he feels understood, he'll be more inclined to let down his guard and reveal something we can use."

Peter began to type, reading off the words as he went. "Your analysis is fascinating. As you know, I have a doctorate in psychology, but what you're suggesting is pretty groundbreaking. I've never looked at the mind that way. I would appreciate learning more, and understanding what led you to your unique conceptual framework."

Neddleman chuckled. "Laying it on pretty thick, aren't you?"

Peter glanced at the printout on the wall, rereading the email message he'd received. The subject line snagged his attention: "FOR WHAT IT'S WORTH." Wasn't that a song title?

Peter opened another browser window and Googled the words. Sure enough, "For What It's Worth" was the title of a Steven Stills song done by the Buffalo Springfield around 1967, a couple of years before the shootings at Kent State.

Peter told MacRae and Neddleman about the song title.

"Nineteen sixty-seven?" Neddleman said. "You saying this guy's in his fifties?"

"Not necessarily. The song's become a classic nailing the zeitgeist of a very scary time. It makes sense that someone like him would resonate to it. Maybe it's a hook I can use . . ." Peter typed a few words from the song as the subject line in his message: LOOK WHAT'S GOING DOWN. He smiled to himself, adding at the bottom: "Were you the guy I talked to at the Crosby Stills and Nash concert, Fleet Center, 2000?"

He typed his name and waited while Neddleman read over his shoulder. "What the hell," Neddleman said.

Peter clicked SEND.

• • •

As Peter drove up Mass Ave toward Harvard Square on his way to the Pearce, he could hear Neddleman's sneering voice: *Philosopher King. Marshal. The Maw.* As he'd pointed out, it was intellectual bullshit. Peter wondered if his new pen pal owned a scooter. Had he been in the military and learned about explosives? Would he swallow the flattery and answer Peter, or sniff out the baited hook?

He took his usual detour down Dunster Street and came screeching to a halt, nearly hitting a car pulling out of a parking spot. How many times had he cruised this street, dying for a parking spot and finding none? It wasn't fair. A car and an SUV were backed up behind him, and the car had its blinker flashing. The driver wanted the parking spot. *Finders keepers*, Peter thought, feeling like the proverbial dog in the manger. Besides, he did need a cup of coffee.

He zipped into the spot, nose first. It took a couple of back-and-forths to get close enough to the curb. A scone would be nice, too, Peter thought, pumping a couple of quarters into the meter. As he headed up the street, he passed a meter man writing up a Volvo that had overstayed its welcome. Cambridge could probably meet its yearly municipal payroll on parking violations alone.

Peter walked past John Harvard's Brew House, under the watchful eyes of Jerry Garcia and John F. Kennedy depicted in stained glass. In its dark, woody interior there was cathedral-style stained glass portraying an equally odd assortment of modern luminaries, all in mock-ancient attire, from Wayne Gretzky to Humphrey Bogart to Richard Nixon.

But he was after coffee, not beer. First he'd pick up a paper at Out of Town News. The pit surrounding the entrance to the Harvard Square T station, filled with tourists and buskers on weekends, was quiet on a weekday morning. A burly fellow in a red-and-blue plaid flannel shirt stood alone in front of the tourist kiosk, holding up a copy of *Spare Change*, the newspaper for the homeless. Peter fished out a dollar and bought a copy. A woman in a greasy green parka squatted on the sidewalk near the subway entrance, a Dunkin' Donuts cup on the ground in front of her along with a hand-lettered sign that said PLEASE HELP. And below that: I COULD BE YOU. As Peter stepped around her, a man dropped a few crumpled dollar bills into the cup. Peter noticed his hand. It was shaking slightly, and the skin was pale, nearly translucent. The man stooped alongside the woman, talking to her, his back to Peter. Something about his silhouette made Peter stop. It was the ears. The man had unusually large ones. Peter pivoted and backtracked. Now he recognized that nose, squashed against his face. The man was holding a stack of flyers, the top one dense with printing.

First a parking spot on Dunster, next the local street preacher whom the police had been looking for. A hospital bracelet on the man's wrist suggested why they hadn't been able to find him. Peter considered calling MacRae but discarded the idea. He didn't want to give Harvard Harry time to evaporate.

"Harry?" Peter said, trying to sound like he knew him.

The man's head jerked up. Under a too-large tweed jacket, Harry's white T-shirt was emblazoned with the slogan WORDS MEAN NOTHING. And below that were the words ACTION IS, with the final words tucked into pants that were held up by twine threaded through his belt loops. His clothes seemed clean, his shoes worn at the heel but polished. The lower part of his face seemed paler than his weathered cheeks, as if he'd recently shaved off a beard.

Harry's look morphed from surprise, to confusion, to fear. Before he could flee, Peter said, "No flag today?"

That threw him. He looked down, as if he expected a flag to materialize in his hand.

"Bastard took it," he muttered.

"That's too bad. Hey, where've you been, anyway?"

Peter held out his hand. Almost automatically, Harry handed him a leaflet. The headline on the page was DEVASTATE TO LIBERATE.

Harry's eyes narrowed. Who was this weirdo? Peter could almost hear him asking himself.

"I was just going to get myself a cup of coffee," Peter said. "Want to join me?"

Harry shot the homeless woman a questioning look. She gave Peter a sharp appraisal, then she shrugged at Harry. She didn't know who he was, either.

Harry scanned the busy intersection, finally reopened to traffic, maybe looking for cops or divine intervention.

"Yeah." He licked his lips. "I could use some coffee."

The Toscanini's near Harvard Square was barely a storefront. Famous for ice cream, they also sold coffee and pastries all day. Harry followed Peter inside. The air was thick with the aroma of coffee layered over the pungency of chocolate and vanilla.

Harry ordered black coffee and Peter paid for that and a vanilla latté. Peter got them both scones. Harry must have been a regular because, without being asked, the clerk reached under the counter, pulled out a handful of nondairy creamer packets, and tossed them to Harry. Peter winced. That stuff was an insult to good coffee.

They took over two stools at the window counter overlooking Mass Ave and Harvard Yard.

"You didn't recognize me, did you?" Peter said.

Harry stirred two packets of the white powder into his coffee and set the extras in a little stack by his cup. He slid Peter a glance, his gray eyes sharp, and he had one foot on the ground, his behind perched on the stool, like he was hedging his bets.

"I'm Peter Zak. I live around here." Harry's eyes registered no recognition. "Well, why should you know me? You're the celebrity. Always out there with your flag. The conscience of Cambridge, really."

Harry stirred his coffee faster, smiling into it. At close quarters, Harry didn't smell bad, just a little stale, like he'd worn his clothes too long. Peter could see the wristband was from Cambridge Hospital. John Doe 22 was the name printed on it.

"So. You've been under the weather?" Peter asked.

"They're all liars," Harry said as he calmly took a sip, sighed, and settled onto the stool as if he meant to set awhile. "They tried to poison me."

"Did they?"

Harry gave a quick glance at the light sculpture overhead. "Fish bones," he said. It did, indeed look like blue fluorescent fish bones hanging against a black ceiling. Geek art.

"So they tried to poison you?" Peter asked, trying to get the conversation back on track.

"Meat."

"Meat." Peter repeated the word. He had no idea what Harry was talking about. That's when Peter noticed that Harry's flyer said, in smaller letters under the headline, "A Beginner's Guide to Animal Liberation." Was he a PETA recruit? Peter mentally lowered the likelihood that Harry was the A-bomber. A rabid antivivisectionist would be more likely to target research labs at Harvard where they were breeding mutant fruit flies, mice, and who knew what-all other unnatural beasties. On the other hand, schizophrenics weren't known for their clear thinking. Convoluted logic could be used to justify anything.

"So how'd you end up in the hospital?"

Harry gave a furtive glance, side to side, and held his hand up to shield his mouth. "I should have seen it coming. First they send someone around to cover up my posters. Saboteur. I told him that was my corner, my pole. But he just laughed. Called me"—Harry rubbed a spot on his forehead where there was what looked like an inch-long scar, still pink, with suture marks around it—"capitalist scum." He picked at his wristband. "Prison. I was a hostage," he said, his mind caroming to unconnected thoughts.

"So he took your flag?"

Harry nodded, his eyes filling up with outrage. "Grabbed it off me and hit me with it." Harry gave a sly smile. "But I got him back. Knocked over his scooter. Showed him."

A man on a scooter who was covering over Harry's flyers with his own? Peter tried not to show his excitement. Maybe Harry'd had a confrontation with the A-bomber.

"He had a scooter? You remember what color it was?"

"White. Except where I bashed it with my foot."

Peter had a pretty good idea what had happened next. Harry's bleeding. He gets taken to Cambridge Hospital, gets his head stitched. As far as he's concerned, the doctors and ambulance attendants are all part of the conspiracy, so he has to protect himself. They ship him to the psych unit for evaluation. He won't give his name to the "enemy," not in a million years, so the police don't know where he is. Weeks later, he washes up back in the Square, clean-shaven, flag broken, just another weirdo street preacher.

Harry leaned forward and looked up and down the street. "They're after me again."

"They are?"

"That's what Linda told me. Came around five or six times, looking for me, asking questions." Harry gouged a wad of paper napkins from the table dispenser and slipped them into his pocket. "Hit men."

If Harry's story was true, then that nondescript white scooter the police were on the lookout for had a ding or two in it. The police would want to talk to Harry, have him look at suspects. But Harry was a wily creature, hard to catch. The whiff of a blue uniform and he'd make himself scarce.

While Harry picked raisins out of his scone, Peter excused himself and went into the men's room to call MacRae, leaving the door open a crack so he could keep an eye on Harry.

"Did you get an email?" MacRae asked before Peter had a chance to say anything.

Peter admitted that he hadn't yet checked. When he told MacRae where he was and whom he was with, MacRae exploded. "You keep telling us you're not a profiler—has anyone mentioned to you that you're not a detective, either? And how do you know it's him?"

"He's shaved off his beard, and he's pale. But I recognize him. I've seen him before. He's been in the hospital all this time."

Now Harry was thoughtfully dipping a piece of scone in the coffee. Peter shrank back as Harry glanced over in the direction of the men's room door.

"I don't think he's your bomber. But he may have had a run-in with him." Peter told MacRae about Harry's altercation with a man on a white scooter. "If Harry was admitted to Cambridge Hospital as John Doe 22 on the same day as the law school bombing, then maybe the bomber broke his flag and—"

"Don't let him out of your sight," MacRae said. "We're coming over. Give me ten—"

"No uniforms. And try to keep a low . . ." The words died as Peter looked out again. Harry was gone. So were the extra packets of creamer. All that was left was a pile of raisins.

• • •

MacRae was apoplectic when Peter told him Harry had taken off.

"Great. He's probably gone underground again. Do me a favor, stay out of my investigation!" he thundered, and hung up.

Peter stood there, staring at the phone. MacRae was the one who'd asked *him* for help, he told himself, but that sounded like a pretty lame defense.

Peter raced back to the Harvard Square T station, hoping to find Harry. Harry's woman friend was still sitting on the sidewalk. Peter dropped a dollar bill into her cup. She mumbled thanks, and looked at him through a fringe of stringy hair. Her eyes were watery, and she smelled of urine and mothballs.

"Linda?" Peter said, hoping this was Harry's "Linda." The woman's face registered nothing. "Has Harry been back through here?"

Her gaze narrowed, but it wasn't in response to his question. It was something she saw over his shoulder. He turned. A dark sedan had pulled up in front of the newsstand and a tall, mocha-skinned man in jeans and a sweatshirt got out of the passenger seat. Neddleman. Across the street, in front of the Coop, a pair of uniformed officers were talking to passersby.

"Don't know any Harry," Linda said, her face impassive.

Neddleman stood by the entrance to the T station, giving Peter the eye. Peter went over to him.

"He was right here, talking to that woman, Linda's her name, I think—" Peter turned to show Neddleman where, but Linda had vanished, too.

He showed Neddleman Harry's flyer.

"Animal rights." Neddleman grunted in disgust. "I hate Cambridge."

Neddleman took the flyer by the corner and slipped it into an evidence bag. He gave Peter a hard stare. "Now would you get the hell—" He stopped. "Shit." He reached behind Peter and lifted a piece of paper taped to the low brick wall surrounding the area in front of the subway station. It began:

Societies without government enjoy an infinitely greater degree of happiness. Under pretense of governing they have divided

us into wolves & sheep. The jaws of commercial consumerism
devour us and leave us corrupt.

The text went on rambling about how we'd all been turned into rapacious consumers, and on into sexual profligacy and moral degeneracy. At the end was a circled A, but this time with a slash through it. What was that supposed to mean?

Flyers had gone up days before each of the previous bombings. Sure enough, there was another one, posted under the window of the jeweler's on the corner. Another was plastered to the side of the tourist kiosk. Christ, they were everywhere. Peter tried not to acknowledge the urge to yell "TAKE COVER" at the top of his lungs and sprint to his car to get the hell away from there.

That's when he noticed that Neddleman seemed unperturbed. In fact, he was chuckling to himself and shaking his head.

"What's so funny?"

"You gotta laugh because what else can you do? We found these damned things stuck to the Longfellow Bridge. We found 'em in the Kendall T station. On a Green Line train. They evacuated the Coop when a customer discovered one in the top floor men's room. Turned out they were in all the restrooms, men's and women's. Even found a copy at Louis." Louis Boston was an exclusive men's store on Newbury Street. "That's the problem when you go public with stuff like this. The wannabes crawl out of the woodwork. Now we've got choruses crying wolf, and we don't know which one means business."

18

ANNIE CAME out of her office at three that afternoon. Jackie was standing by her desk with her coat on, putting on lipstick.

"You leaving early?" Annie asked. She cringed at her own words. She was starting to sound like Verna Lovejoy, the woman who had run the downtown office where Annie worked for a summer when she was eighteen. Every time Annie arrived at a minute after eight, or got up to leave for lunch five minutes before noon, Miss Lovejoy got that smug, sanctimonious look on her face, raised her eyebrows, and exhaled, making a little sound like she'd chomped down on a miniature whoopy cushion. The old battle-ax. Scary, the woman had seemed ancient, but she'd probably been about the age Annie was now. Unmarried, no kids, no life outside of work, and . . . Annie shuddered. There were entirely too many parallels.

"It's fine," Annie said. Of course it was fine. She'd promised Jackie that as long as she did the work, she could have whatever leeway she needed to keep her life in order. Jackie was certainly holding up her end of the deal—she'd eliminated the backlog of paperwork, reorganized their files, reduced their list of deadbeat clients by half, and come in just about every day to ask Annie if there was anything else she could do.

"I'm finished with everything. I've got some errands to do before I pick up Sophie," she said, her voice sounding a little too bright. She dropped the lipstick into her purse and left.

Annie watched from the office window as Jackie emerged from the building entrance. She hesitated a short way up the street, looked up and down, then got out her cell phone and continued walking. About halfway to the light at the corner, a station wagon eased up alongside her. Jackie waved and ran over to it. The passenger door swung open. Annie shrank back as Jackie gave a furtive look over her shoulder, back toward the office. When she looked again, Jackie was gone. So was the car. Annie had a good idea who'd been driving.

This is not your problem, Annie reminded herself, trying to squash the irritation she felt. It was Jackie's life. Staying away from Joe wasn't a condition of employment, certainly not a condition of friendship.

Annie sat down to work. Jackie had stuck a Post-it to her computer monitor: "HOURS!" Jackie couldn't bill the clients if Annie didn't log her hours. Annie had fallen nearly three weeks behind.

She pulled out her date book, opened the spreadsheet Jackie had prepared for her, and began transferring her chicken-scratched notes. She logged one week's hours and kept going. When she got to a week ago Tuesday, she logged the four hours she'd spent that morning doing a background check on a client's prospective business partner. What had she done in the afternoon? Right. That was when she'd taken off to go to the zoo with Abby and Jackie, the same afternoon that the bomb went off at the county courthouse at a time when Joe Klevinski was having a job interview. Supposedly.

Annie logged the rest of her hours and closed the file. Jackie had also left her a pile of a half-dozen transcribed affidavits. She picked the top one off the pile and stared at the neatly stapled pages. She needed to read it and write a summary, but her gaze wasn't focused on the words. She was thinking about the first Mrs. Joe Klevinski. Annie mulled over Jackie's words: *What kind of mother takes her son away from his father like that?* How hard had Klevinski tried to find her? Annie wondered. Had he hired an investigator? It wasn't all that easy to disappear completely. Too bad the first Mrs. K wasn't around. Talking to her might have convinced Jackie that Joe wasn't going to change.

Or maybe not. Maybe no one could find her because she was dead. Dead people were actually pretty easy to find. Annie opened a browser window and typed in the URL for the online Social Security Death Index. She didn't know her first name, so all she typed was KLEVINSKI in the LAST NAME field. Fortunately, that was a fairly unusual last name. A list came back. She scanned it, looking for women in the right age range. There were none. Not officially dead.

Annie went back to reading the affidavit. The words blurred across the page. Idly, she opened up an online directory. She typed in KLEVINSKI and MA. Back came Joseph Klevinski in Cambridge; the address was the apartment Jackie lived in, the one she'd made Joe move out of. There were also a Carl Klevinski in New Bedford and an Elaine in Franklin. Maybe that was her. Or maybe she'd gone back to using her maiden name, or remarried. There were entirely too many possible scenarios.

Annie knew this was a waste of time. She was procrastinating, putting off the busywork she hated. But she was curious. She widened the search area to the entire United States, and dozens of names came back. There was Anna in North Carolina. C in Union, New Jersey—it was usually women who were listed by first initial.

An androgynous Dana from Paramus, New Jersey. Scrolling through the list, she noticed there was also a Joseph in Toledo. Little Joey would be twelve. Kids that age sometimes had phones listed in their own names. She printed the list.

Through the open office doorway, Annie could see Jackie's desk with its bowl of hard candy and framed school photograph of Sophie. If Joe and his first wife had been living in Cambridge, then undoubtedly they'd been to family court, right across the street from the district courthouse, less than a mile from Annie's office. If there'd been a restraining order, there'd have been a hearing. Divorce and custody hearings, complaints for protection—all she had to do was pull the records, and *voilà*, she'd have a first name, a maiden name, a social security number. Armed with that information, the rest would be easy. Like making a chink in the tough hull of a coconut, just a few more gentle taps would send fissures all around, releasing the meat inside.

Annie checked her watch. The family court records office was open for another hour. With traffic starting to back up, she'd get there faster on foot. She switched her boots for sneakers, put on her jacket, and tucked her wallet, a pad, and a pen into her pocket. She turned out the lights and locked the office.

Her cheeks stung from the wind as she ran up narrow, tree-lined Third Street, past converted red-brick industrial buildings and handsome old row houses. The sky was dark with clouds, the treetops swayed and quivered in stiff wind gusts. The horizon lit up, and far off there was a roll of thunder. No time to go back for an umbrella.

Fat drops of rain pelted her as she ran past the yellow sawhorses that blocked off Thorndike Street and stretched across the front of the district courthouse. She ran around to the front of the probate court building on the next block. Family court records were there on the second floor.

Rain came down more steadily as Annie ran past the wide granite steps leading to the base of four massive brick columns that framed the building's original entryway. The modern entrance was a purely functional wooden door in the side of the base of the steps. Two men and a woman were huddled to one side, smoking.

She made it inside just as the sky opened up in earnest. She was surprised to find a line of people backed up into the narrow, high-ceilinged entry tunnel. They were waiting to go through security. That was odd. This late in the day it had usually cleared out.

Annie squeezed past, waving her court ID. When she got to the front, she realized the cause of the backup. They'd started photo-graphing visitors. The line must have been out onto the street and around the corner earlier in the day.

She got to the staff entrance and handed the security officer her court ID and key card. He was a fresh-faced kid, his hair slicked back. Security had been tightened here, too. He wanted to see a sec-ond ID. She showed him her driver's license. He looked back and forth from her to the photo. *Okay, so I had a bad hair day* — she knew better than to crack the joke. She gazed out into the lobby while he wrote her name in a logbook. Another new procedure. The people who packed the benches of the crowded, stuffy room looked as if they were waiting for trains, not their day in court.

"Ma'am?" the security guard said. "I said you can go in now."

Ma'am? Sheesh. Annie strode past the snack bar that filled one corner of the lobby and took the stairs to the second-floor records room. She had plenty of time; usually the lines were shorter this late in the day. When she reached the doorway, she stood there in dis-may. The low-ceilinged room with its counters and crowds of people looked like Filene's Basement during a sale. A sign hung over one counter: DIVORCE. Over another: PATERNITY. She half expected to see PANTYHOSE over the counter where more than twenty people were lined up to request records. No way she'd get to the front of that line and get what she needed before the place closed. Damn.

She'd just turned to leave when the lights flickered, and there was a crash of thunder that shook the floor. There were screams as the place went dark, then silence. *Another bomb?* The thought swept through the building like a foul-smelling wind.

It seemed like minutes, but it was probably only seconds before the lights came back on, and a rumble and hum as the building's assorted systems came back online. There was nervous laughter.

Annie stood at the second-floor balcony and looked down on the round tables that crowded the center area of the main floor. She hated to go home empty-handed.

"Pain in the ass," a man grumbled as he walked past and headed down the stairs. "Figures it would happen right when I get to the front of the line," a woman said to another as she brushed past.

In the good old days, when Annie had just started doing this kind of work, there were no computers to crash. You looked up what you wanted in a master index and then checked out the ledger you needed. Now, with the index online, everything ground to a halt when the computers burped.

Annie returned to the records room. Just a few patrons and the staff remained inside. Lightning flashed again, and rain poured in sheets down the windows.

"Annie? Annie Squires?" Annie thought she recognized the man's voice. She turned. Did she know this florid man wearing a three-piece suit who seemed to know her? "You don't recognize me, do you?"

Then it dawned on her who he was. If he'd been wearing his cop's uniform she'd have recognized him instantly. Instead of shaking his offered hand, she hugged him. Then she stood back and took in the pinstripes. "You're not a lawyer now, are you?"

He chuckled. "Lawyer? Me? Hell no. I got a nice desk job, though. That's my office." He pointed to a door that said CHIEF CLERK, and below that CHARLES AYRE.

"No kidding," Annie said as she remembered what her Uncle Jack had said about how Charlie had a knack for helping out the right people.

"How's Jack?" Charlie asked, his face solemn with concern.

"He's pretty good," Annie said, and brought him up to date on how her uncle had moved into a nursing home. She didn't tell him that Uncle Jack rarely recognized her or her mother when they came to visit.

"And yourself?" he asked. "You still in the business?"

Annie knew what cops and ex-cops thought about her business, the business of helping defendants. "Actually, I was here hoping to pull some divorce records. It's for one of our clients who's also a friend. A good friend." She gave Charlie a sideways look. "She's being harassed by her ex. He was married before, divorced. I thought there might be prior restraining orders. You know, that kind of thing."

"A friend?" Charlie said, and put his index finger under Annie's chin and studied her face.

Cripes, he was looking for bruises. She laughed and pulled away. "No, it's not me. Really, it's not."

Charlie shepherded her into his office. There, from one of the walnut bookcases that stood tall between arched windows overlooking Cambridge Street, he grabbed a CD. He explained to Annie that he kept his own copy of the records index since the network was "slow as molasses." He slid the CD into his PC and brought up a window.

Annie wrote down "Joseph Klevinski" and Charlie typed in the name. He shook his head and clucked to himself at what he was finding.

"This guy's a piece of work."

A few minutes later, armed with notes written on a scrap of paper, Annie returned with Charlie to the main room. He pulled a half-dozen ledgers of court records and made her promise to return them to their spots.

"Gonna have to throw you out of here in twenty minutes, or I'd make you tell me what you've been up to. Next time you come, you give me a call. We'll get some coffee," he said, and left Annie to her work.

PETER COLLECTED souvenir copies of the wannabe A-bomber flyer as he walked back to his car on Dunster Street. The damned things were posted everywhere. Peter unlocked his car. Despite his detour for coffee and encounter with Harvard Harry, he had plenty of time to get back to the Pearce for his final appointment with Rudy Ravitch before discharging him. He got into his car. He knew he should have called the police the minute he'd spotted Harry. MacRae and Neddleman had every reason to be pissed at him. No, he wasn't a detective, as MacRae so helpfully pointed out.

A car horn jolted Peter from his thoughts. A silver Honda was pulled up alongside him, and the driver was jerking his thumb at him. *All right, all right, I'm going,* he thought as he started the car.

He made it around the corner and back up to Mass Ave. Then traffic came to a halt. He heard what sounded like chanting, and someone shouting through a bullhorn. Shit. A demonstration. He crept closer. Traffic was narrowed to one lane to make room for double-parked police vans. The Cambridge Common swarmed with demonstrators, an odd assortment of what looked like college students and older people, women mostly, waving hand-painted signs and shouting "Freedom, Freedom!" LIBERATION FROM RIGHT WING TYRANNY was written on one sign. OUR DEMOCRACY IS IN DANGER, said another. A woman who looked a lot like one of Peter's mother's mah-jongg friends was holding a placard aloft. When the woman turned away, he could see that printed on the other side was a campaign poster for Ralph Nader.

As police officers frantically assembled yellow sawhorse barriers along the edges of the Common, a crush of demonstrators spilled out into the street. A young man in a Harvard sweatshirt waved a sign in Peter's windshield—AMERICAN DICTATORSHIP. RED ALERT. BIG BROTHER IS AMONG US. MacRae would love this.

Peter hit the steering wheel in frustration. There wasn't a damned thing to do except put the car in neutral and call Gloria. At least she could let Ravitch know he was running late. After he made the call, he flipped on the radio and tried to relax.

Finally the traffic began to move, first in fits and starts, then at a steady crawl. As soon as he could, he turned off and cut through to Mount Auburn. He might have made it with minutes to spare if it hadn't been for the security backup at the gate. Instead, by the time he'd parked, he was fifteen minutes late.

Peter ran the length of the parking lot, up the winding road, then up the hill to the unit. It was dark and overcast, and leaves were blowing across the sky like flocks of starlings. Winded, he let himself in the side door of the unit. Kwan just stood there watching, poker-faced, as Peter stood in the hallway catching his breath. He knew Kwan was dying to make some smart-alecky remark.

He picked up Ravitch's chart at the nurses' station and took the elevator to the third floor. He hurried up the hall past Kwan's office.

Kwan had left his door open. Peter paused, the administrator in him kicking in. He pushed Kwan's door shut and made a mental note to remind the staff about safeguarding patient privacy. They could be fined $250 for every patient file left unlocked.

He continued to his office, expecting to see Ravitch waiting for him in the chair in the hall. The waiting area was empty. Maybe Ravitch had given up and gone downstairs. Peter got out his keys, unlocked the door, and entered his office. He'd just put down his briefcase when there was a tap at the door. It was Ravitch.

"Sorry I'm late," Peter said. "I didn't see you."

"I was in the bathroom," he said, indicating the men's room at the opposite end of the hall. He took a seat. "Hey, Doc, these pills you have me on? They supposed to make you sick?"

Peter ducked under the overhanging eaves and sat at his desk, ignoring the blinking red message light on his phone. He turned on the desk lamp and examined Ravitch's face. His skin was pale and pasty-looking, and there was a skim of perspiration on his upper lip. He flipped open Ravitch's chart. Kwan had prescribed Paxil for depression and Ativan for anxiety.

"Stomach ache, diarrhea?"

Ravitch gave a doleful nod.

"Unfortunately, those are some of the side effects of what you're taking. Keeping you from eating?"

"I wish," Ravitch said, looking down at his paunchy stomach. "I'm hungry all the time."

Unfortunately, that was another side effect.

"How about bad dreams?" Ravitch asked.

That wasn't from the drugs. "Tell me about them."

"They're about Leon. Leon and me." Ravitch took a deep breath, held it, then exhaled. "Like last night, I dreamed I'm outside the courthouse and this guy comes out, lights up a cigarette, takes a puff.

Then he turns back, opens the door, and I want to tell him to put out his cigarette, there's no smoking inside. Turns out he's not going in. He throws the lighted cigarette into the lobby. Only it isn't a cigarette, it's a bomb."

Ravitch rubbed his hand back and forth across his mouth. "That's not even the worst. Couldn't get back to sleep at all after this one." He cracked his knuckles and stared down at his hands. "I was the bomber." As if in sympathy, a distant roll of thunder rumbled.

"So *you* were the bomber?" Peter said, keeping his voice even.

"Uh-huh. I had it in a paper bag with my lunch. I took it out, and it was like, you know, one of those cartoon bombs, a bowling ball with a lit fuse on top? And I gave it to Leon, and"—Ravitch's mouth twisted into a grimace and he clenched his hands together—"and he takes it from me, and you know what he does? He bites off the fuse. I try to tell him stop, but he's already bitten into it, like it's an apple, and then he just stands there chewing. Then he hands the rest of the bomb back to me. I'm panicked. I want to throw it outside, bury it, but when I look down I see there's nothing but a pile of ashes in my hand. And I want to run away because I know what's going to happen. And I want Leon to come with me, only the bomb's inside him now."

Peter sat back. There were pills for depression, pills for anxiety, but not a single goddamned pill for guilt. All he could do was offer a sympathetic ear.

Ravitch went on. "So I don't know what to do, and I'm pleading with Leon, Tell me what to do. And you know what he does? He says to me, 'Don't sweat it, Rudy. Life's too short.' When I wake up, I can still hear his voice ringing in my head, and I'm soaking in my own sweat."

Peter waited before saying anything, respecting the feelings and the story he'd just heard.

"You've been through a terrible trauma, and these dreams, they're your mind's way of coping. You wanted to rescue him, so you keep having dreams in which you try to make it come out right." He could explain it, but he couldn't fix it. Medication and a good therapist could get Ravitch through the weeks and months to come, but they'd never fully put these issues to rest.

Before the hour was up, Peter had made the necessary referral for follow-up care and promised to write a letter supporting Ravitch's claim for disability.

"Hey," Ravitch said as he was leaving, "one good thing: I quit smoking. Haven't had a cigarette all week. Haven't wanted one. Did you do that? When I was hypnotized?"

"No, you did that yourself. Congratulations."

Ravitch shook his head in wonder. "I been trying for years. Helluva way to quit."

. . .

Ravitch left, and Peter checked his phone messages. Rain beat on the window and clattered on the copper roof overhead. There were a dozen calls, most of them routine hospital business. He jotted notes to himself as he listened.

"Hey, you promised to get back to me. I know you're been busy . . . hey, who isn't?" The high-pitched voice with a slight lisp sounded familiar. The man identified himself as Walt Waxman, reporter from the *Boston Phoenix*. Peter remembered the earlier call.

"I just have a couple of questions. Is there a profile of the type of person who does this kind of thing?" His voice had turned to a monotone, as if he were reading. "Why is he quoting American patriot Thomas Paine?" A pause. "Do 'raptor' and 'maw' suggest the influence of violent computer games?" Peter could hear papers shuffling. "Is there —"

Peter pressed SKIP and the voice cut off. Didn't the police have an official press liaison this guy could pester?

The next message was from Neddleman. "Call me back," and a phone number. That was it. Peter knew he'd want to know if there'd been a reply to his email.

Peter logged in and checked. Twenty-two new messages. He scanned the list. There it was. Peter felt a grim sense of satisfaction. CANARY911 had taken the bait.

The subject line was DON'T KNOW WHAT'S HAPPENING, DO YOU, DR. ZAK? That was a corrupted phrase from Bob Dylan's "Ballad of a Thin Man."

```
You are so transparent. Plans are taking shape that
you, misguided soul, would never imagine. You look
right at Us and see nothing.

What is the end game? Prison? Death? This life only
keeps Us from higher pursuits. As a poet once said,
"You want to hang me, OK, poke me, shock me, just
gonna last for three minutes, five minutes, two
minutes, then you're dead." Death would be Nirvana.
Prison bliss. Instead We are torn asunder, ripped
apart.

Our government is the potent, the omnipresent
teacher. If the government becomes a law breaker,
it breeds contempt for law; it invites every man to
become a law unto himself; it invites Anarchy.

We are merely the agent of change. The work contin-
ues. This purging must be finished. First the
spawn. Then the workers. And now the drones where
they sit, swollen and glowing scarlet with their
```

own self-importance, obsequious parasites fawning
over their Queen, or should I say King.

The Fleet Center? That is a place only the Maw
could drive Us.

Peter forwarded the email to Neddleman and called.

"Interesting. You haven't answered him yet?" Neddleman asked
after he'd read it.

"Of course I haven't. I called you as soon as—"

"Yeah, right. Well, there's that at least." There was silence on the
line. Peter could imagine him rereading the message. "You know
who he's quoting?"

"Bob Dylan. 'Don't know what's happening—'"

Neddleman snorted. "Not that. I meant that other part. 'You want
to hang me, poke me . . .' It's that kid, the DC sniper. That's what he
said to the police when they asked him if he thought he'd be exe-
cuted. This guy hasn't an original thought in his head. I wonder who
else he parrots. Timothy McVeigh? Osama Bin Laden?"

"I agree with you about one thing," Peter said. "I don't think this
is about anarchy, per se, or any organized movement. It's a load of
pseudointellectualized philosophy, all in the service of a really schizophrenic delusion. This person feels trapped between this maw of
his and—what does he call it?—the marshal. This has nothing to do
with people outside of himself. He's blowing things up because he
believes he can restore balance and bring his world back from the
maw." Peter skimmed the message on his own computer screen.
"He's going to keep doing this."

"So, is there any good news?"

"Only that he's talking."

"But what the hell does it mean?" There was a long pause.

It sounded as if Neddleman had his hand over the receiver and was talking to someone. "We're having a status meeting later tonight. Any chance I could get you to come over? I'd like the other members of the task force to hear your thoughts on what we're dealing with here."

"Sure." Peter would have to break a dinner date he had with Annie, but she'd understand. "But you know, I'm not—"

"I know, I know. You're not a profiler. But this guy has tuned into you, for some reason. We need your expertise on board."

THE RAIN had stopped by the time Annie walked back to her office from family court. It had turned colder, and the intermittent drizzle had turned to an occasional flurry of snow. She zipped her leather jacket, turned up the collar, and walked back along Third Street holding her arms crossed in front of her. She'd found what she was looking for, and most of it was predictable.

Brenda. That was Joe Klevinski's first wife's name. Née Mulvaney. Married him when she was just eighteen years old. Now she'd be thirty.

Annie had a page of scribbled notes. After four years of marriage and three restraining orders, Brenda had filed for divorce, saying her husband threatened to kill her and their son. Klevinski was awarded only supervised visits with his son. That must have pissed the hell out of him. They were back in court twice, wrangling over visitation rights. He began threatening the social worker who drew the short straw and had to supervise the visits. Six years ago there was another skirmish in court, and Klevinski lost all rights to visit his son. Then nada. Zilch. The paper trail ended.

What had happened after Klevinski lost his visitation rights? The silence seemed ominous. Annie found it hard to swallow that he'd clicked his heels together, saluted, and left Brenda and Joey to get on with their lives. Maybe they'd gone into hiding when Brenda realized that court order or no, there was little to protect them from such a determined and violent abuser.

At least now Annie had a name, a social security number, and a prior address in North Cambridge. She also had the name of Brenda's divorce attorney, Rachel Bernstein. Annie knew her. Bernstein had occasionally referred clients.

Annie quickened her pace back to the office. Hurrying made no sense — Brenda Klevinski had been missing for years. Still, she broke into a run. There was a chance Bernstein hadn't yet left her office for home.

She found the number, called, and was relieved when Bernstein answered. Yes, she remembered Brenda Klevinski. No, she hadn't heard from Brenda in years. Not since the last custody hearing.

"I know you probably didn't have a personal relationship with her, but I wonder if you had a sense of whether Brenda Klevinski was afraid of her husband. Was she desperate enough to go into hiding?" Annie asked.

Rachel Bernstein didn't answer right away. "She was afraid of her ex. And yes, enough afraid that she'd want to run away."

Want to run away? Annie sensed a note of hesitancy in her answer. "But?"

"I just thought it was odd, that's all. She didn't pay my last bill. I do a lot of work for people who don't have much money. This case was through Legal Aid, so it wasn't a big-ticket item. It happens. It's just that I can usually tell who's going to stiff me."

Annie hung up the phone and sat in the semidarkness trying to digest what she now knew. So, she thought, addressing the shadowy figure she imagined sitting across the desk from her, have you changed your name? Pulled your life together? Were you just flat broke and that's why you didn't pay your attorney? Or did you need every penny you had to make your escape?

What about Joey? Was he all grown up and in junior high now? Hanging out with a crowd, downloading music from the Internet and wanting to get himself tattooed? Would he ever meet his spunky half-sister?

Annie's computer glowed, inviting her to take the next step. If only Annie could find Brenda and convince her to share what had really happened, maybe that would show Jackie what kind of man she'd married. She set to work.

First she ran a social security trace. Back came information, an address that hadn't been updated in ten years. As far as the U.S. government was concerned, Brenda Klevinski was alive and well and living in North Cambridge. That must have been where she'd shared a home with Joe. The only prior address was Worcester. Maybe that was where she grew up.

Next Annie went to a crisscross directory and typed in the North Cambridge address. Paul Shortsleeves was listed as living there now. A boyfriend or husband? Seemed unlikely. If Brenda were still in North Cambridge, then why would Joe tell Jackie that she'd run off. Still, it was possible that Paul Shortsleeves or one of his neighbors had known Brenda.

When Annie entered Brenda's prior address in Worcester, "S. Mulvaney" came back. She felt the familiar rush she got when two pieces of information meshed. Mulvaney was Brenda's maiden name.

Annie chewed her lip and gazed at the computer screen. *Move ahead, take the next step,* her inner voice urged. She wanted to jump in her car and drive over to North Cambridge and have a chat with Paul Shortsleeves or whoever was living in the apartment Brenda and Joe had once shared. She checked her watch. It was rush hour. Should she call first?

The phone rang as she was reaching for it.

"I got another email," Peter said without so much as a hello. "Sounds like he's planning his next attack."

Annie's stomach turned over.

"He's teasing us with hints about what he's going to do next. The task force wants me to come help them sort out what it means. This evening. I know we were going to have dinner. You don't mind, do you?"

Annie felt a guilty pang. She'd been so caught up in tracking Brenda Klevinski that she'd forgotten their date.

"It's okay. Actually, I thought I'd—" she started. She knew Peter had qualms about her hiring Jackie. He thought she was too involved in Jackie's life. You couldn't be friend, employer, and counselor all at the same time. On top of that, Peter thought Joe Klevinski was bad news. If Peter weren't so sweet on Sophie, no doubt he'd have raised a stink about Pearl babysitting her in the afternoons. Problem was, Peter was right. Klevinski was a bomb waiting to go off. That was why she had to gather whatever information she could to convince Jackie to stay away from him.

"I thought I'd work a little more, talk to a few people, then go home and take a hot bath. I'm pretty pooped."

It wasn't a lie, not really. Besides, he had a full plate. He didn't need to be worrying about what she was up to.

• • •

Ten minutes later Annie was on her way. She took Hampshire Street to Porter Square, up Mass Ave, then cut over to side streets. With any luck, by the time she got to his North Cambridge house, Paul Short-sleeves would be home from work, settled in front of the TV having a beer.

The address turned out to be a modest triple-decker, a lot like Annie's. The lights were on in the windows on all three floors. Only a few peels of pale blue paint remained on the front steps, and what must have once been a shingled façade had gray asbestos siding slapped over it. The house next door had had a makeover, complete with stained glass and skylights. A sign planted in the flower bed by the front steps proclaimed the house protected twenty-four hours. The house on the other side was falling-down decrepit and had a sign planted in front, too, stuck in the patch of dirt that passed for a front lawn: FOR SALE. Even teardowns in this neighborhood could fetch upwards of half a million. The world had gone nuts.

Annie climbed the front steps and crossed the dark front porch. She got a penlight from her bag and turned it on. SHORTSLEEVES was handwritten on a piece of weathered masking tape above the middle doorbell. She rang. A dog barked from above.

The barking got louder, and there were sounds of paws scrabbling down steps and heavier footsteps. Someone peered out through the small glass panel in the door.

"Who are you?" came in a man's voice from the other side of the door, barely audible over the dog's snuffling and yapping.

"Mr. Shortsleeves?" Annie said.

There was no answer.

"My name is Annie Squires. Sorry to bother you, I was looking for Brenda"—Annie wasn't sure which last name to use—"Mulvaney."

"There's no one here—"

"Brenda Klevinski?" Annie tried.

The dog sneezed and fell silent, and there was whispering from behind the door. "Are you a friend of hers?"

Annie didn't hesitate. "Yes. I know she lived here a while back. Is she in?"

There was the sound of more whispering, then shuffling. The lock clicked open. When the door opened, an elderly man and woman peered out at her. The man had thick white hair, and his brown cardigan hung from stooped shoulders. Despite the woman's blond hair, she was probably about Annie's mother's age. She had on a white apron covered with dancing green apples. The fierce beast she held in her arms was a squirming white toy poodle. The house breathed out the savory smell of roasting chicken.

"She doesn't live here anymore. But if you find her, would you let us know?" the woman said.

"Sure, but—" Annie said, feeling thoroughly confused.

"It's been so long," the woman said, her voice fretful. "We meant to take it all to the post office, but then, well, you know how it is, one thing and another."

"Pardon me?" Annie said.

"Her mail," the man said.

Mr. and Mrs. Shortsleeves explained that when they moved into the apartment six years earlier, there had been a small but steady stream of mail for the former tenant. For weeks they left it out for the mailman to return.

"We were here about a month when a big envelope came from Sears," Mrs. Shortsleeves said. "It was photographs. You know, family portraits. I handed it to our mail carrier myself. I wanted to be sure that she got the package. That's when he told me she hadn't left a forwarding address. I felt so bad, knowing those pictures were going to get thrown away. I was sure she'd have wanted to have them."

The stream of mail dwindled, they told Annie. But still, every couple of months, there'd be something else. They knew there was no point in giving it to the mailman, and they couldn't bring themselves to throw it away, so they'd set it aside. Annie's heartbeat quickened at this news.

"If you find her, would you tell her? We'd much rather see her get her mail than send it back. They might not even take it after all this time," Mrs. Shortsleeves said.

"I'll let her know," Annie said, trying to sound nonchalant. "I'm sure I'll track her down soon." Annie made as if to leave, then hesitated. "I suppose I could, I mean, if you'd like me to take it to her . . . if you wouldn't mind?"

"Oh, would you?" Mrs. Shortsleeves said.

Mr. Shortsleeves was less easily gulled. He gave Annie a penetrating look as if he were trying to see down into Annie's soul and determine if she was trustworthy.

"I'd be glad to take it," Annie said. "And if I don't find her in the next couple of weeks, I'll bring it to the post office myself. I promise."

Mrs. Shortsleeves whispered something to her husband. He whispered back. It was decided. They led Annie up to the apartment. The door was standing open. Annie stepped inside and waited in the living room.

This was the apartment where Joe and Brenda Klevinski had lived together, where their marriage had gone sour. This was where Joey had grown from baby to toddler to little boy. She looked around. Had Joe Klevinski been the idiot who covered the living room walls with ersatz wood paneling. It made the room, with its handsome bay window, feel closed in and claustrophobic.

Mrs. Shortsleeves put the dog down. It ran circles around Annie, sniffing at her pant leg and growling. Probably smelled cat. Annie scratched the dog's head and pushed it firmly away.

Mrs. Shortsleeves opened the door to a coat closet while Mr. Shortsleeves carried over a stepladder.

Annie moved to the window. She could imagine Brenda standing there, looking out. The corner lot across the street was neatly divided into rectangular spaces, now a tangle of spent tomato plants and withering squash vines. A community garden. Had Brenda had a plot there? Had she helped Joey plant carrots and radishes?

"Here it is," Mrs. Shortsleeves said, pulling a large cardboard box off the closet shelf. She climbed down and handed it to Annie.

Annie lifted the flap—the box was nearly full.

"Thanks," Annie said. "Just curious—when you first looked at the apartment, was Brenda still living here?"

"Oh, no. It was empty. Spic-and-span. Remember, Paul? Brand spanking new kitchen, too."

"Clean as a whistle," Mr. Shortsleeves said. "Mr. Donahue told us the previous tenant moved out without telling him. Only way he knew was the rent checks stopped coming."

"Donahue is the landlord?"

"Was. Now it's his son. Lives up in Andover." Mr. Shortsleeves clucked disapproval. "He's let this place go to hell in a handbasket, that's for sure."

Annie thanked the couple and left. Before returning to her car, she tried the other building tenants. Upstairs were college students. Downstairs lived Hilda Blake, a thickset woman who looked as if she might have posed for the buffalo nickel. She remembered Brenda Klevinski.

"Mousy little thing," she said, sniffing. "Rarely left the apartment. Husband was . . . polite." *Damned with faint praise*, Annie thought.

Through the open door, Annie could see Hilda Blake's living room. Knickknacks crowded every doily-covered surface. There were Hummel figurines, cut glass bowls, a pair of lamps with puffy, stained-glass shades that glowed garish red, yellow, and green. The place made Annie's teeth itch.

"We have only two left! This gorgeous bellaluce fancy cut

ring . . ." said a perky voice from within the apartment. It was the TV—the Shopping Channel.

"You lived right under them. You must have"—Annie hesitated—"heard things."

"I don't listen." Hilda Blake pressed her thick lips together and gave Annie a sharp look. "And I don't gossip. What would be the point, anyway. They're long gone."

"You knew they were divorced?"

Hilda Blake blinked. "Oh. So that's why I didn't hear . . ." She cleared her throat. "No, I didn't."

Hilda Blake's apartment would not have been a place Brenda could come for refuge.

"So you wouldn't have any idea where Brenda Klevinski went when she moved out?"

"He's the one who moved out. Came one night with a moving van and cleaned the place out."

"He moved out at night?"

"Guess he worked days." Hilda Blake shrugged.

Wouldn't want to get mugged outside Hilda Blake's front door. She'd probably just turn up the TV to drown out the noise.

Later that night, while the meatball sub she'd picked up on her way home was congealing in the bag on the counter, Annie sat at her kitchen table. She'd sorted Brenda Klevinski's mail.

Bills were in one pile, offers to open new credit card accounts in another, a pile of quarterly statements from Fleet Bank in another, and finally a pile of miscellaneous junk mail. There were no party invitations or birth announcements, no Christmas cards or letters. Nothing from Joey's school. Not a single handwritten envelope addressed to Brenda Klevinski.

Why were there only three credit card bills but a thick pile of bank statements? She fingered the most recent MasterCard bill.

It was postmarked six years earlier. She pushed aside doubts—ripping off mail was certainly illegal—and opened it. The statement had an overdue balance of $104.30. Where were the subsequent bills? Maybe Brenda paid off the balance and closed the account before she left town, or maybe she changed the billing address.

Apparently she'd never informed the bank of her move. The most recent bank statement was postmarked a month ago, and addressed to Brenda Mulvaney. The account in her maiden name was still open. Not a big deal. Lots of people moved and neglected to close out old bank accounts. When Annie was scrambling to pay bills right after she and Chip went into private practice, she'd done some work recovering inactive bank accounts, often for relatives of people who'd died intestate. Nine times out of ten, her bill exceeded the amount remaining in the dormant account.

Annie tore open the most recent bank statement. She suppressed a gasp when she saw the balance. Brenda's savings account held more than twelve thousand dollars. That was probably a whole lot more than the legal bill she owed Rachel Bernstein.

One by one, Annie opened the rest of the statements and spread them out on the table. Other than monthly interest accruals, the account hadn't been touched in six years.

Tomorrow first thing, Annie promised herself, she'd have a chat with S. Mulvaney, or whomever she found hanging out in Worcester at Brenda's previous address. With any luck, there'd be a relative or family friend who'd take the pile of mail off her hands and offer some reassurance that Brenda was alive and well and keeping a healthy distance from her ex.

But as Annie sat back and surveyed the statements, she found herself increasingly uneasy. Twelve thousand dollars was a lot of money—money Brenda would have needed if she'd run away.

It was ridiculous, really. Brenda had taken off years ago. So why did Annie want answers yesterday? That was easy. She remembered Klevinski cruising down the street, Jackie waving and hopping into his car. *Sophie misses him* had been her excuse. How long would it be before she dropped the restraining order? Allowed him to move back in? By the time the beatings resumed, it would be too late for buyer's remorse. This time, Sophie could get seriously hurt in the cross fire.

Annie glanced over at the bank statements. Not a single penny touched in all these years. Why? The obvious answer was that Brenda either couldn't access her money, or had no more need to. She remembered the neighbor Hilda Blake's comment: *He's the one who moved out. Came one night with a moving van and cleaned the place out.*

Finding out what had happened to Brenda and Joey Klevinski no longer seemed optional. What if . . . Annie felt queasy as she took the next logical step. Maybe it was more than furniture that Joe loaded into that van. Suppose he killed them. It would have been easy to camouflage Brenda's body in a pile of bedding. Joey could have fit into a laundry basket. Then what? Somehow he disposes of them and goes home to Jackie and Sophie? Jackie and Sophie. She remembered hearing an expert talk about killers: *after each murder it becomes easier to kill again.*

She hadn't known how to help her friend Charlotte, and Charlotte's mother had died. The same thing wasn't going to happen to Jackie, not if Annie could help it.

PETER LEANED against the back wall of the room he now thought of as "the situation room" at the police station. He'd much rather be having dinner with Annie at Casablanca, garlicky hummus and pita bread to start, then savory lamb shank with a glass of good zin, and the whole night stretching before them. Instead he was drinking a cup of lousy coffee in a room packed with police officers from Cambridge and Boston, staties, and federal agents.

"How long is this going to take," one of the uniformed officers asked Neddleman, adding a belated "sir?"

"We'll get through as quickly as we can," Neddleman said. He looked taller, somehow, standing at the podium, his steady gaze keeping these guys in their seats. Impatience prickled in the air like static.

Peter tuned in and out as, in rapid succession, officers took turns firing off progress reports. They were checking on white scooters but hadn't found the dented one they were hoping was out there. About a half-dozen faces had been dropped from the gallery of suspects and as many new ones added. They were still looking for Harvard Harry.

An explosives expert got up to speak. He pushed his wire-rimmed glasses up on his long nose and waited until the room fell quiet. "We're dealing here with a homemade bomb," he said. "These types of devices fall into one of two general groups of explosive materials . . ." As he droned on, a couple of officers took out cell phones. Side conversations sprouted.

Neddleman interrupted. "Could you cut to the chase? We need to get these guys home to sleep or back out on the street as soon as possible."

The explosives expert blinked several times as his brain shifted gears. He began again. "The devices used in the law school and courthouse bombings were highly effective devices that use basic materials anyone can get their hands on. Nothing fancy, a bit old-fashioned, a couple of nine-volt batteries and a homemade timer."

He nodded and a projector turned on. A drawing of an open brief-case containing wires and a hodgepodge of batteries, wrapped packets, and a clock appeared on the wall. "This is approximately what it might have looked like. It would have been pretty heavy, maybe twenty or thirty pounds."

Peter would be up next. He tried to study the copy of the email he'd printed out, but found it difficult to focus. He was a neuropsychologist, never met a test he didn't like. He was at home in the hospital, in a courtroom facing a jury, even in jail going one-on-one with a defendant. Here he was completely out of his element, out of his league even. Every single guy in this room knew more about criminal behavior than he ever would. Neddleman had reassured him: that was exactly why they needed him. They weren't dealing with your garden-variety crook.

"Dr. Zak?" Neddleman's voice woke him from his thoughts. It was Peter's turn in the hot seat.

He jerked to his feet and spilled coffee on his pants. He set the cup on the floor and made his way to the front. Neddleman quickly introduced him and handed him the mike.

Officers in the front row sat with arms crossed and show-me looks on their faces. Peter shelved the talk he'd planned to give. They didn't need a lesson on schizophrenia.

"I live on a one-way street," he began. It was such an unexpected beginning that, for the moment at least, he had their full attention. "This morning I get in my car, I look over my shoulder, I back out onto the street, and come this close"—Peter held his open palms an inch apart—"to hitting a red Camaro. I'd looked right at it but it didn't register. That's because I hadn't *expected* to see someone backing *up* the one-way street. I tell you this story because you need to know that this guy isn't what you're expecting. This isn't someone who's getting into bar fights; he's no street creature preaching the end of the world, or a wild-eyed mountain man like Ted Kaczynski. He doesn't smell funny or mutter incantations under his breath. If he did, you'd already have him. Think about how he's managed to slip under the radar. He could look like one of you."

Now it was safe to move on to the psychology. "Okay, so he probably doesn't look like a crazy person. He's probably a schizophrenic, highly organized, with a set of ideals that, as distorted as they might be, he believes will save society. Yes, he's slipping off the edge, losing touch with reality as he becomes single-minded in his mission. He feels no guilt because he believes himself above the pedestrian notions of right and wrong."

Next, Peter turned his attention to the email. "He says, *'This Purging must be finished.'*" Peter pointed to the line on the screen.

MacRae came into the room. He was holding a piece of paper. He scanned the crowd, pausing when he saw Peter. An odd, speculative expression flicked across his face. Then his face went blank. He joined Neddleman in the back.

Peter continued, phrase by phrase, pointing out how it was logical, passionless, and how the bomber was targeting the legal system. "Pay attention to the metaphor . . ." Peter continued, feeling his voice rise as more and more heads turned to watch Neddleman and MacRae conferring. "Forget your preconceptions. He's smart, educated. He's working alone."

"I'm sorry to interrupt," Neddleman said, striding to the podium.

He gave Peter a crooked smile and took over the mike. There was a collective intake of breath. Neddleman held up his hands. "No new attacks. Just new information." He cleared his throat. "As you know, we believe that the bomber may have had a court ID and key card to get past security at the courthouse. We've been checking everyone whose key cards were scanned that morning. So far, we've found four people whose key cards were scanned that morning who claim they weren't there." A murmur swept through the room, and the word *four* echoed off the ceiling. "We've questioned these people. They all say they noticed their key cards were missing in the ten days or so before the bombing."

Peter couldn't believe his ears. He'd been so sure that this was the work of one person, his emailer, a loner with a vendetta against the legal system. He shifted from foot to foot, uneasy, as Neddleman gazed at him like he, of all people, should have anticipated this latest development.

• • •

"Sometimes you get a break in a case and this is what happens," MacRae said, sitting in his cubicle with Peter after the meeting. "It turns every assumption you had on its ear."

MacRae showed Peter the list of people who claimed they'd either lost or had their key cards stolen in the week or two before the bombing. "These key cards were used at approximately one-hour intervals the morning of the bombing, the first one at nine thirteen," MacRae told Peter. "The last one was at twelve forty-eight."

Peter remembered that was about the time Rudy Ravitch said he'd gone on his break. He took out his crumpled copy of the bomber's email and smoothed it open on the table. He looked back and forth from the email to the list of names. A lone, highly organized schizophrenic or a gang of four? It was like a double exposure — there had to be a way to make the two images converge.

He recognized one of the names.

"This guy," Peter told MacRae, pointing to Walter Waxman's name. "He's a reporter. He's been calling me, asking questions about the bomber."

"Yeah, well, that's his job. We questioned him. He works for the *Phoenix*. He was covering the State House that morning. Wasn't anywhere near—"

"Hold on," Peter said. He ran his finger under the words in the email. "*First the spawn.* He bombs the law school. Law students, baby lawyers. *Then the workers.* His next target is district court— working lawyers and court officers." Peter continued to read. "*And now the drones where they sit, swollen and glowing scarlet with their own self-importance, obsequious parasites fawning over their Queen, or should I say King.*"

Peter felt his neck prickling. In his mind he saw an explosion ripping through the top of a huge golden dome, one that loosely speaking resembled an old-fashioned beehive. It made sense. Drones could be lawmakers, a logical next target. And the queen bee, or as the email said, king—that could be the governor.

He shared the thought with MacRae.

MacRae blinked as the realization settled. "The State House?"

22

ANNIE HAD the box containing Brenda Klevinski's mail in the backseat of her Jeep as she drove to Worcester the next morning. The neighborhood where Brenda had once lived was a quiet suburb. The houses up and down the street were identical small, split-level homes, but Brenda's was particularly nondescript. It had white siding, dark green woodwork, and the yews flanking the door were trimmed into perfect spheres. A chain-link fence separated a patch of groomed lawn from the street.

Annie felt anticipation building as she approached the house. Brenda had probably grown up here. Family members were still here.

She rang the bell. The opening notes of "The Battle Hymn of the Republic" chimed back at her. A somber young woman wearing a loose-fitting denim jumper and wooden clogs answered the door. Maybe . . .

"Brenda?" Annie tried.

The woman recoiled as if Annie had struck her. "Brenda—" she stammered. "Brenda doesn't—"

An older man appeared behind her. He was an imposing presence with his stern, craggy face and ramrod stance. "Brenda isn't here. She's dead," he said.

Even though Annie had speculated that this might be the case, she felt stunned, unable to ask the obvious questions.

"Da-ad," the woman said, turning to the man and heaving a heavy sigh.

"Mommy," called a child's voice. A girl about seven years old appeared behind the woman. She was wearing a denim jumper, too. "Can you help me with this?" She held out a piece of three-hole lined paper. "I don't get it." A little boy, a head shorter, joined her. He had on a white shirt and pressed slacks, and he clutched a school workbook with A B C on the cover. His dark hair was slicked back, and a cowlick stuck up in back.

"You kids go back and do your work. Brianna, skip that example and I'll be there in a minute to help." The kids lingered, their sharp eyes on Annie. "Scoot now." They disappeared.

The woman turned back and studied Annie with a calm expression. Annie suddenly felt self-conscious in her faded jeans and leather jacket, like she'd arrived at a formal event in her PJs.

"Why are you looking for her?" the man asked.

Usually Annie had some version of the truth prepared for obvious questions like that, but she hadn't counted on facing this pair. If there'd been just one of them . . . As if sensing her dilemma, the woman turned to the older man and put her hand on his shoulder. "Dad, why don't you let me handle this?"

Annie was surprised when he didn't protest. Just before he turned away, his eyes filled with tears.

"I'm Maureen, Brenda's sister," the woman said.

Go with the unvarnished truth, Annie decided. She introduced herself, and explained that she was a friend of the woman who was now married to Brenda's ex-husband.

"Ex?"

She told Maureen that Brenda and Joe had been divorced, that six years ago Brenda had disappeared. Annie admitted that she was a little baffled at finding herself on something of a mission to find out what had happened. She knew that, in part at least, it was to gather information that would convince her friend that Joe Klevinski was a dangerous man.

"I'm sorry. I realize none of this makes any sense."

"Not everything in this life has to make sense," Maureen said. She gave a quick glance over her shoulder and stepped outside with Annie on the front steps. She pulled the storm door closed behind her.

"I haven't seen Brenda since she left home years ago. She and my father, well, you see what he's like. Back then he was a hundred times worse. Brenda got pregnant. When he found out, he went berserk. They had a terrible fight. He threw her out on the street with nothing, just what she was wearing. Now, as far as he's concerned, she doesn't exist."

"You didn't try to keep in touch?" Annie hoped it didn't sound like an accusation.

"I was only fourteen."

"And your mother, did she—?"

"My mother died when I was a little. My dad's the one who raised us."

Annie understood how Brenda Mulvaney could have been attracted to someone like Joe Klevinski. Like her father, he wanted things his way. Peter would call it a repetition compulsion, or some such psychobabble. Or maybe there was something genetic—a lemming gene. Either way, same result: however hard you tried to escape your past, you were doomed to relive it in Technicolor. She wondered if her friend Charlotte had survived her father's abuse only to end up in an abusive marriage of her own.

"She never tried to get in touch," Maureen said. "And I didn't know how to find her. Of course, I always wondered what happened. I thought she'd come back, someday. She has a son?" Annie nodded. "If she needs help . . . if you find her . . ." She searched for the right words.

"I'll try to let you know, without making a ruckus here. You don't by any chance have a picture of her?"

"He tore them all up right after she left."

"Would there have been a high school yearbook picture?"

"I guess so. Worcester High. But we don't have a copy."

Mr. Mulvaney glowered at them through the storm door. Annie took a card from her pocket and slipped it to Maureen. "If you think of anything, here's how to reach me."

What had she been thinking, anyway? Annie chided herself as she took the Pike back to Cambridge. If it was going to be that easy, she'd have found Brenda and Joey already. She could still check the junior highs around the Cambridge and Worcester area to see if Joey was registered—she'd call the school offices pretending to be a dentist's assistant who needed to let Joey Klevinski know that his dentist appointment for that day had been canceled. But she had a nasty feeling that she was going to come up goose eggs again. Otherwise she'd reached a dead end, used up all the resources she had at her disposal. To get any further, she needed official status. Whatever was still out there to find, an official police investigator could get without breaking a sweat. When she crossed Route 495, she took out her cell and called Mac.

"MacRae here," Mac said, picking up his cell phone after the first ring. His voice was sharp. He'd been so short-tempered lately, like the A-bomber had taken a few strategic tucks in his shorts.

"It's me. You got a minute?"

"Not really. I'm about to go into a meeting."

"I need some advice. Help, maybe."

"You?" Annie could imagine him staring at the phone in stunned silence.

"Long meeting or short?" she asked. Before he could answer she added, "I'll be there in about thirty minutes."

She hung up before he could argue.

• • •

There were Jersey barriers outside the police station to keep vehicles away, and a new security setup at the door. Annie took off her boots and passed through the metal detector. The guard checking her backpack found her penlight and emergency container of Mace. He made her show her permit to carry, then confiscated the Mace and gave her a receipt so she could get it on her way out. The penlight he let her keep.

She crossed the lobby and went up the stairs. Usually she recognized most everyone there. Not today. The place had become the nerve center for the A-bomber investigation and it was crawling with uniforms and suits. She found MacRae in his office talking on the phone. He motioned for her to sit.

"That's great. Listen, I gotta go," he said. "Let me know when you get back."

When he hung up, he gave Annie a big grin. "How the hell are you?"

"What's with you? I didn't know your face still did that."

"Yeah, well, we got some good news for a change. That crazy guy that hangs out in the Square with a flag handing out leaflets? The one your friend Peter sent underground after finding out that he had a confrontation with the bomber? We got him. He showed up for a reading last night at the Harvard Coop, if you can believe it. He came to heckle that guy who invented the red-meat diet. And that's not all. Looks like we've got a bead on the bomber's next target."

"You do?"

"You must not have listened to the news this morning. The State House. We've got it locked down. Finally we can do something instead of sitting here waiting to get hit."

He looked at his watch. "So you said you needed advice? For the next three minutes I'm at your disposal."

Annie told him about her search for Brenda and Joey Klevinski, and how she'd come up empty.

"Klevinski?" MacRae said, recognizing the name.

Annie told him she'd been married to one of the A-bomber suspects.

"Nine people killed, we've got a credible threat against the State House, and you're wasting my time with a woman who ran off six years ago?" MacRae shook his head. "She's probably sitting pretty on the beach in Miami, thinking Thank god no one from my old life has tracked me down. So long to lousy husbands, bad debts—"

"Mac, she's got twelve thousand dollars in a savings account here. Hasn't touched it since she disappeared."

He considered that for a moment. "I'm not going to ask you how you know that."

"She was disowned by her family, kept isolated by her husband. As far as I can tell, she had no friends, no job. She had a little boy. He'd be twelve years old." She let that sink in. Mac had a son about that age who lived with his ex. "Someone has to care what happened to them."

MacRae rolled his chair up to the desk and started typing on his computer. "You know I shouldn't be doing this."

"Yeah, but you're a decent human being and you like it when I owe you one. Brenda Mulvaney Klevinski," Annie spelled the name as MacRae typed. She gave him the social security number.

He paused for a moment, eyes on the screen. "Let's see. No missing person's report." He typed some more, then waited. "No car's registered in her name." More typing. "Sheesh. No driver's license even. No criminal record, either." He typed more and waited, tapping a pen up and down on the blotter. "Looks like she took out a couple of restraining orders, but you already know that."

"How about a detailed credit report? All I could get was the short version."

"You're pushing it."

A police officer stuck his head in the door. Annie knew him from way back. "Hey, Annie," he said. To MacRae he added, "We're ready for you."

"Be there in a sec." MacRae said, continuing to type.

"Don't say I never done nothin' for ya," he said, pushing back a minute later.

"Consider this your good deed for the year," she said. The printer beside his desk groaned to life and the pages began to print.

Annie noticed two telephone numbers tacked to the wall over MacRae's desk. They were Peter's office and home numbers.

"One more thing," Annie said. "Do me a favor, don't mention this to Peter."

MacRae handed her the printout and gave a Cheshire-cat smile. "I wouldn't think of it."

• • •

Annie drove back to her office. She had Brenda Klevinski's credit report safely stowed in her backpack. What was in it had surprised her. Brenda was continuing to use a MasterCard issued to "Brenda Klevinski." The billing address had been changed to a post office box in Brighton, and at the end of last month there was an outstanding balance due of $1,850.

Up to that moment, Annie had been sure Brenda had vanished without a trace, something which wasn't that easy to do if you didn't have a lot of cash. It had seemed more and more likely that she'd been killed. Discovering an active credit card should have allayed her fears, but it didn't make sense. For one thing, credit card companies charged an easy 20 percent interest rate. Why wasn't Brenda using the money in her savings account to pay off the balance?

She cruised up Mem Drive. Traffic was light as she passed the BU Bridge.

And for another thing, if Brenda felt safe enough to go into Brighton Center and check mail in a post office box, then why . . .

Blue flashing lights and the brief whoop of a siren disturbed her thoughts. She glanced in the rearview mirror. The cop behind her wanted her to stop. What was his problem? She was barely doing forty. Pain in the ass.

Annie pulled over, flipped open the glove compartment, and got out her registration. She got her wallet from her backpack, opened it, and stared at the little plastic window where her driver's license should have been. It was empty. She checked the billfold, in the other wallet compartments. *Why now?* She rummaged in her purse, coming up empty.

There was a tap on the window. Annie squinted up at the officer, praying that it would be a familiar face. It wasn't. He had his hand out. She rolled down the window and passed him her registration.

"I can't seem to find my driver's license. I know I have it, it's just not where it should be. You know, I keep it in my wallet . . ." Annie broke off. *Stop babbling,* she told herself.

He had wraparound sunglasses on under his cap. She couldn't see his eyes, but his mouth was a humorless line. He examined her registration. "This is out of date. The registration sticker on your license plate is expired."

Annie groaned to herself. Now she remembered. She'd gotten something from the Registry of Motor Vehicles, an envelope she'd opened and left in the pile of mail on her hall table.

"I'm sorry, Officer. I've been meaning to get to it—"

"And your driver's license?"

"I have a license. I just don't *have it.* You see, I—"

There was no point in continuing. The officer walked back to his cruiser, taking her out-of-date car registration with him. Annie could see he was talking on his two-way radio. Probably running her plates.

A half hour later, Annie was standing at the curb, waiting in an impotent fury for a tow truck to come get her car. It was being impounded, and she had a ticket in her pocket that was going to cost her. It would have been poetic justice if Joe Klevinski had been driving the tow truck, but when it finally showed up, the driver was a stranger.

Annie called Abby only after failing to reach Chip and Peter. Abby sounded overjoyed to be called to the rescue. She said she'd be right over. It would give them a chance to talk about the wedding.

Great. That was the reason she'd been avoiding Abby, so she wouldn't have to make polite noises while her sister droned on about wedding plans. Why couldn't she just have eloped like she did the first time?

"You don't think I'm going overboard, do you?" Abby asked when they were riding along the river. "It's Luke's first time."

"You can do whatever you want. It's your wedding."

She zoned out as Abby bubbled on about calla lily bouquets and raspberry-filled wedding cake. On the river, an eight skimmed past. She could almost comprehend what Peter saw in the sport. Made it look so effortless when it so wasn't.

Abby fell silent. They were stopped at an intersection, and the turn signal ticked as they waited for the light to change.

"Annie? You're okay, aren't you? I mean, you're not angry with me or anything?"

"Of course not. What makes you think that?"

"You've just been so, I don't know, weird and distant. You like Luke, don't you?"

The light changed and Abby inched the car into the intersection, waiting for a break in the traffic.

"I like Luke a lot. And I'm happy for you. Really I am. I'm sorry, it's just that I've been so preoccupied with work."

"Everything okay between you and Peter?"

Annie felt her back stiffen. Everything was *fine* between her and Peter. Besides which, it wasn't anyone's business but theirs. "Peter's great."

"That's a big relief, because I've been wanting to ask you something."

Uh-oh. Annie knew what was coming.

• • •

"She's going to make me wear puff sleeves, I just know it," Annie said, grousing to Peter. That's what he got for calling her back at the office, hours after she'd sent out an SOS. "Or strapless, even worse. Maid of honor, phooey. I'll probably have to wear high heels, dyed to match. Get my hair done. Wear makeup." It felt good to rant. It had been that kind of day. "I hate makeup. And pantyhose?" She made a gagging noise. "Between that, and getting my car towed—I mean what a royal pain in the ass. And now I have to pay god knows how much to get my car out of hock and more to get a new driver's license."

"Maybe you left it somewhere?"

"You'd think so. I've been trying to . . ." Annie gazed at her backpack sitting under her desk. She lifted it onto the desk. "It's gotta be in here somewhere." She dumped out the contents, slid her fingers into all the compartments where the license might have gotten stuck. If someone stole it, she'd have expected her wallet to be missing, too. Everything else was where it should be. Insurance ID, credit cards, and . . .

"Shit. My court ID is missing too." It came back to her. "They've got all these new procedures at family court. The guard took my license and court ID, wrote my name down on a list. I don't remember him giving them back to me."

"You were over there today?"

Annie felt a twinge of discomfort. She still hadn't told Peter about trying to track down Brenda Klevinski.

"Yesterday, just doing some research for a client."

It was just a little lie, barely a fib even. Still, she didn't like telling it.

23

AFTER PETER hung up the phone, he sat there staring at it. Abby's upcoming wedding had Annie unglued, totally discombobulated, to use one of his mother's expressions. Marriage. It was a topic Annie had never pressed him on, and he'd never pressed her, even though they'd been seeing each other for nearly two years.

He gazed over at the spot on his bookshelf where he used to keep a photo of Kate. He'd put it away because he got tired of explaining to well-meaning visitors, acquaintances who noticed the picture and asked if that was his wife. Kate would be laughing at him now, her arms folded across her chest. He could almost hear her teasing voice. *You don't know what you want. But that's okay because neither does she. You two make a perfect pair.*

Peter checked his watch. He had another five minutes before he had to be at a budget meeting. He listened to his phone messages, then scanned his email. Nothing new from CANARY911. He gathered up the papers he needed, and mused about how easy it was for a security guard to fail to return someone's ID. Peter had once inadvertently left his plane ticket and driver's license at an airport security checkpoint. Nearly missed his plane. On top of that, they'd treated him like it was his fault.

He picked up the file containing his budget spreadsheet and left his office. If Annie hadn't gotten stopped for running that red light, it might have been days, weeks even before she realized what she'd lost. Just like those people the police were investigating whose key cards were scanned the morning of the district courthouse bombing, but who insisted that they weren't there.

As Peter started for the elevator, he noticed Kwan had left his office door open again. He'd forgotten to yell at Kwan about yesterday's lapse. Fortunately, no one was hanging around in the hall today. Peter pushed the door shut.

He knew he should get to his meeting, but he stood there, feeling as if a swarm of dots were buzzing around his head, waiting to be connected. Yesterday, when Kwan left his door open, Rudy Ravitch had been waiting in the hall for Peter. He gazed toward the men's room, half expecting Ravitch to materialize, knowing full well that he'd been discharged just the day before.

You look right at us and see nothing. That's what CANARY911 had said. A courthouse security guard like Ravitch was ideally positioned. He could have harvested key cards in the days and weeks before the bombing, then scanned them in that morning to lay a false trail. He could easily have brought a bomb in with him and left it in the lobby. When it was about to go off, he could have gone out for a smoke. Maybe he'd underestimated the power of the explosives and stayed too close to the building.

Peter had spent two or three hours alone with Ravitch. He'd seemed genuinely grief-stricken. Also blue-collar and relatively uneducated, not at all Peter's image of CANARY911. Could it all have been an act? It was possible. Panic attacks could be faked. Ditto hypnosis. But how could he have pulled off the email? Patient rooms at the Pearce didn't come equipped with computers, and there were none in the public spaces. Peter glanced back at Kwan's now closed door and saw the answer. Ravitch could easily have helped himself to Kwan's computer.

Forget the meeting. Peter returned to his office and picked up the phone.

"Of course we ran background checks on the security guards," MacRae said when Peter reached him. "Why do you ask?"

"I, uh . . ." Peter said, stammering. "I was just wondering if you checked on all the security guards." He knew this didn't answer MacRae's question. Peter had been racing ahead, full bore, without considering the ethical issue: Rudy Ravitch was his patient. He couldn't divulge anything about their sessions.

"Why do you ask?" MacRae said, repeating the question with emphasis.

"I just had this niggling doubt and I thought it wouldn't hurt to ask. I mean, it would be real easy for a security guard to forget to give back key cards and IDs."

"Is this any security guard in particular?"

He couldn't give MacRae Ravitch's name. "I just think you guys should be paying attention to people who blend in. That's what our emailer is telling us. Any kind of uniform is camouflage. All people see is the outfit. If someone deliberately took those key cards, then he has to have had opportunity. That means he's been hanging around the courthouse. Security guards are there all the time. If it's not a security guard, then someone whom the guards wouldn't notice if he passed through several times in short order."

"Like a forensic psychologist? Lawyer? Investigator?" asked MacRae.

Peter caught the sarcasm. "Cop. Homicide detective. Yeah, anyone like that."

The minute Peter hung up his phone, it rang. It was probably Gloria wanting to know where he was. Their meeting should have started five minutes ago.

He picked up the phone. "Hold on to your shirt. I'm on my way."

"You don't have to get snippy with me." It was his mother. "And I wasn't expecting you."

"Sorry. I thought you were someone else. Listen, I can't talk. I'm in a rush."

"So I gather. This won't take long. Sunday is Sophie's birthday. So we're throwing her a little party, and she most especially wants you to be there, though I'm sure I couldn't say why. So you should be here at noon. You can help me decorate."

Decorate? Definitely not Peter's strong suit. "I need to check—"

"So check. Then you'll be here." Click.

• • •

Peter wasn't surprised when Ravitch called him the next afternoon. In the two hours since the police had been to his house and questioned him, Ravitch had started smoking again, and downed three beers to beat back the anxiety that built up inside him.

"Why are they after me?" Ravitch's voice was slurry. "I didn't do anything. They're asking me about where I was this other day, it's like a month ago. How should I know? Then I realize they think I'm the bomber. That I'd kill my own friend." Peter could hear Ravitch blowing his nose.

"I doubt if you're being singled out. They're probably checking everyone."

"The worst thing is, I feel like"—he hiccupped—"I feel like I did it.

Like I should have noticed something or someone that wasn't normal."

They continued talking. Peter's other phone line beeped, but he ignored it. If Ravitch had done nothing wrong other than go out for a smoke, then of course there was no basis for these intense feelings of guilt. But guilt didn't require a reality base to thrive.

Peter had his own share of guilt at the moment, not quite as undeserved. True, he hadn't given MacRae Ravitch's name, or divulged anything from their therapy sessions. But it was because of Peter that the police were grilling security guards. He knew police scrutiny would only exacerbate Ravitch's already tenuous state, and that Ravitch had a tendency to somatize, to act out his issues. Smoking, turning to alcohol, becoming depressed—those were predictable outcomes. Peter hoped the investigators would quickly eliminate him as a suspect.

Now Peter's red message light was blinking.

"You know the cognitive behavior therapist I referred you to is great at dealing with this kind of stuff. Call him." Peter said, trying to extricate himself from what he knew could turn into an hour-long therapy session if he let it.

"But I'll have to start all over at the beginning, explaining—" It sounded as if Ravitch was weeping.

"I'll call and fill him in."

Peter extracted a promise that Ravitch would schedule an appointment with the new therapist as soon as possible. After he hung up, he checked the message. It was MacRae.

"Thought you'd like to know, Rudy Ravitch was taking a lunch break when the law school was bombed."

Damn. Was a lunch break long enough to get from the courthouse to the law school and back? Easy if you had a scooter.

Annie took a cab to the Registry of Motor Vehicles first thing the next morning. She had the cabbie wait while she renewed her registration, then had him continue to family court where she retrieved her license from lost-and-found, then on to the tow lot just off the Southeast Expressway. Fifty bucks for the registration, nearly a hundred in towing charges, sixty-five for the taxi, and there was still the damned ticket. For that she'd have to show up in court. At least she had her car back.

It was late morning when Annie parked on the street, a block from the post office on Harvard Street in Brighton. She'd come equipped with quarters to feed the meter all day. She'd hoped to get there earlier to stake out Brenda Klevinski's PO box.

Annie slipped a high school yearbook photo of Brenda out of her bag. She'd gotten it from an Internet company that specialized in yearbook photos. Give them a name, a year, a high school, and a credit card to charge the hundred-dollar fee, and back came a digitized image. At seventeen, Brenda had been pretty, with wide-set mascaraed eyes and dark hair teased into the pouffy bangs they all wore back then. Annie's god-awful high school graduation picture with her hair done up the same way could be zinging around on the Internet, too. Pretty scary. She wondered if Brenda had done her hair in the girl's john before school, and rolled up her skirt like Annie's friend Charlotte whose father never let her out of the house without a head-to-toe inspection. Mr. Florence forbade Charlotte to wear makeup, short skirts, high heels, or lacy underwear. He wouldn't have his little girl dressing like a slut.

Around the chin and mouth Annie could see Brenda's resemblance to her sister, Maureen. Brenda could have changed dramatically in the intervening years, but at least the photo was a start.

Annie stuffed her hair into a Boston Red Sox cap, zipped her leather jacket, put on a pair of sunglasses, and walked to the post office. The squat, gray granite building had wide double doors. She found the PO box where Brenda Klevinski's MasterCard bills were being mailed. She peered in through the little window. Looked like just a day or two of mail. That was good. Meant someone was checking it regularly.

"Excuse me." She jumped at the sound of a woman's voice. It was an elderly woman in a pink quilted car coat. Annie stepped aside so the woman could get to her box.

Annie got herself a cup of coffee from the Herrell's on the corner and took it to her car. When a spot closer to the post office opened up, she moved into it. She was putting more quarters in the meter when a young woman got out of a minivan and walked toward the post office. Dark hair, slight build. She carried her shoulder bag clutched in front, like she needed it for protection. Could have been Brenda.

Annie followed the woman inside and pretended to address an envelope at one of the counters. The woman waited on line to buy stamps. When her turn came, she chatted with the postal clerk. She was a regular. She barely glanced at Annie, and left without opening a PO box. Not Brenda.

Thank God for Herrell's, Annie thought as she made her way over there two hours later. She didn't mind buying a chocolate chip cookie in return for the right to pee. When she came out, she ducked back into the post office, just to be sure the mail hadn't disappeared while she was relieving herself. It hadn't.

By seven o'clock that evening, her backside ached from sitting. Coffee cups, used napkins, and two empty bottles of water made the inside of her car look like a trash heap. She gave up and went home.

Next morning at eight, she was back. She put on her baseball cap again, got out of her car, and entered the post office, praying that the mail was still in the slot. She had no desire to do an overnight stakeout. She peered in. Looked exactly the same as it had the day before.

The post office was deserted. Windows didn't open until 8:30. She could see her car across the street, parked behind an old black Chevy wagon like her father's cherished car, perfectly positioned for the day. Time for coffee. Herrell's was open. This morning there was a line. She couldn't risk missing Brenda, so she turned to go. She'd come back when they were less busy.

She'd reached the door when she heard a familiar, harsh voice. "Takes a friggin' hour to get a cup a coffee in here." She turned back. It was Joe Klevinski and he was holding a large coffee and coming right at her, head down, shoulders set like a charging bull. He muttered as he brushed past her. Her heart leaped as their eyes met briefly, and she could feel sweat prickling under her cap.

He didn't pause for an instant. There was not a flicker of recognition in his eyes. She watched him leave, then followed at a discreet distance.

Sure enough, he went into the post office. She didn't dare go in and watch. She went back to Herrell's and watched through the window. When he came out, he had a fistful of mail. He darted across the street. Then he paused and stood there for a moment. Annie couldn't see his face, but it looked as if he was gazing at her Jeep. He turned back toward Herrell's. Annie shrank back, her heart pounding. When she peered out again, he was gone.

Shaken, she made her way back into the post office. Brenda Klevinski's PO box was empty.

PETER WAS in the middle of what felt like his first normal day in weeks. Morning meeting, walk rounds, interviews with a couple of applicants for the post-doc position they had open. He was about to break for lunch when MacRae called.

"I'm really sorry to bother you again," he began. "We've got Harvard Harry down here, but he won't go in and look at the lineup."

So? Peter wanted to say. *Why is this my problem?*

"You know how to deal with . . ." MacRae paused. Peter imagined the words he might have used. *Crazies. Nut cases.* ". . . oddballs."

"I could have told you—" Peter started.

"I'm sure you could have, but it's too late for that now. Could you come down?" There was a long pause. "Please." Another pause. "I've got someone coming over there to pick you up."

"You what?"

"I figured it would be easier. You won't have to find parking, and—"

There was a tentative knock at Peter's door. It pushed open and there was a police officer.

"He's here," Peter said into the receiver.

"Be nice to Officer Brady. There's things he'd rather be doing than chauffeuring you over here."

"There's things I'd—" Peter started, but MacRae had hung up.

Officer Brady drove with the blue lights flashing and the siren going. Peter rode up front, imagining what a thrill this ride would have been when he was a kid. They slowed on the approach to intersections, then zoomed through red lights, crossed over into the lane for oncoming traffic. The usual thirty-five-minute ride took fifteen. A dream commute.

MacRae greeted them in the lobby.

"I have to be back in forty-five minutes," Peter said.

"We'll have you out of here in twenty," MacRae said, and led Peter to an interrogation room. Harvard Harry was there, curled up in a chair pulled into a corner.

"Harry?" Peter said.

Harry gave a quick glance in Peter's direction and then tucked his head back down. "I hate raisins." At least he remembered Peter. That boded well for him as an eyewitness. "They look like dead flies."

Peter sat in the other chair. "All they want you to do is try to identify the guy who took your flag," he said, trying to sound his most trustworthy.

Harry grimaced. He was letting his beard grow out, and he wore the same tweed jacket he'd had on the last time Peter saw him. His white oxford shirt looked rumpled but clean.

"Gestapo," Harry muttered. "SS. They've got me, now they'll never let go."

"No one's got you. They just wanted you to look at some suspects. Didn't they ask nicely?"

Harry snorted derision. "How do I know I can believe *you*? How do I know it's not a trick? And besides, why should I help them? All they do is harass me. They sent me to that place where I was a prisoner for weeks. They made me eat"—Harry's lips curled in distaste—"meat. And sugar. Sugar's poison. So's flour and so's rice. Isn't that why they call it ricin? It's got rice in it." Harry snickered at his own joke.

Peter knew he was dealing with a delusional system, immune to fact. But it could be bent in other ways. "Didn't the police officer tell you? They're sorry for harassing you."

Harry didn't look impressed.

"And the police want to help get your flag back for you, and get the guy who did it."

Harry uncurled a little and narrowed his eyes at Peter, like he was using X-ray vision. Peter knew he'd scored.

"Just to prove it," he said, pressing his advantage, "I can get the police detective to come in right now and tell you he's sorry."

"Apologize?" Harry said, tasting the word. Peter could feel him hovering.

"Would that help?"

"A cop's going to apologize to me?" Harry's face broke into a broad smile. He thought that was a swell idea.

MacRae wasn't nearly as pleased. "Apologize? For what?" he said when Peter found him in his cubicle.

"It doesn't matter for what. It's not real. Just apologize for what Harry thinks the police did to him." MacRae gave Peter a sour look that got sourer when Peter added, "Be nice, and do it wearing a uniform."

"Humoring a lunatic," MacRae muttered as he shrugged on a borrowed uniform jacket. "Ridiculous. Loony tune . . ." He fastened the buttons and tugged on the too-long cuffs. "This better work. How good an ID are we gonna get from him, anyway?"

"You'll get a fine ID if he really *sees*. I wouldn't put Harry on the witness stand, but he'll do as well as anyone identifying the person he saw, provided you can get him to cooperate. His memory is intact, attention and concentration just dandy. He's a schizophrenic. He filters what he sees through a distorting lens so it all fits into the grand conspiracy. The trick is to manage his paranoia about being in a police station. At every step, he's going to suspect it's a trap."

MacRae trudged down the hall.

"Repeat after me," Peter said, "I'm really sorry."

"Would you shut up," MacRae shot back.

MacRae sucked it up and managed to apologize without choking on the words. In fact, he gave a pretty good demonstration of official contrition. Enough to convince Harry, anyway, to look at the lineup.

Peter and McRae shepherded Harry down the hall.

"Now you know the room is going to be dark," Peter explained. Even for someone who wasn't paranoid, entering a small, darkened room with a bunch of strangers in it could be intimidating. "That's because of the one-way glass. It's dark on our side so we can see into the other room where the suspects are, but they can't see us."

MacRae held open the door. Already inside, standing in the shadowy room, were Neddleman and a man in a suit whom Peter took to be the DA.

Harry paused on the threshold. MacRae looked exasperated, like he wanted to drop-kick Harry into the room. Peter motioned to him to cool it. Finally Harry slid sideways inside and, hugging the wall, made his way around to the edge of the one-way glass. He waited there, his ear to the window frame.

Five men were lined up in the adjacent room, visible through the glass. Peter recognized an unhappy-looking Rudy Ravitch. Next to him was a fellow who looked familiar. It was the man Peter had watched MacRae interview. James Tietz. Had he been so pale before? Now there were hollows under his eyes. Peter remembered his long-standing vendetta against officialdom. Here was a man who was not a schizophrenic, but he distrusted the police every bit as much as Harry.

Peter didn't recognize the other three men in the lineup, though he assumed they were faces from the gallery of photos in the situation room.

Harry inched forward so he could just see through the glass. His arm snaked out across the window and whipped back. Harry watched. No one in the lineup flinched. Harry did it twice more. Then he walked to the middle of the window. With his face nearly touching the glass, he wiggled his fingers behind his ears and stuck out his tongue. Finally, he stretched his arms up over his head and pressed his palms to the glass. Peter could imagine the caption to the picture: SPLAT! Still, no one on the other side of the glass reacted.

Harry took a few steps back. Peter put his hand on Harry's shoulder and exchanged looks with MacRae before he said anything. "See anyone you recognize?"

"Sure," Harry said. Peter could feel a collective intake of breath. "That." Harry pointed to a man on the end, heavyset and dark. "He gets coffee at Peet's in the morning." Peet's was a coffee joint in Harvard Square. "Takes the T. And that one." Harry indicated James Tietz. "He was at that so-called hospital where they kept me locked up."

"I mean, do you see the man who took your flag?" Peter said.

Now Harry took his time. He looked at each man in the lineup, his gaze lingering on Rudy Ravitch. Ravitch's brow was glistening with sweat. Then Harry studied James Tietz. Tietz looked tired and uncomfortable. He raised his arm and coughed into the crook of his elbow. When he put down his arm, Peter noticed what looked like cold sores, one at the corner of his lip, another on the end of his nose. In the harsh light, the sores looked like they were crusted over with putty, like he'd tried to cover them with makeup. Tietz had more sores on the backs of his hands.

When Harry finished his survey of the suspects, he turned his attention to the men in the observation room with him. He took his time giving Neddleman the once-over. Next he scrutinized McRae, then the DA, and finally Peter.

"He's not here," Harry said. "Figures. I didn't think you were going to get my flag back."

• • •

After the lineup, Peter waited in the hall. He suppressed a smile as he watched Harry take his good sweet time putting on his coat. Then Harry asked where was the men's room. Five minutes later, he ambled past, torturing the uniform assigned to escort him out by meandering through the hall, sticking his head into office after office. He stopped to commune with the soda machine. He cadged some money off his escort and got himself a Coke.

Neddleman stepped into the situation room and motioned for Peter to follow him. He pulled the door shut, then stepped over to the bulletin board with the head shots of active suspects.

"The man that Harry said takes the T and goes to Peet's?" Neddleman said, indicating the photo of one of the men Peter had seen in the lineup. "He's a janitor at the law school. Harry probably does see him around the Square, maybe even at Peet's."

"Which suggests that Harry's right about Tietz, too," Peter said. "Did you notice, that guy doesn't look well. He's got some kind of cold sores on his face, and also on the back of his hand. Maybe Harry did see him at Cambridge Hospital. Could be that's the reason he wouldn't tell you where he was at the time of the courthouse bombing."

MacRae made a note. "Maybe he's being treated for something he doesn't want his boss and his coworkers to know he's got."

Cambridge Hospital. Peter knew it had an AIDS out-patient clinic. He hoped they'd have a hard time finding out if Tietz was one of its clients. Patient confidentiality should count for something.

"So none of the men in the lineup took his flag?" Neddleman asked with a weary sigh that almost made Peter feel sorry for him. "I suppose negative progress is still progress."

Peter had to get back to work. He glanced at his watch. "Getting late," he said.

"Thought you'd be interested in these," Neddleman said, ignoring the hint. He spread out four photos on the table. "These are the men who had their key cards stolen. Notice any similarities?"

They were all men in their thirties or forties, all with dark hair, two with glasses and two without, not one of them distinctive-looking.

Peter realized what Neddleman was getting at. Maybe the A-bomber had stolen photo IDs of men who approximately resembled himself.

"How do you think he managed to get all those key cards?" Peter asked.

"As you pointed out, this could easily have been pulled off by one of the security guards. Any reasonably nimble pickpocket could have done it, too. The IDs could have been lifted in the courthouse caf. People use key cards to get a discount, then half of them eat with their IDs sitting on their trays. All you'd have to do is stroll by and help yourself."

He told Peter that they had the State House "battened down tighter than a drum." The governor was scheduled to address a joint session the following Monday. "We'll have uniforms all over the place, ultratight security, snipers up in the gallery. We're not taking any—"

Peter broke in. "Listen, this is all fascinating, but I gotta get back."

"Of course. I'll get someone to take you, and thanks for the help with Harry." Peter shook his offered hand, and Neddleman held on. "There's one thing I wanted to ask." Here it came, the reason he was being so chatty and nicey-nice. "It's critical that we know when this maniac sends you another email."

"I'll let you know the minute I do."

Neddleman dropped Peter's hand. "With all due respect, if past performance is any indicator, you don't check your email more than a couple of times a day. That may not be enough. If we could get access to your account, then we could monitor it and . . ."

Peter understood that Neddleman was concerned about public safety, but still, how could he make such a suggestion? As if doctor-patient communications were no more sacrosanct than transactions on eBay. He tried to keep his voice calm. "That's impossible. Patient confidentiality is at issue, and the hospital is on a secure network."

"We won't read your email, just monitor it, screen for messages from CANARY911." Neddleman's informality had been transformed into military stiffness.

The arrogant sonofabitch. "Are you kidding? I'd get fired, and rightly so."

Neddleman gave Peter a hard, impassive look. "I *can* get a warrant."

It seemed incomprehensible that the police could get a court order to check his email. Wasn't privacy guaranteed in the Constitution, not to mention HIPAA regulations and doctor-patient privilege?

"Then you'd better get one," Peter said, and picked up his jacket.

Neddleman was barely breathing. He had his hands clasped in front of him, and one finger was going up and down like a metronome.

Time to deescalate. They were talking about messages from someone who didn't care how many people he killed. Peter consciously unfolded his arms and softened his stance. "Tell you what, you got a computer with Internet access? I'll check it right now. And again when I get to the Pearce. And then every few hours."

"Every hour. And when you're sleeping?"

"I only sleep about six hours."

Neddleman gave a grudging nod. "We'll see how it goes."

Like a good soldier, he went into Neddleman's office and checked his email. No new messages from CANARY911.

Neddleman promised a squad car would pick him up in front of the police station in ten minutes. Before leaving, Peter took a detour to MacRae's cubicle, intending to blast him for getting him snarled up in this mess. But as he got near, he heard voices. MacRae wasn't alone. The other voice was a woman's. Peter paused to listen more closely. It was a very familiar woman's voice, too low to make out the words. He strode past, giving a quick sideways look just to confirm. It was Annie. She and MacRae were leaning toward each other over MacRae's desk. He had his hand over hers.

Peter headed for the exit. He had no right to be angry, he knew that. Annie and MacRae had a long friendship going back to when they were kids. They'd grown up in Somerville, gone to the same high school, and law enforcement ran in their families. Still, he'd have been happier if Annie had told him why she was going to be visiting MacRae. What were they doing holding hands, anyway?

• • •

Annie knew she was losing it. She lowered her voice to a whisper, but she had her hand balled up in a fist. It was all she could do to stop herself from banging on MacRae's desk, or better yet, his thick head.

"I know there isn't a missing person's report," she said. "Brenda Klevinski has been estranged from her family for years, and why would her ex-husband want anyone to look for her when he probably killed her? She and her son could be buried in the basement of that house."

MacRae put his hand over hers. "You don't know that. Annie, calm down."

He could be so damned patronizing. Annie eased her hand away. "What if I get her sister to file a missing person's report?"

MacRae leaned his chair back. "After what, five years? That's not going to count for much. She's over twenty-one."

"Don't you get it? Her ex-husband has her mail delivered to a PO box. He's using her credit card to make it look like she's still around. And there's a bank account with twelve thousand dollars in her maiden name that I'm sure her ex doesn't know about because the bank statements go to the house she hasn't lived in for six years. I'm telling you, Brenda Klevinski is not alive and well and living in Reno."

"Annie, has it occurred to you that we have an awful lot going on right now? If the mayor's wife went missing, we'd have a hard time freeing up personnel to do a serious investigation."

"If it turns out that Brenda Klevinski's ex-husband killed her and, because you're too busy to give this any bandwidth, his wife and little girl get hurt—"

MacRae held up his hands in surrender. "Okay, okay. I'll get someone to look into it."

"When?"

"Soon."

"You're not just saying that to placate me."

"YES, I'm saying that to get you off my case." He stood. "I told you, I will put someone on it. Next week, after Monday." When he set his jaw like that, she knew that was the best she was going to get out of him.

Annie got up. "You can be such an asshole."

MacRae leaned forward, his hands on desk. "So can you."

PETER BLINKED into the bright sun outside the police station. Annoying but not surprising, no police cruiser was idling at the curb waiting to take him back to the Pearce. It had only been a few minutes since Neddleman promised a car would be there.

A virtual city of TV vans were camped out near the police station. There was barely room for the chess players and street people who usually owned the benches on the patch of scruffy lawn adjacent to the Central Square intersection. Harvard Harry was there, talking with a man in a dusty overcoat who sat on a bench beside a full shopping cart topped off with a blanket.

"Dr. Zak! Dr. Zak!" Peter groaned, recognizing the high-pitched, lispy voice. Sure enough, the man who came loping over to him had press credentials hanging from around his neck. It was the reporter who'd been pestering him with telephone messages.

"Walter Waxman." Waxman offered a pudgy hand. "Have you got

a minute for some questions?" He was a short, overweight man, a little soft around the edges, with dark, thinning hair.

"I'm not answering questions. Talk to media relations. That's their job."

Waxman peered at him, eyes intense through smudged Clark Kent glasses. He held up a microcassette recorder. "Dr. Zak—"

"Please, get that thing out of my face."

Where the hell was his ride? He glanced back at the police station. Annie was coming out the door and across the sidewalk, heading toward him. She held her jacket closed and had her head down.

"Would you get lost, please," he told Waxman. Annie drew level with them, her back hunched, her body tight and closed. "Annie?"

Her head jerked up. She glanced back to the police station, then at Peter. "What are you doing here?"

"I was helping them . . ." Peter started. Waxman took a step closer. The last thing he wanted was to give this idiot inside information.

"You a friend of Dr. Zak's?" Waxman said, all innocence.

"Annie Squires," she said, before Peter could stop her.

"This man is a reporter," he told her, raising his eyebrows.

Annie eyed the press credentials.

"You're one of the detectives?" Waxman asked.

"It's none of your—" Peter's words were interrupted by a high-pitched wail.

"Traitor! Traitor!" Harvard Harry was standing on a bench and pointing directly at them, screeching. "TRAITOR!"

"A fan of yours?" Waxman asked, deadpan.

"I'm parked across the street," Annie said. "Let's get out of here."

Annie's Jeep was just a half block up on the other side of Mass Ave. They walked to the intersection. When the traffic let up, Peter put his arm around her and they crossed. It felt good walking with his arm around her shoulders, hers around his waist. Like coming home. With her long legs, she could easily match him stride for stride.

He told her about the lineup, how Harvard Harry hadn't identified anyone as the man who'd bopped him on the head and stolen his flag.

"Harry's pretty pissed at you," Annie said when they reached her car.

"He seemed okay when he left the police station. Go figure. I guess the atmosphere out here is enough to set anyone off." He took her hand. "So what are you doing here, anyway?" He tried to make the question sound casual. What he really wanted to know was why the hell she and MacRae were holding hands.

Annie gave him a steady look, and his stomach sank as he felt her weighing her answer. "I asked Mac to do a little research for me. I was just following up."

"Research? Isn't he flat-out, investigating the bombings?"

"That's what he says. So I was twisting his arm a little."

That's all? Peter wanted to ask, but he stopped himself. Jealousy was ugly and counterproductive.

"So, I got invited to Sophie's birthday party," Annie went on.

He didn't point out that she was deliberately changing the subject. "Right. Sunday. Come early. You can help us decorate."

Annie did a double take. Her look said *You, decorate?* "I'll be there. But I have to leave early for church."

It was Peter's turn for a double take. In all the time they'd been seeing each other, Annie had never once mentioned church. He'd always assumed she was a thoroughly lapsed Catholic. Maybe it had to do with the upcoming wedding.

"You going for Abby?"

"Thank god she's not tormenting me with that, too. No, I promised

Chip I'd go with him. It's an annual thing at the cathedral. Anyway, it's a lot of pomp and circumstance, and hey, we can all use a little divine guidance these days. If I don't like what they say, I can always join the picketers outside."

Peter knew he needed to get back to work, but another minute wouldn't hurt. He took her in his arms and examined her face. He could feel the tension in her body.

"You okay?" he asked.

Annie put her arms around his waist. She paused a second, like she was thinking about how to phrase her answer. "Just a case I'm working on. It's got me worried. Same old, same old."

"Anything I can do?"

She smiled and shook her head. "Nah. I'm sure it'll sort itself out."

She tightened her arms around him and he pressed her hips into his. He could smell her sweet, fruity scent. More than anything he wanted to bag the day and go somewhere they could be alone and re-assure himself that everything was all right.

An older woman walked by pushing a double stroller holding a pair of identical tow-headed toddlers. She cleared her throat and looked down her nose at Peter and Annie with distaste.

Annie pulled away. "Oh dear. Mustn't set a bad example." She gave him a peck on the cheek, got into her car, and left.

Peter crossed back over to the police station. He zigzagged through media encampments, keeping his head down to avoid eye contact. Harry was still there, talking with his friend on the bench and sipping his Coke. There was still no cruiser waiting to take him back to the Pearce. Damn. He checked his watch. It should have been there by then. He marched back toward the police station, gearing up to hassle Neddleman. He had no intention of waiting there half the day.

"TRAITOR!"

Peter didn't look around. He knew Harry had spotted him. Nothing wrong with that guy's short-term memory.

He reached for the front door and began to pull it open, and stopped. Where was Walter Waxman? He turned and scanned the sidewalk, the grass, the benches outside the police station, ignoring Harry's accusatory finger and continued screaming. Why wasn't Waxman out there trying to interview Harvard Harry, or buttonholing police officers. Peter could see Waxman's intense, nearly cross-eyed gaze, his glasses, his features indistinct like a blurry photograph — it was a face he'd seen before.

"TRAITOR!" Harry screamed again. Now Peter knew why.

• • •

Neddleman was with the DA when Peter burst into his office. "You still here? I told them to send a car to pick you up." He reached for the phone.

"Harvard Harry recognized him."

Neddleman and the DA stared at Peter like he had a few screws loose.

"I was waiting for your damned cruiser, which by the way has not shown up, and I'm telling you, Harry recognized the guy who stole his flag. This reporter comes over to me and Harry starts screaming 'traitor' at me, like he thinks I'm communing with the enemy."

"A reporter stole his flag?"

"Where are those pictures? The ones of the people whose key cards were stolen."

Neddleman tossed Peter the file folder. He opened to the photo of Walter Waxman. The dark-haired man in his thirties wore dark-rimmed glasses and had a muscular, taut face with broad cheeks and squinty eyes.

"I'm telling you, that's not him."

"That's not who?"

"That's not the guy outside wearing *Boston Phoenix* press credentials and passing himself off as Walter Waxman. The one Harry recognized."

Neddleman jumped to his feet. "Why the hell didn't you say so?"

Peter ran to keep up as Neddleman hurried down the hall and into the office area. Neddleman rounded up a half-dozen officers and they stood in a group while Peter described, as best he could, the suspect's face, the glasses, his stature and paunch. He told them where he'd seen him last.

"Wearing?" Neddleman asked.

"Press credentials." For the life of him, Peter couldn't remember what else the guy had on. "Harry could tell you." Neddleman looked at him, disgusted. "But the guy's gone now. Must have realized Harry recognized him."

"Why didn't you tell us sooner?"

"I didn't put it together. I thought Harry was just being, well, Harry."

"Anything else?"

"Yeah. Two things. I've seen him before. He was in the coffee shop near the district court right after the bombing. He left without paying his tab. And I recognize the voice. It's kind of squeaky. He's called me on the phone, left me a message with questions about the A-bomber, like he was a real reporter."

"So we've got him on tape, maybe," Neddleman said, his voice hopeful.

Peter couldn't remember if he'd deleted the message. "I can check."

Neddleman dispatched the officers to look for the man pretending to be Walter Waxman, and to nab Harvard Harry, who'd been promoted from crackpot to star witness.

Peter called his own voice mail and went through the old messages. He was relieved to find the message was still there. Neddleman put it on speaker phone.

"Hey, you promised to get back to me," began the high-pitched voice. As the man purporting to be reporter Walter Waxman read off his questions, Neddleman sat back, sipping coffee. "Is there a profile of the type of person who does this kind of thing? Why is he quoting American patriot Thomas Paine? Do 'raptor' and 'maw' suggest the influence . . ."

Neddleman snapped forward. He listened through to the end, then replayed the message.

"That confirms it." Neddleman said. "There's nothing about raptors or maws in the content we released to the public. Those words were in the email message sent to you. He's our guy."

Peter realized he wasn't going to get back to the Pearce anytime soon. He sat with a police sketch artist picking from eyebrows, chins, and hairlines until a drawing was completed. Peter examined it. This pudgy, innocent-looking guy was the A-bomber. He'd long ago learned that there was no such thing as "the face of a killer." Ted Bundy's twenty-eight victims trusted the notorious serial killer, who came across as handsome and charismatic, a showered and shaved Ivy-Leaguer. The man who'd killed Kate looked like a blond, blue-eyed Boy Scout. Here they were, dealing with a terrorist who resembled a potato dumpling.

WHEN ANNIE got back to the office, Jackie was on the phone, hunched over the receiver, her body turned away from Annie. "Yes, I know you like mustard on your sandwich. I just forgot . . . Right, no mayo, white bread."

Annie poured herself coffee. So Joe had moved back in. Jackie hadn't told her as much, but she wasn't surprised. She wondered if he liked his sandwich cut in triangles with the crusts trimmed, too.

"I'm sorry." Jackie took a tissue and wiped a tear from the corner of her eye. "Uh-huh."

Annie poured coffee for Jackie. How pathetic was that, to be bullied to the point of tears over a ham sandwich?

Jackie blew a kiss into the receiver and hung up.

Annie brought the coffees over and sat down across from Jackie's desk. Jackie forced a smile. "Thanks, Annie. Oh, and I have a message for you. Joe wanted you to know, he's sorry for making such a mess of things."

I'll bet he is, Annie thought.

Jackie went on. "Really. He wants to make things right."

"He's moved back in?"

Jackie nodded. "I was just now talking to him. He's shopping for a birthday present for Sophie. Isn't it sweet, Pearl offering to throw her a little party? She's been so generous."

Annie didn't feel like playing along. "What about the restraining order?"

Jackie looked down into her lap and twisted the tissue.

"Has he started hitting you again?" The words were out before Annie could stop them.

Jackie hunched her shoulders and turtled her head.

Annie felt a pang of guilt. She was battering Jackie, too. "I'm sorry, but . . . no, I'm not sorry. I have to tell you, I think this man is even more dangerous than you imagine."

"Annie, I know you think you're helping me. But would you just back off?" Her voice broke. "Please."

Annie couldn't stop herself. "Do you really think his first wife just upped and disappeared?"

Jackie lifted her head, defiant. "She did. She took Joey and she —"

"Vanished into the ether? Leaving no word of where she was? No forwarding address for mail? Without ever getting in touch again?"

"But she has been in touch."

Annie felt her mouth fall open. "She's . . . You've seen her?"

"No, we haven't seen her. Not since they left. But Joe hears from her. Sure. How do you think he pays child support?"

"Child support? He . . ." Annie found herself at a loss for words as her mental image of Brenda Klevinski resurrected itself from the grave.

"He just mentioned the other day that he was paying a tuition bill for Joey. She's got him enrolled in a parochial school near Ann Arbor."

Michigan? Annie tried to take a step back and digest this new information. Had she let her flat-out loathing for Joe Klevinski fire her imagination? Was Joe Klevinski picking up mail from the PO box that was Brenda Klevinski's MasterCard billing address simply an innocent arrangement designed to maintain child support from a safe distance? Sounded pretty convoluted, more like something Joe made up when he realized Annie was onto him.

She retreated to her office and rummaged through the pile of papers on her desk, looking for the printout she'd made of the dozens of Klevinskis she'd found listed in the country. She paged through. Not a single one in Michigan.

Annie itched to get a look at the latest credit card bill and see for herself if there were any tuition charges. But how? Then she remembered that she'd been able to look up her own credit card account on the Internet. She'd had to request a password; with that and the account number, she'd been able to log in, and there it had been in all its glory, her last six months of profligate spending. She could do the same thing now, call and request a password for Brenda's account. All she had to do was find out the credit card company's customer service number. She blew on her fingertips, like a safecracker confident of her skills, and began to type.

Annie had no trouble convincing the phone rep that she was Brenda Klevinski. After all, she knew Brenda's account number, date of birth, social security number, mother's maiden name, and mailing address. The only fly in the ointment was that she couldn't get the password over the phone. "For security reasons," the woman said, it had to be emailed. Annie promptly opened herself a Yahoo account under the name BRENDAK5000 and had them send it to her there.

When she got into the online listing for the account, she found the balance due was up to four grand plus a hefty finance charge. She scanned the items in the last month. There'd been almost daily charges in the twenty-dollar range from Nasty Pete's, an appropriately named bar in North Cambridge; other charges were from Shell and Exxon stations in the Boston area, a couple of hits from CVS, another from Best Buy. Nothing remotely resembled a parochial school tuition payment, and nothing at all from Michigan.

Child support my ass, Annie thought as she printed the account activity. She put the pages into a file folder and set the folder in her top desk drawer. But what now? Short of digging up the basement of the house Brenda had shared with her husband, she'd run out of ideas. She had nothing even approaching a bloody glove to wave at the police. Maybe she should confront the guy and spook him into revealing something. Or tell Jackie what she knew to get her to stay the hell away from him. Jesus, the woman had not a single ounce of sense. Any idiot could see — Annie stopped herself mid-rant. She had to be careful. Her actions could easily backfire and put Jackie and Sophie in greater danger.

She yearned to talk to Peter, ask his advice. He'd met Jackie and Joe Klevinski. He knew the psychology of abuser and abused. That was precisely why his advice, from the beginning, had been *MYOB.*

She sat back in her chair. MacRae had promised to assign someone to look into Brenda Klevinski's disappearance. Next week. He was good for his word. She'd just have to wait.

• • •

Peter opened the Saturday morning paper with a mixture of dread and anticipation. On the front page was the drawing of the A-bomber he'd helped the police artist construct. He wondered if this guy would look at the drawing and feel the rush a flasher gets from being seen. After all, that was what he'd been doing, sending email messages and masquerading as a reporter—flashing himself at the world, asking to be caught. In the A-bomber's vocabulary, it was the "Marshal" outing the "Maw."

Peter spent most of Saturday at the Pearce, catching up on what he should have done Friday—seeing patients and completing paperwork. He checked at least once an hour for email from CANARY911, and each time dutifully reported to Neddleman that he'd received nothing. He knew the police weren't expecting the A-bomber to strike until Monday, but still he kept checking CNN for breaking news.

Peter opened his email one last time later that afternoon, before going over to Toys "R" Us to find a present for Sophie. Still nothing.

He thought the shopping trip would be a welcome distraction, but after ten minutes wandering up and down aisles, being bombarded by the Chipmunks' squeaky-voiced singing on the sound system and assaulted by a mind-numbing array of choices, he was tired and cranky. He bypassed a stuffed, voice-activated Pomeranian that walked and yipped on command; a Russian-speaking doll wearing a pink tutu; and a dancing hamster. Who came up with these toys, anyway? What happened to good old train sets and building blocks?

He made his way over to the Building and Models aisle and found Tinkertoys and Lincoln Logs. Sheesh, today's versions were made of plastic. The train sets that looked anything like the ones he remembered started at a hundred bucks. At the end of the aisle, a toddler lay on the floor screaming and kicking his chubby legs, his face beet red. Sensory overload. Peter could relate.

He meandered some more and found himself in an aisle chockablock with art supplies. The make-it-yourself tattoos snagged his attention. Did they have pierce-it-yourself kits for kids, too? He briefly considered bathtub finger paints, but suspected that Jackie wouldn't appreciate them. Then he saw the display of markers, ten feet of shelf space, floor to ceiling, packed with every type of felt-tipped pen imaginable—fat ones, skinny ones, ones that sparkled, others that glowed in the dark, still others that laid down a trail of jelly. He took heart. Sophie loved to draw. When he saw the spiffy-looking yellow-and-blue nylon tote that held a hundred felt-tipped pens in assorted shapes and sizes, he knew that was it. He bought it, along with a pair of oversized pads of paper, six rolls of Lifesavers, and a bag of balloons. He waited while the paper and markers were gift wrapped in twirling pink ballerinas.

He returned home exhausted. A full day at the Pearce was less stressful. *Check your email*, his conscience hectored. He poured himself a glass of wine from the open bottle of zin on the table. His computer was on a table in the corner of his living room, a modern anomaly in the cozy space filled with books and turn-of-the century mission oak furniture.

He jiggled the mouse, then opened a browser window and logged on to the Pearce's email system. He scanned his new messages. He took a sip of wine and started to relax; then he saw it—a message from CANARY911. He dropped into a chair. He could hear that soprano voice reading along:

Subject: The evidence is clear that you've been
       scheming

Peter recognized the words from an obscure ode to paranoia that Tom Paxton wrote called "Mr. Blue." This guy was hypersensitive to all referents to paranoia out there, and had taken them as his own anthems.

He read the body of the message.

The embers of Our pyre definitely seem to be heat-
ing up. Soon, We lop off the head of the beast,

drive a dagger into the heart of the King. There
will be an inferno. Momentary, for sure, then
stillness at last.

Need to sleep. Days and nights are stretching
again, soon they turn upside down. Then the purging
will be done. Red segues to Black. We can rest, the
Maw sated, the Marshall subdued, the Philosopher
King in his proper place in the ascendance among
Our unholy trinity, and god can go back to his
playacting.

Still think this is a singalong?

Peter forwarded the message and called Neddleman.

"Good," Neddleman said. "What he's saying—it's all consistent.
He's planning to strike again Monday, when the governor speaks at
the State House. We'll be ready for him."

Something in Neddleman's tone sounded off. Peter wondered if
the confidence was real or bravado.

27

ANNIE DROVE to Peter's Sunday morning to help with the preparations for Sophie's party. This was the kind of fall day New England was famous for, maple trees an intense orangey red against a brilliant blue sky. A cop was directing traffic in front of a church at Mass Ave and Orchard Street. Annie found herself scanning the group of pedestrians crossing the street and others milling about in front, looking for the man who Peter said was the A-bomber. She and Peter were the only two, aside from Harvard Harry, who'd actually seen him. But she hadn't been noticing, and had only a vague memory of an overweight, geeky-looking guy wearing horn-rimmed glasses, with press tags dangling from his neck.

Annie's birthday gift for Sophie was wrapped in birthday paper and sitting on the passenger seat. Annie had never been much into toys as a kid; what she'd lusted after was a horse, a real one. She'd read everything she could get her hands on and knew all about saddles and bridles, grooming, even mucking out a stall. Her most cherished gift from that time had been a pair of red cowboy boots and a cap-shooting rifle. She ended up buying Sophie exactly what she'd have wanted: a realistic, eight-inch-high, molded plastic model of a horse. It reminded her of the mare whose shimmering flanks she'd stroked when Uncle Jack took her to the stables south of Boston where the police kept horses for mounted patrols. It had tossed its long mane and whinnied as Annie, half-filled with terror at the sheer size of the beast, approached. It stood while Annie stroked its neck and inhaled the scent of warm horseflesh, hay, and manure.

She arrived at Pearl's to find the house transformed. All the lights were on, and purple and pink streamers had been strung across the living room and dining room ceilings. She smelled freshly baked cake. Mmm. Homemade cake was a treat she hadn't enjoyed in years. And maybe real icing that didn't come from a can?

Mr. Kuppel and Peter sat on the sofa, surrounded by a dozen balloons. Peter was struggling to tie off a fully inflated blue one shaped like a baseball bat. Mr. Kuppel's red face matched his flannel shirt as he strained to get a yellow balloon to inflate. When he saw Annie, he gave her a feeble wave.

"So what happened to good old-fashioned helium?" Annie asked.

"Damn," Peter said as his balloon went spiraling through the air, making a vaguely obscene noise. It landed in the corner.

Annie went over and picked it up. She remembered one of her birthdays, she couldn't have been more than four years old; she'd watched, fascinated and terrified at the same time, eyes squinched and her hands over her ears, as her dad blew up balloons. She'd watched one after the other, each one getting so big she was sure any moment it would burst.

Annie blew into the blue balloon. It began to inflate. Halfway there she paused, her fingers pinched over the end. "Such a fascinating concept. You put your mouth on the end and blow. What will they think of next?"

Peter cracked up and winked at Annie. "Who knew the package had a hundred and forty-four of these babies?" he said, starting on a red one.

"Hello, Annie dear," Pearl called from the other room.

"I'm too old for this nonsense," Mr. Kuppel said, heaving himself up from the sofa.

Annie went into the kitchen and gave Pearl a kiss. Pearl's cheek was cool under Annie's lips, despite the flush on her face.

"You need any help with the cake?" she asked, indicating the two round, golden layers resting on wire racks on the counter.

She glanced at the newspaper on the counter, too. A small, front-page story was about the church service she was going to later that day.

"You could ice the cake," Pearl said. She dumped potato chips into a bowl. "There's food coloring in the closet. Can you add a touch of red to the icing? Sophie wants pink. She's coming early to decorate it herself."

Annie lifted the dishcloth covering a small bowl on the counter. Vanilla butter cream, her favorite. Annie found the food coloring and mixed in two drops of red. That turned the icing a raspberry pink. Pearl set one of the layers on a plate and handed Annie a narrow rubber spatula. Annie iced one layer, then set the second layer on top and iced it.

From the living room came the sound of a balloon fart, followed by Peter's "Shit." Annie loaded her finger with leftover frosting and went out to him.

The pile of blown-up balloons was now at about twenty-five. Peter's glasses were crooked on his nose, and one of his shirttails had come loose.

"You look like you could use a treat," Annie said, offering up her finger.

Peter smiled and looked around. They were alone. He took her finger in his mouth and held it there much longer than he needed to if all he wanted was that kind of treat.

"That's quite enough," said Pearl, from the kitchen door.

Annie whipped around and felt herself blushing. She realized Pearl was referring to the balloons.

Pearl held out a ball of string and a scissor. "Make two bundles," she said. "And hurry up. It's nearly noon."

"Slave driver," Peter muttered.

He and Annie cut lengths of string and attached them to the balloons. He tied them together in two bundles. Annie got up on a chair and hung one bunch from the dining room light. She was getting up on the piano bench in the living room to hang a second bunch when the doorbell rang.

"Sophie. It's about time," Pearl said, bustling down the hall to the front door.

Annie could hear Sophie's high, excited voice. Then Jackie's. Sophie rushed into the room, oohing and aahing over the decorations, then the pile of presents.

"Oh, Daddy, look," Sophie said.

Annie froze. Joe Klevinski entered the room carrying a Sophie-sized package and a bouquet of heart-shaped, red Mylar balloons. Clearly on best behavior, he was clean-shaven, and had on a brown corduroy suit jacket over a white shirt. His dark hair was combed neatly back. He put down the package.

Annie finished tying the balloons in place and got down off the piano bench. Klevinski stared at her. She checked the buttons on her shirt, and smoothed her pants.

Pearl eyed Joe Klevinski with disapproval. She looked as if she was about to give him a piece of her mind when Sophie came over and slipped her hand into Pearl's.

Pearl's face softened. "Well, if it isn't the birthday girl," she said, beaming at Sophie. She gave her a kiss on top of her head. "You look lovely."

Sophie did a little pirouette, showing off her black-and-white taffeta dress with a floppy red silk flower pinned to the waist. She had on black patent leather Mary Janes with frilly white socks. It was sweet the way she sneaked a shy look at Peter.

"You ready to ice the cake?" Pearl asked. "Better shake a leg. Your guests will be here any minute."

Sophie followed Pearl into the kitchen, her dress making a swishing sound. Jackie sidled over to her husband. *The guy had brass balls*, Annie thought, *showing up and acting as if nothing had happened.* There was a long moment of awkward silence as Annie, Peter, and Mr. Kuppel stared at him.

"Listen, I'm real sorry we got off on the wrong foot," Klevinski said with a sheepish smile, shifting from foot to foot. This was probably the same act he used on Jackie. "I know you weren't expecting me, but how could I not go to my daughter's seventh birthday?"

"Eighth," Annie said, the word exploding. Peter clamped his hand on her arm, like a stopper.

"So I can't count." Klevinski held out his hands in a gesture of contrition. "Sophie wanted me to come." That was his trump card. He knew they wouldn't make a stink, because, after all, this was Sophie's day.

"Daddy, look!" Sophie called. She came out carrying the layer cake laden with pink frosting. SOPHIE was spelled out in Lifesavers on the top.

The doorbell rang and soon the house was full of little girls. Annie watched, amused, as Peter organized a game of blindman's bluff—Sophie put one of Pearl's gauzy scarves over his eyes, and he stumbled around the living room trying to tag the girls, who squealed and giggled, giving away their locations. He was such a good sport.

Joe Klevinski watched from the dining room, a sour look on his face. But when Sophie went looking for him to ask him to take a turn as blind man, he was out on the back porch smoking a cigarette.

Pearl announced it was time for cake. They herded the kids into the dining room. Sophie sat at the head of the table under the balloons and streamers, her face glowing.

At least Annie would be able to stay long enough to sing "Happy Birthday." She followed Pearl into the kitchen. Pearl stuck eight candles in a circle around the edge of the cake, and dotted the I in SOPHIE with the one to grow on. She rummaged around in one of the kitchen drawers. "Now where did I—"

"Allow me," Klevinski said. With a flourish, he produced a book of matches from his pocket, struck one, and lit the candles. Then he picked up the cake, and Annie watched him carry it out into the now darkened dining room, taking center stage, like he'd done a single thing other than show up and buy what looked like a perfectly ghastly stuffed animal.

Everyone sang. The girls clapped when Sophie blew out the candles in one puff. With her father flanking her on one side, her mother on the other, she closed her eyes tight to make a wish. Pearl snapped a photo. If you didn't know better, Annie thought, it was a picture-perfect image of the ideal American family.

Pearl brought the cake back into the kitchen. Annie cut pieces and set them onto paper plates that were ferried back into the dining room. Even Klevinski helped. The kids had all gotten their cake, and Annie was cutting Klevinski a piece when she noticed the matchbook on the counter. He must have left it there after lighting the candles. It was from Nasty Pete's, the Cambridge bar that showed up over and over in what was supposed to be Brenda Klevinski's credit card statement.

"Looks delicious," Klevinski said, an obsequious smile on his smarmy face. "Are you the chef?"

Annie wanted to press the cake and ice cream into his face. Instead, she held the plate out to him. When he took hold of it, she didn't let go.

"You can fool your wife and you can charm your little girl," she said under her breath, "but I just want you to know, I'm onto you. If anything happens to either of them, I'll get the police down your neck faster than you can say homicide investigation."

He jerked his head around, looking to see if anyone had heard. Then he gave Annie a hard look. "I don't know what you're talking about."

Annie didn't bother to argue.

• • •

As she drove to the South End, Annie savored Joe Klevinksi's expression. She could see that she'd rattled him, but any satisfaction she felt evaporated as she contemplated him going home with Jackie and Sophie. Annie's stomach contracted. Men like that didn't have overnight transformations. She eased up on the gas. She'd been pushing ninety. The last thing she needed was to get stopped by the cops again.

Sunday traffic on the Pike was a breeze, and it took only minutes to get from Cambridge to the South End. She hit the Southeast Expressway and took the exit near the sentry tower of the Pine Street Inn, a refuge for the homeless, turned onto Berkeley Street, and made her way across. Parking spots on the street were all taken, and enterprising locals had set up hand-painted signs in the parking lots of local businesses: $20 EVENT PARKING.

Two blocks from the cathedral, the street was nearly gridlocked. *Should've bladed over,* Annie thought. The car behind her honked. Boston drivers did that even when it was pointless.

Annie made her way down a side street, and lucked out when someone pulled out of a parking spot a few blocks away from the church. She locked the car and walked up Washington Street. Dilapidated apartment buildings and deserted factories gave way to renovated row houses. It was only in the last few years that this area had begun to blanch and chasten. On the corner across from the cathedral, where there'd once been an A&P, there was now a spanking fresh Foodies Urban Market. ORGANIC PRODUCE said a hand-lettered sign in the window.

The austere, granite, Gothic-style Cathedral of the Holy Cross, Boston's answer to New York's Saint Patrick's, loomed before her. The archbishop himself lived in a small rectory in the back.

She couldn't say why, every year, she let Chip talk her into going to this event for Boston's Catholic lawyers. It was always a media circus. She threaded her way through the picketers—this year there seemed to be even more than usual. One miscreant stood off to the side with a sign that slapped you in the face with the message GOD HATES FAGS. Another picket sign read STATE'S RIGHTS and in smaller print NOT ONLY WHEN YOU AGREE. Another proclaimed GOD IS NOT A REPUBLICAN. Oh yeah, the special guest this year was the U.S. attorney general.

There were police officers everywhere—among the picketers, in front and along the sides of the church. Some were stationed at the gate checking tickets and examining purses and briefcases. The street in front was closed to traffic, and a pair of black limousines with government plates were parked in front of the church.

As she walked into the shadow of the church, Annie recognized a familiar surge of guilt. When she was a kid, she'd gone to confession regularly. She'd had to name her sins in order to be forgiven. These days, this church that seemed to have so much difficulty naming its own sins was no longer *her* church. The ritual and the hoopla, the rules and righteousness and all the rest seemed irrelevant.

She found Chip waiting for her by one of the side doors with passes to get them in. The air vibrated with organ music as they entered the cavernous interior with its soaring ceiling and muted light filtered through the intense deep blues, reds, and greens of stained glass. Her head filled with the sweet aroma of incense, though she couldn't be sure if it was real or a phantom from her memory.

A sign on a stand at the top of the aisle said PLEASE TURN OFF ALL CELL PHONES AND BEEPERS. Annie did. Chip touched a finger to the holy water and crossed himself. When she was a little girl, she'd have felt compelled to do the same.

The cathedral was still half empty. They found seats near the front and settled in to wait. It would be another twenty minutes at least before the service began. The altar glowed as if lit from within.

In the shadowy side aisle stood the confessionals. She remembered kneeling every Saturday afternoon in the closed space. *Bless me, Father, for I have sinned . . .* She'd told Father McDonough how she lied to her mother, hit her sister. She never told him she'd let Billy Pfister touch her *there* and liked it, or how she'd thought about doing more, but still she felt the shame that had been bred into her. By then she realized that Father McDonough, who sometimes couldn't remember her name, wouldn't be offering her much enlightenment. Once, at a counseling session her mother made her attend, she'd asked hypothetically what should she do if she knew someone was hurting someone else? She was dying to confide in him, tell him about her friend Charlotte's parents. That week,

Mrs. Florence had driven them to the movies. She'd been so sore, she'd needed Charlotte's help to get in and out of the car. She'd "fallen" down the stairs, Charlotte had told her. Again.

Was this, just hypothetically, a family member? Father McDonough had asked. She'd felt a surge of protectiveness toward her own parents. She backed away from the subject, or made something up to distract him, she couldn't remember which. In any event, she never got around to telling him, and it still bothered her that she'd never told anyone who might have brought the abuse into the sunlight. That's why it was so hard to watch Jackie Klevinski take Joe back into her life. This time, at least she was speaking up. She was hollering, even.

She closed her eyes and relaxed, yielding to the music that seemed to vibrate up through the seat of the wooden pew. Despite her ambivalence about the Church, there was something reassuring and familiar about being there.

28

PETER STUFFED the last paper plate and cup into a black plastic garbage bag in his mother's kitchen. He went to the door and surveyed the apartment. The place looked as if it had been struck by a bomb. Streamers sagged from the ceilings; the living room carpet was awash in torn gift wrap, ribbon, and crumpled tissue paper; dining room chairs were overturned to form a sort of fort, littered with the balloons that Sophie and her sweet little friends had decided they'd rather detonate than take home. Mr. Kuppel and Peter's mother sat on the sofa looking wasted.

"And I thought I had it bad with boys," Pearl said.

Coffee, that's what they needed. Peter started a pot. The coffee machine began to burble. He sat at the kitchen table and looked at the paper. The sketch of the A-bomber and a news update on the investigation were on page one. In the lower corner was an article about the annual Catholic service for lawyers that Annie and Chip were attending. Sounded like a big deal, what with the attorney general of the United States attending. There was a sidebar explaining its name. Apparently the Lord High Justices who celebrated the first one in England in the thirteenth century had worn scarlet robes, and ever since then it had been called the Red Mass.

Red Mass. *Scarlet* robes. The words swam on the page. *Red segues to black.* Wasn't that what the A-bomber had said in his last message? And hadn't there been something earlier about red? Peter felt a chill roll down his back.

"I gotta go. Forgot I had something to do," he told his mother, who was sprawled on the sofa, her eyes closed. Mr. Kuppel was massaging her feet. "Coffee'll be done in a minute."

Peter let himself into his house next door. It seemed to take forever for his computer to boot up and let him into email. He found what he was looking for in one of the messages from CANARY911:

> This purging must be finished. First the spawn.
> Then the workers. And now the drones where they
> sit, swollen and glowing scarlet with their own
> self-importance, obsequious parasites fawning over
> their Queen, or should I say King.

"Glowing scarlet," that's what he'd remembered. Of course. The A-bomber wasn't targeting the State House and the governor. He had his sights set on the Red Mass at the Cathedral of the Holy Cross, and on the "King" of lawyers, the attorney general of the United States. This time collateral damage would include Chip and Annie.

Peter glanced down at the time in the corner of his screen. The mass would be just getting started. Was it already too late? He tried Annie on her cell phone. No answer. He swallowed the panic that rose in his throat.

As he raced out the door, he called MacRae. No answer there, either. He left an emergency page, started his car, and headed toward the river, going as fast as he dared on the narrow streets. He tried calling Neddleman. This time he left a voice message, tripping over his words as he tried to explain.

He approached the tolls for the Pike. There was a ten-car lineup in the lane that had a toll taker; the three automated lanes were empty. He kept meaning to get one of those damned transponders. What the hell. He zoomed through the automated lane setting off alarms. For once, he wished a police officer *were* lurking there, picking off scofflaws, so he could tell someone what was happening.

Sunday traffic was light, and already the Boston skyline rose out of the horizon before him. At least he could call 911. They always answered. As he was dialing, a black Corvette going about ninety in the right lane nearly sideswiped him. He veered to avoid being hit and the phone flew from his hand, landing somewhere under his feet. He groped for a moment, trying to keep the car steady, then gave up looking for it. He'd be in the South End in minutes.

Peter abandoned the car in front of a hydrant two blocks from the cathedral and ran the rest of the way, listening for explosions and dialing 911. He put away the phone when he saw the police officers standing guard by the yellow sawhorses that barricaded the street in front of the cathedral. Picketers milled across the street, and he tried to see if the phony Walter Waxman was among them. If he'd planted a bomb, Peter was sure of one thing—he'd hang around to see it go off.

Peter approached an officer whose eyes were shaded by the brim of his cap. Without preamble, he announced, "There's a bomb in there." He wondered if the urgency in his voice sounded like hysteria. "You've got to evacuate the place."

The officer didn't flinch. "Can I see some identification?"

"Didn't you hear me?" Peter said, his voice rising. "I said—"

"Calm down, sir." The officer looked uncomfortable, his gaze shifting left and right like he was looking for backup. "Only authorized personnel and ticketed guests are allowed beyond this point. Everything is under control."

"Under control my ass. There's a bomb planted in the cathedral. He's after the attorney general."

The officer half-turned and took out his walkie-talkie. He cupped his hand so Peter couldn't hear as he spoke into it. Peter tried to push past him. He had to get inside, warn everyone. The officer grabbed him by the shoulder to pull him back. "I'm sorry, I can't let you—"

Peter broke free, ran to one of the massive doors and yanked it open. "Everyone needs to evacuate immediately! Stay calm." His voice echoed into the interior. "GET OUT NOW!"

The officer was on him again, gripping him in a bear hug, pulling him away and out to the sidewalk. Peter didn't care. People were flowing out of the church now. He strained to see if Annie and Chip were among them.

From the other side, he felt dark shadows gather around him. He turned. Three large, scruffy-looking men were closing in. One wore a torn, stained T-shirt and jeans. His face was smeared with dirt. Another one wore baggy pants, a dirty overcoat, and had a heavy beard and dark skin. There was something vaguely familiar about him.

"What the hell is going on?" he said, starting to launch a protest, but his voice caught in his throat when he saw a chubby figure straddling a white motor scooter in a driveway diagonally across the street. It was the A-bomber, and he was watching Peter. When Peter locked eyes with him, the man pulled a jacket hood over his head, revved the scooter, and took off.

"There he is. There's your man!" Peter screamed, trying to break free of the officer's hold on him, unable to point. "He's over there. Across the street."

The bearded man turned to look. Peter watched, dumbstruck, as the man whipped a walkie-talkie out of his overcoat pocket and started running toward the scooter, shouting and pointing as he went. His two buddies followed, weaving around churchgoers fleeing the cathedral.

There were sirens, and a police car screeched from an alleyway across from the cathedral, followed by two more. But they didn't get far, as they were quickly swallowed up in the crowd of people who'd emptied out of the cathedral and were milling about in the intersection. By the time a path was cleared, the scooter was gone.

The bearded man in the filthy overcoat returned, fuming. "How many times do I have to tell you? Stay out of my investigation!" He took off his coat and threw it on the ground. "Do you need it in writing? I can get a court order. Or maybe I should just hold you for obstructing an ongoing investigation." He grabbed hold of the corner of his beard and yanked. The whole thing came off in one piece. Wincing, Neddleman added, "Jesus Christ, and we almost had him."

• • •

"Why the hell didn't you tell me?" Peter asked Neddleman.

They were outside the cathedral. Chip and Annie had gone home after Peter assured them he'd be fine. The crowds had gone, and the only people left were a few genuine homeless men drinking in the entryway of the lone empty storefront across the street.

"You told me you were sure he was after the State House. How was I supposed to know you were staking him out here?" Turned out the police had combed the church the night before and found a bomb taped to the underside of one of the front pews. A far more powerful device than its predecessors, it could have killed hundreds and maimed one of Boston's historic landmark churches.

"Frankly, I didn't want you getting in the way. And this just proves I was right."

Peter felt disgusted. If Neddleman had leveled with him, the A-bomber would have been safely behind bars. "Like hell it does. Just proves you have your head up your ass. You want my help, which by the way you've gotten plenty of, but you don't trust me."

"It's not my job to trust you."

"It's your job to find this guy, to do whatever it takes to bring him in."

Neddleman didn't argue. "Damn. And we *knew* he'd be hanging around to watch." He peeled a piece of adhesive off his chin, rolled it in a ball, and flicked it at the curb.

Neddleman's cell phone rang. He pulled it out. "Yeah?" He nodded. His eyes lit up. Whatever it was, it was good news. He listened some more. "Call if you get anything else." He hung up.

He hesitated a moment, then said, "They found the scooter. Downtown. Maybe he got careless and we'll get some prints. I hope." Neddleman cracked his knuckles and his face hardened with determination. "We're going to get him. Eventually."

• • •

Peter lay spooned together in bed with Annie in her bedroom that night. He kissed her shoulder and hugged her so the curve of her back fit snug into his chest. The dozen red roses he'd brought were in a vase on the dresser. Annie had been speechless when he'd presented her with them.

"I was afraid they were going to arrest you," Annie said.

"Good thing they didn't. Horizontal stripes aren't my thing," Peter said, trying to keep it upbeat. He'd barely gotten past his fury at Neddleman for leaving him in the dark. Now he was trying not to think about how bereft he'd have been if he'd lost Annie. "The worst part is he's still out there. I don't think he'll stop now. He's craving attention, and that's what he's got. Damn. If only I'd—"

"You're not a mind reader," Annie said, cutting him off. "You did what you had to do, so don't beat yourself up. They wouldn't even know what they were looking for if it hadn't been for you. They'll get him."

Peter had no doubt that they would get him, as Neddleman said. But would *eventually* be before or after the bomber performed his next trick? There was no point in poring over the coulda-shoulda-wouldas, to use his mother's expression.

Peter ran his hand down Annie's side, into the curve at her waist, over the swell of her hip. This was what mattered. This, and the way he and Annie fit perfectly together. You had to figure out what was important to you and then pay attention to it—that was what he told his patients.

"This is nice," he said. He kissed her neck. "So what's going on in the real world?"

"Real world? You mean the wedding from hell?" Annie laughed. "Abby left me a message that Luke's dropping by the office tomorrow with a couple of maid-of-honor dresses for me to try on. At least she's not making me go shopping in one of those stores." Annie turned around to face Peter. She kissed his forehead. "Did you and Kate have a big wedding?"

"We—" It surprised Peter that this was something they'd never talked about. Kate hadn't wanted a big wedding. She'd worn a white lace Mexican dress and sandals, a garland of tiny roses around her head, and a veil made from a length of white chiffon she'd painted with flowers. No bridesmaids, no ushers, just a judge who was a friend of the family. "We got married on the Vineyard at a little inn in Aquinnah. Just my mother and father, my brother, Kate's father, her sister, Kwan and Gloria, of course, plus a few friends. It was nice."

"That's where you went after . . . ?"

It was awkward, finishing that thought. "After her murder" sounded melodramatic. "After her death" made it sound like a nonevent, like Kate had just keeled over with a sigh like an old tree that lost its grip on the earth.

"Not far from there. I scattered her ashes on a bluff along the Moshup Trail overlooking the ocean—funny, the place is called Zack's Cliffs." Peter felt his throat tighten and his eyes fill with tears.

Annie kissed him, a tender kiss this time, on the mouth. She ran her fingers through his hair, and her eyes searched his. "You've never brought me flowers before. Thank you. The roses are beautiful."

"I wanted you to know—"

Annie kissed him again. He was grateful she didn't press him for an ending to the sentence.

Annie barely recognized Jackie's voice on the phone Monday morning. "I feel terrible," she croaked. "I have a cold."

It was the first time Jackie had ever called in sick. Annie quickly cataloged the day's work. Chip would be out taking depositions. Annie had planned to catch up on paperwork and make phone calls. And, of course, Luke was coming over with the dresses for her to try on. One fewer witness to that indignity was probably a good thing.

"You sound terrible. Stay home. Take care of yourself. You need anything?"

"No, I'm okay. By the way, Sophie loves the horse."

"I'm so glad. I was sorry I couldn't stay to see her open her gifts."

"She's been playing with it and drawing it. Slept with it on her pillow. How did you know?"

Annie felt herself smiling. "Just a lucky guess."

They chatted a little longer. Annie told Jackie that Peter had given her roses for the very first time.

"Red roses?" Jackie excused herself and sneezed. "You know what that means? Love. Passion. Yellow is friendship. White is purity."

"Believe me, that's not the kind of thing Peter would know."

Jackie laughed. "I wouldn't be so sure." Her laughter was cut off by the sound of a man's voice in the background. "Listen, I got to go," she whispered, and hung up.

What did the color of the flowers Joe sent Jackie signify? Annie wondered. Repression? Intimidation?

Annie wrote PLEASE RING on a piece of paper and taped it to the outside of the office door. Then she locked it and settled into her office to work. When the phone rang, she let it go to voice mail. By the time the doorbell rang three hours later, she was feeling proud of herself. She'd managed to plow through most of what she'd hoped to get done.

She opened the door. Luke was standing there in work boots, blue jeans, and a flannel shirt over a white T-shirt. He held aloft a long garment bag. She took it and gave him a kiss. He exuded an earthy, rich scent, almost like manure.

"Sorry, I hope it was okay to come dressed like this. I came from work."

"Horses?" Annie asked.

"Actually, this morning it was elephants. One of our volunteers didn't show up and I ended up . . . well, you don't need to know that. Suffice it to say, when someone doesn't show, the work doesn't go away." He gave a wry grin. Despite how outrageously handsome he was, she could definitely get used to this guy.

"Well, thanks for this," Annie said, indicating the garment bag. She laid it down across a chair and unzipped it. She suppressed a groan. The first dress was lime-green satin with a dropped waist and flounced skirt. Perfect for Drucilla, Cinderella's ugly stepsister. At least it didn't have puffy sleeves. The second one, a pink silk number, did. In spades. The third dress was a soft lilac. It was like something you'd see on a Grecian urn, gathered bodice with the fabric twisted into a graceful S-curve, a single thin shoulder strap. Annie held it up. The flowing, two-layered skirt fell in ripples.

"That's the one, isn't it?" Luke said. "Abby thought you'd like it."

Annie didn't want to ask how much it cost. "It's amaz—" she started. Was she being set up? Were the other two dresses put in there so that when she got to "Door Number 3" she'd be so grateful to see something reasonable that she'd shut up?

"I've got to bring back whatever you don't want so Abby can return them. You got a minute to try it on?"

Annie carried the dress into her office. She closed the shades and stripped down. The underslip slid down over her like a second skin. The dress itself was soft and silky, pure luxury. It could have been made for her. Not too short, just a little roomy in the hips. Her sports bra didn't exactly do it justice. She twisted her hair up and walked up and down the office on the balls of her socked feet. The hems of the two gossamer layers fluttered as she moved. There was no mirror in the room, but the damned dress made her feel knock-down-dead gorgeous.

The doorbell rang. Annie lifted the corner of the window shade and peered out. A big old Chevy station wagon was double-parked at the curb. Last thing she wanted to do was greet a potential client in this getup.

She wiggled out of the dress and underslip. She pulled on her jeans. As she was buttoning her shirt, she opened the door a crack. She heard Luke and another man's low voices. Then the sound of the office door closing.

"Just a delivery," Luke called. "He was going to leave them outside on the landing."

Annie came out. Luke was holding a vase of red roses. More

passion? When it rained it poured. Annie pulled a rose from the vase and smelled it. They'd even removed the thorns from the stems.

Luke picked up the card that had fallen on the floor. "They're for you." He handed Annie the card. "Who's Petey?"

Annie read the card. Sure enough, it said LOVE, PETEY. She pressed the card to her chest and doubled over, laughing. What a lunatic Peter was. She had roses at home, now more at work. And signing the card *Petey*? She wasn't sure she wanted to know what kind of epiphany he'd had about their relationship.

"Where do you want me to put these. They're heavy as all get-out."

"Just put them over . . ." Annie stopped. Heavy? A flower delivery that was left on the landing? And let's face it, Peter bringing her one bouquet of roses was pretty earth-shattering. Two? That was thoroughly out of character. And she *had* seen a Chevy wagon like the one parked outside recently; she remembered because it reminded her of her father's beloved old car. But where?

Smell the roses, an urgent voice cried out in the back of her head.

"Put them down," Annie cried as she backed away. Luke looked at her, baffled. "Drop them! Now!"

It felt like slow motion as she lunged, knocking the vase of flowers out of Luke's hands. She watched the base crack, revealing a tangle of wires and batteries.

"Get out of here! Run for it!" Annie shouted.

She was out on the landing, Luke at her heels, when she felt the shock wave hit her from behind, and for one blinding instant she knew it was too late.

• • •

The organ music sounded to Peter more like a bellows. He sat beside Annie in church as the processional came up the aisle. In the lead was a man in red robes and a tall, pointed bishop's hat. A golden censer trailing curls of smoke swung from the pole he carried, but the odor was more like rubbing alcohol than incense. As the bishop came closer, Peter realized the robes weren't red cloth, they were smeared with blood. Peter watched mesmerized as blood trickled down the man's face and dripped from the censer. The figure moved steadily up the aisle, the censer swung closer and closer. The bishop took another step and Peter could see his face. It was Harvard Harry, grinning maniacally, and the wheezing organ sounded like *traitor, traitor, traitor*. A yellow canary fluttered around the censer as it swung back and forth. One more swing, and it would hit them and explode. Peter jerked himself awake.

He was in a chair in Annie's hospital room. He tried to stretch. Every muscle in his body complained. Annie looked exactly as she had when he'd finally succumbed to sleep at about three in the morning, on her back, unconscious, her skin the color of chalk, her head swathed in bandages, the tube in her nose connected to oxygen. One arm had an IV drip, the other was in a cast.

He rubbed his eyes and blinked. It felt like he had sand in his eyeballs, and his mouth tasted like he'd been chewing on an old tire. The sky outside was just turning light. When Peter had rushed over to the hospital yesterday afternoon, Luke had been awake and in stable condition in a room down the hall with Abby watching over him. He'd been behind Annie and taken the brunt of the explosion. Annie had been hit in the head by flying debris, and broken her wrist. She still hadn't regained consciousness. He wanted to be there when she did.

Peter's mother and Annie's mother had been there last night, keeping watch. At midnight he'd finally managed to convince them that they didn't all need to stay.

Annie *would* regain consciousness, Peter told himself. Her skull was intact, and her vital signs were good. He'd hounded her doctor into letting him see her MRI. No brain damage.

He closed his eyes. When he opened them again, the sun was slanting in through the window, and a nurse was taking Annie's blood pressure.

Peter stumbled into the bathroom and pissed the three gallons of coffee he'd drunk the night before. He washed his hands. His haggard, unshaved face stared back at him from the mirror. The bags under his eyes had bags, and he looked groggy and startled at the same time. He threw water in his face and toweled off, then squeezed some toothpaste out onto his finger and rubbed it over his teeth. He rinsed out. That felt marginally better.

He took out his cell phone and thought about turning it on. He knew there'd be scores of messages, calls he didn't want to return. The hell with them.

He went back into the room. The nurse was gone. He pulled the chair close to the bed and took Annie's hand, the side that wasn't broken. He held it.

"Hey, you," he said. "Come back. I know you're in there." Annie's chest rose and fell gently. "See, here's the thing, you have to come back. It isn't optional. Because I want you here with me." Still nothing. "I'll even go blading—"

Peter stopped and jerked to attention. He felt gentle pressure from Annie's hand. Her eyelids fluttered. She gazed at him from half-open eyes, and a smile played on her lips, followed by a wince of pain.

She murmured something, but he couldn't make out what. A wave of relief washed over him. "Welcome back." He pressed his lips to her fingertips.

She gazed at the cast on her arm, a look of confusion on her face. She groped the bandage on her head.

"You remember what happened?" he asked.

She relaxed into the pillow, her eyes unfocused. She said something that sounded like *the most beautiful dress*, but he couldn't be sure. Her eyes closed.

"Annie? Annie?" But it was no use. She was out again.

"Hey," came a voice from the doorway. Peter looked up. It was MacRae.

Go away, Peter wanted to tell him. *She doesn't want to see you. And I certainly don't, either.*

"How's she doing?" There was genuine concern on MacRae's face.

"Broken wrist. Concussion. Abrasions."

"She wake up yet?"

Peter admitted that she had.

"That's great news."

Peter glanced at the clock. It was barely eight. "You're here awfully early. I'm surprised they let you in." Peter could hear the confrontational edge in his voice.

MacRae crossed his arms over his chest. "I tried you at home. On your cell. I thought you might be here." Peter rubbed his chin, feeling the thick stubble, as MacRae gave him an appraising look. "You look like hell."

Peter couldn't help smiling. There was something comforting about still being able to trade insult for insult with this bozo.

MacRae added, "I thought I'd come by, see how Annie's doing—"

"Well, now you've seen her you can—"

"—and to let you know, we've got him in custody," MacRae said.

Peter stopped. He closed his eyes, and felt the bones in his neck crack as he rolled his head back and around. At least there was that. There wouldn't be any more bombs.

"I only wish we'd found him sooner," MacRae added as he perched on the edge of the bed and gazed at Annie. "God, I feel awful about this."

"So who is he?"

"His real name is Richard Blankstein," MacRae said. He eyed Peter.

"Never heard of him."

"We identified him from prints on the scooter. He was waiting for us in his apartment. Had a little suitcase packed, like he was going on an overnight to his granny's, if you can believe that. We've got him in a holding cell. Won't talk to us, won't talk to an attorney." MacRae chewed on his lip. "He wants to talk to you."

"Sonofabitch." Peter spat out the word. Talk to him? He wouldn't have trusted himself within thirty feet of the guy. "Yeah, well, you can tell him I'm otherwise occupied."

MacRae waited a few beats before adding, "Peter, the only thing he's saying is that there's another bomb. It's set to blow tomorrow."

Why was that his problem? "Sounds like you've got your work cut out for you."

There was a moan from the bed. "Peter?" Annie was struggling to sit up.

Peter sprang to her side, pushing MacRae over. "Hey, hey. Lie back. I'm right here."

Annie sank back. Her eyes seemed unfocused. "You sent me roses. So lovely. You never did that before."

Peter jerked his head for MacRae to leave. "You mind? I'll talk to you in the hall in a couple of minutes."

MacRae left without an argument.

"See, they're right here," he said.

He pulled a rose from the vase on the table by the window. Annie's mother had picked up the flowers from Annie's apartment the night before when she went to pack Annie an overnight bag.

He placed the rose on Annie's chest. She fingered it and smiled.

"Do you remember the explosion?" Peter asked.

"Explosion? At the cathedral? The bomb, it didn't go off."

Peter wasn't surprised that Annie didn't remember. That was pretty normal with a head injury. "There was a bomb at your office. You and Luke . . ."

The rose fell to the floor. "Luke? Is Luke okay?"

"He's right down the hall. Abby's with him. He's going to be fine."

"I remember roses. You sent me roses again." Annie smiled. "Petey."

"Huh?"

"The card that was in the flowers. You signed it 'Love, Petey.' "

Now he knew she was delusional, or maybe she was getting a little too much Valium through the IV. He told her that the A-bomber had been arrested and wouldn't talk to anyone but him. That there might be more bombs.

MacRae cleared his throat from the doorway and looked at his watch. "You coming?"

"Not if you don't quit bugging me. Would you just get lost for a couple of minutes?"

MacRae withdrew.

Peter wasn't sure Annie had absorbed what he'd been telling her. "I don't want to leave you."

"No choice," Annie murmured.

He knew she was right. "I'll call your mom. She was going to come back in a couple of hours but—"

"Don't." She put her hand on his arm. "I can wait. I'll be okay."

"But what if you need something?"

"Nurse call button." She groped at the side of the bed, found it, and waved it at him.

Nurses didn't always answer their call buttons. Peter found Annie's cell phone in her backpack and turned it on. He programmed it.

"All you have to do is push one to call me. Okay?"

"Mmm."

"What did I just say?"

She licked her lips. "Just push one." Her voice was thick with sleepiness.

"Show me." He set the phone on the mattress beside her, pulled his own phone out of his pocket, and turned it on.

"You're such a pain." Grimacing, she raised her head and propped herself up on one elbow. She pressed 1, then SEND. A moment later, the cell phone in his pocket vibrated.

"I'm putting it under your pillow, okay? That way you won't have to reach." He slid the phone in place and kissed her on the forehead. She was already nodding off. "So you know how to call me, right?"

"I'll just put my lips together and—" She took a breath, pursed her lips, and blew.

Cracking jokes was a good sign.

Peter followed MacRae out to the hospital parking lot.

"You want to follow me to his apartment?" MacRae asked.

"Apartment?"

"Neddleman thought you'd want to see where this guy lived before you talked to him."

Neddleman had been smart sending MacRae over to ask Peter if he'd talk to—what was his name?—Blankstein. Could that be his real name? Seemed like an excellent *nom de guerre* for someone who wanted to remain unknowable.

It annoyed the hell out of Peter that Neddleman was right, he did want to see Blankstein's home. Experts could identify the species of bird just by examining the nest. People were the same. What you kept, what you tossed, and how you organized your surroundings, all of that was as revealing as a set of Rorschach responses.

30

WALL-TO-WALL BOOKS, magazines, and CDs—that was what feathered Richard Blankstein's one-room apartment on the top floor of a triple-decker in one of the few Cambridge neighborhoods that was still largely industrial buildings and rundown homes. The building had six apartments but only five doorbells. Apparently Blankstein was a pebbles-on-the-window kind of guy, or else he never had visitors.

Peter stood in the apartment with MacRae, trying to get a sense of the man who'd just tried to annihilate the person he loved most in this world. The room was tidy, but not obsessively so. There was a mattress on the floor, a steamer trunk, a card table, a workbench, and a state-of-the-art stereo system. Dark green blankets were nailed over windows that would have looked out over the back of the building.

"The neighbors rarely saw him," MacRae told Peter. "He works nights, a cashier at the BP station at the corner of Prospect." Peter knew the place. It was one of the few local gas stations where you could fill up twenty-four hours a day. The cashier worked in a little

Plexiglas booth about the size of a fat man's coffin, just enough room for a TV and a space heater.

Peter snapped on the pair of latex gloves that MacRae handed him, and gingerly lifted the lid of the steamer trunk. If there'd been anything unpleasant in it, he reminded himself, the police would have collected it as evidence. Inside were neatly folded underwear, socks, and sweaters. Reminded him of the trunk his mother had packed him for summer camp. More clothing hung on a metal clothing rack by the front door. There were a dark blue zippered parka, a tweed sport jacket, a half-dozen pairs of pants, shirts, and a suit with wide lapels.

"Computer was there," MacRae said, indicating the card table with a metal folding chair. "We took that in. And a laminating machine. The kind you use to dummy up fake IDs. We also found the stolen key cards."

Under the windows was an old workbench with a battered copy of *The Anarchist's Cookbook* lying on it. Underneath were boxes with spools of wire, batteries, covered coffee cans, assorted electronics. Peter shot MacRae a questioning look.

"We got the volatile stuff out of here," MacRae said. "He had a five-gallon tank of gasoline, black powder, hydrochloric acid. Lucky he didn't burn the place down or asphyxiate himself."

Peter scanned the floor-to-ceiling bookshelves. There were several biographies of Thomas Jefferson. Looked like Blankstein had the complete works of L. Ron Hubbard, the founder of Scientology, next to *The Archetypes and The Collective Unconscious* and *Synchronicity* by Carl G. Jung. Four shelves were devoted to science fiction, mostly paperbacks, shelved alphabetically, from *The Hitchhiker's Guide to the Galaxy* by Douglas Adams at one end to works by Roger Zelazny at the other. There was one of Peter's favorites, Zelazny's *The Dream Master*. It was about a therapist who cures his patients by entering their dreams. Now there was a world-class be-careful-what-you-wish-for.

There were magazines, neatly stored in plastic upright files. *The New Republic; The Nation; Harvard Law Review.* He pulled out a copy of *Reason* from a few months earlier and flipped through. The glossy news and opinion magazine that looked like it had a libertarian bent was a library copy. Great swaths of text had been highlighted in yellow, and one article, "Coercion vs. Consent: A reasoned debate on how to think about liberty," had its corner dog-eared. Peter put the magazine back.

Richard Blankstein lived a Spartan lifestyle, Peter thought, mentally scratching his head and taking note of what was not there. No photograph albums, no framed photos, no letters or cards, no knickknacks.

He poked his head into the kitchenette. There were a two-burner stove and microwave. Not a dirty dish in the sink. He opened a cabinet. Two boxes of Cheerios and cans of soup. The small refrigerator held a carton of milk and some American cheese. The freezer was stuffed with frozen burritos. Blankstein wasn't going to be one of those prisoners who complained about the food.

So what else was there to see? He stuck his head in the bathroom. It was pretty bare. Just a bar of soap. Blankstein had probably packed his shampoo and toothbrush.

Peter returned to the living room and did a slow 360. What was he missing? Bookcases, bed, computer work area, workbench, kitchen, bathroom.

"No garbage cans?" he said to MacRae.

"Yeah. We noticed that, too. We went through the garbage outside the building. Nothing."

Blankstein kept his clothing on a metal rack and in the steamer trunk. So what would he keep in his closet? There didn't seem to be one in the apartment. Not possible. Every apartment had a closet. Peter rolled the clothing rack aside. Sure enough, there was a closet door. He pulled it open.

That was bizarre. Surely there was some force of nature that made miscellaneous objects crawl into empty closets. But the only thing that had crawled into this one was a small, threadbare, oriental prayer rug.

Peter sniffed. What was that familiar yeasty smell? He reached up and pulled the chain of the overhead light. The closet walls were papered in white and blue flowers. The wallpaper had been slapped up by an amateur, on angle, the seams overlapping. He touched the wall. It was moist. Now he recognized the smell. Wheat paste.

"Hey," he called to MacRae. "Did you notice? These walls were just recently papered."

He stepped aside so MacRae could take a look. "I'll be damned." MacRae took hold of the corner of the sheet covering the back wall and pulled. The paper came clean away revealing a plaster wall, dense with writing. MacRae pulled off the paper on the adjacent closet walls. These were covered with writing as well.

"Must've taken him quite a while to write all this down," MacRae said.

Phrases popped out at Peter. "Legalistkill Juggernaut," "Highway robbers in suits," sneered forward-slanting, sloppy cursive writing. "I am a true Seeker," "I cleave to no system"—these phrases were written in a hand as upright and restrained as the words themselves. Elsewhere, in careful printing, it said, "We must take control," and "The Consumer must be persuaded to stop."

Three handwritings, three different tones of voice. Peter realized what he was looking at. This was an extended, semiarticulate dialogue among the Maw, the Philosopher King, and the Marshal, the three characters Blankstein had referred to in his email. There was no coherent narrative flow, but the thoughts seemed loosely connected.

In one place, the printed words "Law must be neutral" were followed by the barely legible "But the nail that sticks up gets smashed down." Then came the carefully written response: "We thank you for the reality check."

Though he searched and searched, there was nothing in the scrawling hand of the Maw, or the aseptic printing of the Marshal, or the perfect penmanship of the Philosopher King about the bombings. Nothing about law schools or cathedrals, court buildings or law offices. No hint of what the next target would be.

Did Blankstein work the way the average person would, from top to bottom, left to right? Near the floor on the right-hand wall was written: "No apologies. We are nothing more than a grotesque mirror image of a Society bent on self-destruction. We wish to remove from our present prison to another more amenable address to complete the Work at hand."

All that was missing was THE END. Peter could imagine Blankstein sitting cross-legged on the bit of carpeting, unrepentant, writing these final lines before papering over the interior of the closet, his overnight bag packed. He'd run out of walls on which to write. A prison cell would give him three big empty ones, blank slates on which to start anew.

• • •

Annie lay in the hospital bed after Peter left. She was still trying to wrap her head around what Peter had been telling her. She remembered working in her office that morning; then Luke arrived. She remembered trying on the dress. The doorbell rang. Then what? Peter said there'd been a bomb. Luke was hurt. She'd been hurt, too.

She reached up and touched the gauze. Thinking made her head ache. She could feel one kind of pain in her scalp on top of her head, a tightness, probably stitches. Had they shaved off some of her hair? She didn't want to know. But the worse pain was a throbbing in her right temple, and also in her arm, where the slightest movement caused arcs of pain to radiate from her wrist.

She groped under her pillow. No, she didn't need her cell phone. She needed the nurse call button. She found it hanging on the side of the bed and pressed. Minutes later, she heard squishy footsteps.

"Anne?" The nurse, a tall, lanky woman with long dark hair, wore flowered scrubs, almost like comfortable pajamas, and sneakers.

"Annie," Annie said. "I hurt. My head, my arm." She was embarrassed to find tears pricking out of her eyes. Anger surged through her. She wanted to rip out the IV. How long were they going to leave these damned tubes in her nose? She felt raw and chafed all over, shivery with cold.

The nurse checked the chart. "I'll see if I can get you something." She covered Annie with an extra blanket and hurried off.

Annie stared at the ceiling. *Breathe,* she told herself. *Relax.* Getting tense and upset only made pain worse. *One hundred, ninety-nine, ninety-eight.* On each count she inhaled, then exhaled, emptying her lungs.

"Annie?" It was Abby. She looked pale, wrung out. The powder-blue suit she had on looked as if she'd slept in it. She perched on the edge of the chair. "Peter told me you woke up, but when I came in earlier, it looked like you were out again. You doing okay?" She touched the bandage on Annie's head. "You're not, are you?"

"I will be. How's Luke?"

"He's cut up, and bruised. Cracked a couple of ribs. Collapsed lung."

"Hang on to him. That one's a keeper, no joke intended."

"I'm trying to," Abby said, tears streaming down her face. "I'm so glad you like him."

"I do."

Abby left when the nurse returned. She injected the contents of a hypodermic syringe into the IV line. Afterward, the nurse poured water from a plastic pitcher into the glass on the bedside table. Then she gently pressed Annie's wrist and took her pulse. Already Annie felt warmer.

The nurse stood over her, smiling. "It's working, isn't it?"

Annie nodded. She imagined the pain, like some disgusting yellow discharge, draining from her head and out her ears. Jackie would have been proud of her. The power of positive thinking, she'd have said—never mind that it was backed up by the power of Demerol, or codeine, or whatever wonderful elixir the nurse had sent flowing into her.

She closed her eyes and let herself float. She didn't doubt it had happened, but still she had no memory of a bomb, or of anything unpleasant except that lime-green satin dress. That she remembered. It was something a Muppet would wear. Pumps in her size dyed that color? She tried not to laugh.

She remembered Luke holding a big bouquet of red roses. *Who's Petey?* he'd asked, picking up the card off the floor. The delivery man had wanted to leave the flowers on the landing, the delivery man who'd arrived in a black Chevy wagon.

Amazing that there were still cars like her father's old tank still on the road. The world was full of doppelgangers like that. Flowers at home, flowers at work. The nurse who reminded her of Jackie Klevinski, a long, solemn face, hair tied back at the nape of the neck. And Jackie reminded her of Charlotte Florence. And Charlotte's father reminded her of Joe Klevinski.

Her mind looped, and looped back, returning to the black Chevy wagon. A car like that had been parked behind hers when she staked out the Brighton post office. And somewhere she'd seen a car like that not long ago. Where . . . ? But the thought slipped away. She felt herself drifting, and for some reason she smelled pot roast. She wasn't hungry, really, but the smell was comforting.

31

As ANNIE said, there was no choice. Still, Peter had to force himself to follow MacRae to the massive police headquarters in Roxbury. As he walked to the rear entrance from the parking lot, he saw himself reflected in the glass exterior. His suit jacket was rumpled and his face was gray with stubble. He groped in his pocket for his tie, then abandoned the effort. Putting on a tie would be like sticking a Band-Aid on a concussion. At least he didn't have to run the media gauntlet at the main entrance.

MacRae shepherded him through security and upstairs to an office. Neddleman was waiting.

"Thanks for coming," Neddleman said, standing when Peter entered. He didn't bat an eye at Peter's appearance. "Coffee?"

God, he could use a cup. Maybe that would make the world snap into focus. "Please."

Neddleman poured a cup from the pot in the corner. "Milk? Sugar?"

Peter shook his head. Straight caffeine, that was all he needed. Neddleman handed him the cup.

"I know this is difficult." The guy oozed sympathy. Probably kept his emotions in a jar along with his hair gel. "It'll be just the two of you. No wires. No hidden cameras. No one-way glass. That's how he wants it. We have enough evidence to hang him, so all you need to do is find out if and where he's got more bombs."

If this was so simple, then why couldn't they do it without him? Peter took another gulp of coffee. It was good and strong. He felt his head clear.

Neddleman's gaze went back and forth from Peter to MacRae. "You okay with this?"

Peter drained the cup and handed it back to Neddleman. "Can we just get it over with so I can get the hell out of here?"

Peter followed MacRae down the hall and up a flight of stairs. MacRae pressed a buzzer in the wall, and a door swung open. MacRae led the way past a guard desk and down an antiseptic corridor. He stopped in front of a door with a small window in it.

"He's in there."

Peter peered through the glass. All he could see was a table and two chairs. He pulled the door open. He heard Blankstein humming before he saw him, sitting cross-legged under the table. He had his eyes closed. As he breathed out, he made a sound like the wheezy bellows in Peter's dream.

So this pathetic excuse for a man was responsible for so much anguish, so much terror, so many deaths. Mary Alice Boudreaux, Rudy Ravitch's buddy Leon Gauss, the other victims whom Peter knew only as statistics. Annie and Luke had almost been added to the list. And there would be more if Peter couldn't get him to tell where he'd hidden the next bomb. How much easier it would be to just insert a cattle prod into this man's ass and see if the information didn't miraculously pop out of his mouth. Not to mention how much more satisfying the whole process would be. It was a very narrow chasm, barely a crack, really, between humanity and depravity.

Peter steeled himself. He sat in a chair and pushed back from the table so he could see Blankstein.

"Hello, Richard."

Blankstein's eyes snapped open. "Hello, Peter."

"You know I have to tell the authorities everything you tell me," Peter said, issuing the obligatory Lamb warning, "and it can be used against you in court. You'd be better off talking to your own attorney."

"Scum. Blow the buggers up."

"Isn't that why you're here?"

Blankstein laced his fingers, closed his eyes, and resumed humming.

"You like small spaces, don't you? I saw your closet."

The humming stopped.

"You going to do that in prison? Talk to the walls?"

A smile spread over Blankstein's face. "They have a wonderful library, did you know that? Books, magazines. And a network where you can order—"

Peter brought his fist down on the top of the table. "Why'd you try to kill Annie? You just want to add more notches to your belt?"

Blankstein covered his head with his arms and cowered. "Who's Annie?"

"That's the way you do it, isn't it? Don't give a fuck who gets hurt."

"I thought you understood."

"Well, I don't. I'll never understand. Doesn't it bother you that—"

"It never bothered them, why should it bother me?"

"You—" Peter took a breath. *Easy does it,* he told himself. No point in indulging blind anger. "Them?"

"The police. The lawyers. The judges."

Peter tried to muster a sympathetic tone. "They didn't help you?"

"They don't help anyone but themselves."

"You asked them for help?"

Blankstein resumed rocking and humming.

"Is that why you're blowing them up, because no one listened to you?"

"No one listened."

"You called them."

The humming was louder now.

"Why did you call them?"

"The closet was safe."

Peter stopped himself from asking why. He wasn't here to understand, or unburden. He wasn't here to assess sanity, though he hadn't the slightest doubt that Blankstein was insane, in every sense of the word. He was here to get information, pure and simple.

"So you started, what, planting bombs to destroy the people who wouldn't help you?"

"They deserve to die. Society is corrupt. Depraved. Buying, spending. Raping the environment. Pillaging our legacy. It has to stop."

"You taught yourself how to make bombs?"

"Just read the book. Find the recipe." He made a sound like a bomb exploding and grinned.

"But there's more to come, isn't there? You're very clever. They'll never know what you've planned."

Blankstein held completely still. "That's why you're here, isn't it? It's not because I wanted to talk to you. It's because they want you to find out where I left it."

"It?"

"The bomb."

"Just one?"

Blankstein giggled. "Maybe."

"Where?"

"Why should I tell you? I'm going to plead guilty anyway, so what's the difference? One more bomb to finish the work. One more bomb and the Maw is forever quieted."

He had a point. Guilt was guilt. Except that Richard Blankstein felt nothing that the rest of humanity would have recognized as guilt. Lives didn't matter to this man, not even his own. And from a legal perspective, whether he killed nine or nine hundred, so what? Even if he got the death penalty, he'd only get zapped once. With a decent defense attorney and an expert psychological evaluation, he could get a life sentence, get his three square a day, and lose himself in the prison library. Prisoners even earned law degrees from their jail cells. They had rights, though Ashcroft had made sure that not everyone who was incarcerated did. Foreign terrorists . . . That gave Peter an idea.

"I shouldn't tell you this, but they're going to charge you with terrorism. Send you to Guantanamo." The lie rolled out without even a second thought. Richard Blankstein was not his patient, not his client. He was a pseudointellectual schizophrenic without a conscience to govern his ideals. "They'll lock you up in a little cage out in the sun. Just bars. No walls to scribble on. No books. I hear the guard comes by every four hours or so with water, just to be sure you don't fry out there."

Blankstein stopped rocking. "They can't do that. I'm an American citizen."

Peter choked back a laugh. "Were. They're taking that away from you, too, because you've committed terrorist acts. That's what your lawyer would be telling you right now. They're capable of anything.

"And here's what else your lawyer would be telling you. You're holding the cards, because you know where the bomb is planted. All you have to do is tell me. That's it. Tell me, and like magic, I promise you that you won't be getting a one-way ticket to Cuba. Then you can go ahead, plead guilty, enjoy yourself. I hear they serve burritos on Thursdays at Walpole."

. . .

Neddleman was ecstatic when MacRae relayed Blankstein's claim that he'd salted a bomb in the downtown skyscraper One Beacon Street, where the Supreme Judicial Court of Massachusetts was temporarily housed. Within minutes, he'd ordered the building evacuated and searched.

Sitting with MacRae in his office afterward, Peter was in no mood to be high-fived. He'd crossed a line. He'd deal with the guilt, just not right now. There'd been no choice, he knew that, but that didn't change the fact that he felt like he'd soiled himself, violated the principles he lived by.

In a contest of ideals, Blankstein was best in show. He had his principles and acted accordingly, intellect before emotions. Blankstein had picked his enemies: Harvard Law School, where tomorrow's lawyers and judges were born and were nurtured; the courts where they practiced their deceit; the attorney general of the United States, the Satan in charge. All in the name of societal change. If some poor souls got annihilated in the process, tough nuts. They were sacrificed to a greater good.

It all made sense—all of it except the last bomb. Blankstein probably had some convoluted rationale for targeting a practicing attorney and an investigator who should have been small potatoes, unworthy of his attention. Still, the lack of symmetry troubled Peter.

"Just curious. Were there any flyers found around Annie's office?"

MacRae nodded. "Cars parked on the street had these in their windshields." He took out a sheet of white paper, a Xerox of a page printed with a broad-tipped marker. It was printed in all caps.

And beneath that, a circled A.

Peter almost laughed. "That's short and sweet. Lacks some of the finesse of his earlier work, don't you think?"

"We're looking at it," MacRae said, a hint of defensiveness in his tone.

"All caps? Handwritten? And that symbol at the bottom looks more like a stop sign than an anarchist symbol."

"Yeah, I know." MacRae looked like he had a bad case of indigestion.

"You sure Blankstein was responsible for the last one? I mean, Chip's law office? Doesn't seem grandiose enough for him."

"We're exploring the possibility of a copycat. We've talked to Chip about who might have had a grudge against his firm."

Peter didn't doubt that the list would be long. Chip and Annie had been working for the public defender's office for years before they went into private practice, and they'd had their share of unhappy clients. Ralston Bridges, who'd killed Peter's wife, was a case in point.

"Have the investigators reported on what they found in Annie's office?" Peter asked. "I mean, is it the same kind of bomb?"

MacRae told him the preliminary report was inconclusive.

"You don't know if they found any"—Peter cleared his throat; it felt so silly to be asking this—"flowers. Roses, for example. In the office, I mean."

MacRae didn't scoff at the question. Instead he turned to his computer. "I'll pull up the report." He typed something in and waited. Typed some more. Then he looked over at Peter. "Red ones?"

32

THANK GOD for drugs. Annie's vision was hazy, and the only pain she felt was a dull throb in her head, distant, like it was that clock on the wall that had been banged up. She'd been out for an hour. Still, she felt like one of those dead balloons at Sophie's party. It was nice, really, that Sophie and her friends didn't cower in the corner, shriek, and cover their ears when a balloon burst. She closed her eyes.

The sound of footsteps kept her from slipping under again. Maybe the nurse was coming to check on her. No, those were hard footsteps, like leather shoe heels. Peter? She hoped it was Peter.

She felt a hand on her arm. She was glad he was back. Sun streamed in through the window behind the man who bent over her. But it wasn't Peter. The man wore green scrubs. An orderly? She let her eyes close and began to drift. Then she noticed the smells. Cigarette smoke, stale beer, and sweat. She forced her eyes open.

"So, did you like the flowers? I know you've got a thing for red roses." The man was holding one of her roses. Peter's roses. He pressed it into her face. The sweet smell of roses mixed with the rubbery smell of his latex glove. She struggled to push him away, and pain shot up her arm, clearing the narcotic haze that threatened to smother her like a warm, moist blanket.

"You just couldn't mind your own business, could you? Bitch." The man's fingers tightened on her arm. She knew it couldn't be Charlotte's father, but that's who she saw. "You had to stir up trouble. Turn my wife against me. Fill my daughter's head with nonsense."

"I didn't do anything. I couldn't—" she said, barely able to muster a whisper as he leaned on her chest. She tried to bring her knee up into his groin, but only succeeded in pushing him off balance. She groped for the nurse call button but it was no longer there. The door to the room was shut.

He came back at her, holding her down, his face in hers. It was Joe Klevinski. "If at first you don't succeed," he said. He pulled out a hypodermic syringe, and with his teeth removed the plastic sheath from the needle.

Annie screamed, butted his head, and sent him staggering back. Then she rolled onto her side and tried to free her legs. It felt as if she were moving through sludge. When he came back at her, she got off a solid kick to the groin.

Klevinski fell back and doubled over in pain. He knocked over the vase of roses. The glass broke and water spilled out onto the floor. *They're heavy as all get-out,* Annie remembered Luke saying as he offered her the roses that were delivered to her office. She could see that vase hitting the ground and cracking, revealing wires inside like a nest of vipers.

She only had a few moments before he'd recover and be on her again. She had to get away. She rolled away from him, but the rail on that side of the bed was up. *All you have to do is push one to call me.*

She groped under the pillow for her cell phone, pressed 1, but before it even rang, Klevinski knocked the phone out of her hand. She tried to scream again but he had his hand over her mouth.

He was on top of her now, his knee rammed into her. Annie felt her chest compress under his weight. She struggled for breath as he pressed down.

She tried to shake her head free of his hand, or bite him, but she couldn't. She knew what she was supposed to do, she'd taught the women in her class how to defend against this kind of attack. Press up and throw him off balance. But she couldn't press, she could barely breathe.

"Pathetic pussy," he said. She could taste the rubber of the glove and smell its chloriney scent. "Brenda put up a better fight than this."

The world turned gray around her, as if the lens of an iris were closing.

"Too bad I have to waste this nice junk on you. Nightie-night," he whispered, his hot, moist breath in her ear.

• • •

Peter walked to his car in the parking lot behind the police station. He got in and started the engine. If Annie hadn't imagined the roses, then maybe she hadn't imagined the card. So who had sent it? No one called him Petey except his mother and, to his chagrin, a few of her friends whom he didn't dare contradict. His brother used to call him Petey when he wanted to get a rise out of him. And of course, Sophie Klevinski. For some reason, it didn't bother him a bit when she did.

He put the car in gear and glanced at his watch. He'd go home, take a shower, maybe get a quick nap, and be back at the hospital in time to relieve Annie's mother. He turned onto Ruggles and headed up toward the Fens. He sniffed an armpit. Pretty ripe. Well, that's what he got for sleeping in his clothes. His body ached for a long, hot shower.

He approached the BU Bridge. In a few minutes he'd be in Cambridge. Then, a couple dozen blocks one way he'd be back at the hospital. A half-dozen blocks the other way and he'd be home.

Getting to the bridge from Boston was like threading a needle. Three lanes were supposed to merge into one, only "merge" wasn't part of the local vocabulary. Peter nudged his car forward, cutting off a Land Rover. His cell phone vibrated. He honked as the behemoth came within inches. The driver probably couldn't even see the top of his Miata. The phone vibrated again. He pried it from his pocket and glanced at the readout. It was Annie.

"Hey, what's up?" he said. There was no answer. "Hello?" He looked at the readout again. They were still connected.

"Annie? You okay?" Silence—or maybe not. He heard something. Grunting and muffled voices.

The light turned green. He shot through the intersection, then pulled over and stopped on Commonwealth Avenue. Trying to ignore the car horn blasting behind him, he rolled up the window and cut the engine. He put a finger in one ear, the phone to the other. "Hello? Can you hear me?"

Was that a man's voice? Sounds of struggle?

"Annie!" he yelled into the phone. What the hell was going on? "Are you all right?"

He started the car and peeled out, over the bridge, through the rotary, and up the ramp and onto Mem Drive. Traffic was backed up at the light. He couldn't wait. He leaned on his horn, flashed his headlights, and accelerated into oncoming traffic. There was none of that exhilaration he'd felt riding shotgun in the police cruiser a few days earlier. Cars coming the opposite direction swerved to avoid him.

He sped up to the intersection, honked his way through, then veered back to his own side of the street.

"What's happening?" Peter screamed into the phone.

Then he heard a man's voice. "You won't be needing this anymore." And the phone line went dead.

Peter dialed 911 and turned onto a dog-legged street to cut over. The hospital was only a few blocks away, but he wanted to be there *now*.

"Police emerg—" he heard on the phone, then a crackling sound and the signal cut out. Damned cell phones. He hit REDIAL, and barreled into the hospital emergency entrance, screeching to a halt beside a NO PARKING sign. He left the keys in the ignition, and hoped the car wouldn't get stolen. He couldn't worry about that now. He raced through the double doors.

A surprised clerk rose to her feet as he stormed past. "Sir, you can't go in there."

"Police emergency," he heard over the phone. He continued to the inner area.

"A patient in room four twenty-three at Mount Auburn Hospital is being attacked," he said into the phone and loud enough for everyone around him to hear.

The dispatcher asked his name. A nurse tried to block his way. "You're not allowed back here," she said, her hands up, a mixture of fear and distaste on her face. He realized he looked like a lunatic in his rumpled suit, red eyes, and day's growth of beard. "I'll have to call security."

"Good idea. Call security. I'm calling the police now, too."

"Please give me your name and location," the voice on the telephone insisted.

"Peter Zak. Get someone over here fast. Mount Auburn Hospital. The patient is being attacked."

"Stop him!" the nurse called as Peter raced toward the stairway exit.

"Room four-two-three!" he shouted over his shoulder.

He slipped into the stairwell and started up. The stairs clanged as he climbed. He hoped there'd be a security guard hot on his tail, but there wasn't.

The operator on the phone asked him to spell his name.

"Would you just send someone over here!" he said into the phone, and disconnected.

He emerged into the fourth-floor hall and hurried down the corridor, past a nurse's station and around the corner. Halfway down was Annie's room. The door opened and an orderly backed out into the corridor. The IV rack clattered as he pushed it along.

Peter checked the impulse to tackle him. Was the man's voice he'd heard on the phone just an orderly? Were the grunting and straining sounds nothing more than Annie shifting from the bed and back on again? Had she just leaned on the phone and ended up dialing 1?

The orderly walked away, down the hall. It was odd how the IV bag dangled from the rack, and how he was letting the tubes trail along on the ground.

"Code Gray, Unit four-two-three," blared the PA system.

Why didn't the orderly double back to the room?

"Code Gray, Unit four-two-three," the message repeated. Still the orderly didn't seem to hear.

"Hey!" Peter yelled after him.

The man gave a quick glance over his shoulder. It was Joe Klevinski.

"What the fuck were you doing in there?" Peter shouted.

Klevinski backed away. He picked up the stand, held it across his body, and hurled it at Peter. He dodged just in time, and the heavy steel apparatus clattered and banged across the floor. By the time he recovered his footing and got the stand out of the way, Klevinski was gone.

Peter ran to Annie's room. He pulled the door open. Annie lay on the bed, flat on her back. Her breathing was shallow, her body limp. There was no blood, no bruises that he could see. The sweet smell of vomit filled the room. Annie was covered in it.

Aspiration of vomitus was his first concern. That could be lethal. He turned her on her side and made sure her airway was clear. He touched her forehead. Her skin was cool and clammy. Her pulse was light and rapid. His gut wrenched. If only he hadn't left her alone.

He didn't know what to do next. Start CPR? The nurse call button had been ripped from the wall. He knelt alongside Annie. Her eyes were barely open, the pupils constricted.

"Klevinski?" he said.

She gave a barely perceptible nod.

"What did he do?"

Annie looked down at the inside of her arm where there was a raw, red spot and a bloody puncture wound. That's where the IV had been attached.

"Drugs?"

Annie's blinked once. He took it for a *yes*.

"That's him!" shouted a man's voice. Peter felt himself being seized by the shoulders and pulled back.

"That's her boyfriend," a nurse said, pointing an accusatory finger at Peter.

A doctor was beside Annie now. He pressed his fingers against her wrist. "She's got a pulse." He pushed open one eyelid.

"She's been drugged," Peter said.

"I can see that." He turned to Peter. "What did you give her?"

"It wasn't me. It was—" He stopped. Why was he wasting time defending himself? Here were caregivers who had the power to help

Annie. He remembered, Annie had said Klevinski was a former heroin addict.

"I think it's heroin," he said.

"You think?"

"Well, I told you I didn't . . . Yeah. Heroin." Peter prayed that he was right. Annie's symptoms jibed with a heroin overdose.

"Narcan. Two milligrams. IV. Now," the doctor said. A nurse rushed off.

Peter stood there feeling helpless. His back was coated with a cold sweat. He barely felt the security guard tighten his lock on him.

When he'd found Kate in her ceramics studio, her throat slit, no amount of CPR or drug antidote could have brought her back. Annie was still there, inert but breathing. Why the hell wasn't the nurse back? Annie seemed to be going whiter by the second, her lips tinged with blue. *Please, don't scare me like this.*

Finally there were running footsteps in the hall. The nurse returned with a cart and handed the doctor an IV bag. Peter winced as the doctor probed the already raw skin inside Annie's arm. He held his breath as the doctor found a vein, inserted the needle, and hooked up the IV.

The second hand on the clock jerked, then jerked again. Peter couldn't remember the last time he'd prayed for anything, but he was praying now. Still nothing. He knew Narcan was used to treat overdoses of narcotics like heroin. That meant it worked for morphine, Demerol. But what if he hadn't given her heroin. What if this was going to make her sicker? What if . . .

Annie took a sharp inhalation of breath and tried to sit up. She swatted the doctor away and gasped.

Peter felt his knees go as relief surged through him. The security guard started to pull him away.

"Annie, tell them it wasn't me."

But Annie was retching off the side of the bed.

The security guard propelled him out of the room. "Tell your story to the police," he said.

There, charging up the hall, were two uniformed police officers and MacRae. For once, Peter was glad to see him.

33

ANNIE TRUDGED up the stairs to her office, cradling her plaster-covered broken arm in front of her. It ached with each step. In fact, her whole body hurt—hips, back, and shoulders—and her ribs complained each time she tried to fill her lungs with air. It was a potent reminder of the bruises she wore all over in shades of gray, black, blue, and magenta, reminiscent of her old parochial school uniform.

They'd made her stay in the hospital for three more days after the morphine overdose, then sent her home with orders to rest. By then Luke was up and around; he'd be going home in a few days, too.

She'd been so relieved when the police arrested Joe Klevinski. They'd stopped him at a border crossing into Canada, the Chevy wagon packed with suitcases. Sophie and Jackie were in the car with him. Now he was in jail awaiting indictment, and MacRae had promised Annie that finding Brenda and Joey Klevinski would become a police priority. Annie hadn't talked to Jackie—she felt awkward calling her, and Jackie hadn't been in touch.

At home, Annie had managed to stay in bed for one day, flipping TV channels and going nuts. Pearl brought over a potted chicken. Annie's mother brought a tuna casserole and Annie's favorite barbecue potato chips. She'd scarfed down the entire bag in one sitting.

The next day she'd paced, wondering if the police were finding Brenda and Joey alive and well in Michigan, or if their skeletal remains were being excavated from the basement of the North Cambridge apartment building where they'd once lived.

Sleep brought her vivid nightmares of explosions and suffocation. When she finally wrenched awake, she'd be gasping for air, drenched in sweat, the smell of creosote and burnt rubber in her head.

That morning, she'd woken up exhausted, determined to go into her office and see for herself. The nightmare images her brain was conjuring couldn't be worse than the real thing.

All she'd done was take a shower, get dressed, put some makeup over the bruises that showed worst, and driven over. But her legs felt like sandbags as she climbed the steps, and by the time she reached their office she had to drop her leather bag to the floor and lean against the wall to catch her breath. There was a piece of plywood nailed over the space in the door where the pebble glass pane had been blown out. *Things can be replaced, people can't,* her mother's voice reminded her. That was right before she'd said, *Give yourself time to recover.*

Annie fumbled with the key and opened the lock. When she pushed the door open, darkness greeted her. It was cold inside, and the windows were boarded over. She gagged on the smell, pine cleaner over layers of smoke. She remembered. Chip told her that cleaners had come to do what they could, and a building engineer had proclaimed the overall structure fit.

She put her hand over her mouth and nose and felt for the light switch. Click. No lights came on. Damn. She fished a penlight from her bag and swept the interior with the beam.

The outer office had been emptied of most of the furniture. File cabinets, buckled and twisted like modern sculptures, were pushed against the wall. Wires dangled from the ceiling where there had been light fixtures. On the floor were two neat mounds of debris, and three orange traffic cones marked the perimeter of a soot-rimmed hole in the floor, about three feet in diameter.

Annie approached the crater, feeling ahead with her foot to be sure the boards were solid. Gingerly, she lowered herself into a crouch. As she reached out to touch the edge of splintered wood, she felt her face convulse, her stomach seize up. That hole was meant to be all that was left of her. But it wasn't herself she was thinking of. It was Mary Alice Boudreaux. She'd been *holding* the bomb, for god's sake. Annie steadied herself. She rummaged in her bag for a tissue. *Get a grip.*

How bad was her office? she wondered. She stumbled to her feet and made her way there. A few shards of wood attached to the hinges were all that was left of the office door. She shone the light around the interior. The windows were boarded over here, too, but otherwise it wasn't nearly as bad. Most of her furniture was still there, except for the lamp that had been her mother's. Its porcelain base would have shattered. A brass reading light had survived.

She sat in her desk chair and leaned back. The cushion smelled slightly of smoke. The file cabinets were still intact, and so was her desk. The computer was gone. Maybe the data on it could be rescued. Or maybe not. She was surprised at how little it bothered her. They'd figure out how to cope. If nothing else, something like this gave you a little healthy perspective on what was important.

She sat there in the silence, the echoes of the explosion still palpable. It was so quiet. No phones ringing, no hum of fluorescent lights and computers. Then she heard a door close. It hadn't occurred to her to notice whether their downstairs neighbors, a realty office, had been damaged or not. Maybe they were open for business.

There were footsteps on the stairs. Annie jerked to attention, sending a spasm of pain through her arm. She felt the adrenaline burst, her heart pounding, though she knew it was ridiculous. Joe Klevinski was in jail. It was probably just Chip or one of the cleaning crew.

Still, she turned off the flashlight and rolled her chair well back into the shadows to where she could see through to the reception area and into the hall. She heard footsteps cross the upstairs hall. A tall, thin figure stood silhouetted against the hall light. Annie breathed a sigh of relief.

"Jackie?" Annie called.

Jackie gave a little scream as Annie flashed the light on her. Jackie held one hand to her chest and the other shading her face.

"Annie? You scared the bejesus out of me."

"That makes two of us."

"It's too friggin' dark in here," Jackie said. "I was hoping I could see if any of my things were salvageable."

"Hang on, maybe I can jury-rig some light in here." Annie said. The hall light worked; maybe the wall outlets out there did, too.

Annie got the brass reading lamp from her office and plugged it into the extension cord that had been hooked to her computer. She snaked the cord out into the hall and plugged it in. She turned the switch, and *voilà*.

"Let there be light," Jackie said. They both started to laugh, but the laughter cut off as they looked at one another.

Jackie's face was bruised, and a cut had been stitched across her cheekbone. Annie knew from the way Jackie was looking at her that the makeup she'd put on wasn't doing such a hot job of covering her own bruises.

Jackie looked away. She went over to one of the debris piles and began to pick through it.

"I'm sorry," Annie said to Jackie's back, not sure exactly what she was apologizing for. Maybe for being right.

Jackie flashed her an angry look. "I asked you to back off. I begged you. But no, you had to back him into a corner. You humiliated him." She stood and kicked at the pile of charred remains. "Looks like everything I care about got blasted all to hell."

She turned and walked out of the office. Annie felt empty listening to Jackie's footsteps receding down the stairs. The front door opened and slammed shut. She knew Jackie wouldn't be coming back.

• • •

Leaves swirled through the air as Annie stared down at the grave. Her arm was still in a cast, and her wrist ached in the cold, though the bruises on her body had turned to shadowy splotches. Peter put his arm around her shoulders and pulled her close.

"I wonder where they're going to bury Brenda and Joey Klevinski," she said. The police had found their remains buried in the community garden across the street from their old apartment, in the plot Brenda had gardened. Klevinski had signed up for it every year since her disappearance. Annie shuddered at the thought: Brenda had literally dug her own grave.

Brenda's sister had come forward to claim the bodies. Annie hoped their graves would be less bleak and anonymous than these, lined up like so many rectangles in an accountant's ledger. Only the small headstone lying on the ground, a stone pillow, identified this space as Constance Florence's grave. *Constance.* Annie hadn't known that was her friend Charlotte's mother's first name. She'd been thirty-seven years old when she died, just three years older than Annie.

"I wish I could have helped her."

"Annie, you were just a kid."

"Yeah, but I knew what was happening." Beyond the wind she could hear trucks rumbling down a neighboring street. "Maybe now at least I've evened the score."

"You could've been killed."

"Jackie and Sophie could've been killed."

"Why didn't you at least tell me what you were up to?"

"You'd have had a fit. I knew you didn't approve of my getting involved in Jackie's personal life."

She felt Peter stiffen. "Since when do I get to approve or disapprove of what you do?"

"So you wouldn't have told me to back off?"

"Well . . ."

"Peter, I've been doing my own thing without checking in with anyone since I was twelve."

"And I don't *want* you to check in. But next time you decide to bearbait a murderer, would you give me a heads-up? Could you just get used to the idea that I'm going to worry about you?"

"I'll try." Annie rested her head on Peter's shoulder. "Jackie quit. She blames me for what happened. She says I backed Joe into a corner." If she could turn back time, Annie wondered, would she really do anything different? "I pushed him, didn't I?"

"You must have scared him good. Who knows, maybe he was back on drugs."

"Uncontrollable rage. You think that'll be his defense?"

"Could be a mitigating factor. I'm glad it's not up to me to sell it to a jury."

Abby could be blaming Annie, too, for getting Luke nearly killed. But she wasn't.

"Did you see, they indicted Blankstein?" Peter asked. "He's pleading guilty. Refused an attorney."

"That'll save the taxpayers a whole lot of money. He's insane, isn't he?"

Peter nodded. A light rain started to fall. They headed back toward his car.

"Looks like they won't have to postpone the wedding," Annie said as Peter started the engine. "Luke will be on crutches. I'll have my arm in a sling."

"You never told me about the dress. Puff sleeves?"

"Not a one. It's gorgeous. Well, it was, anyway. Abby's got a new one on order."

Peter drove along the road in the cemetery, from one flat, featureless stretch of lawn to the next.

"I'd much rather be cremated," Annie said.

"Me, too, actually," Peter said. His hand crept over to hers. "But not until we're both old and gray and have grandchildren."

Annie felt herself flush with pleasure and squeezed his hand back.